Full Figured 6:

Carl Weber Presents

Full Figured 6:

Carl Weber Presents

Electa Rome Parks and Eric Pete

www.urbanbooks.net

Urban Books, LLC
97 N18th Street
Wyandanch, NY 11798

ISBN 13: 978-1-60162-705-6
ISBN 10: 1-60162-705-X

First Mass Market Printing January 2015
First Trade Paperback Printing June 2013
Printed in the United States of America

10 9 8 7 6 5 4 3 2 1

Distributed by Kensington Publishing Corp.
Submit Wholesale Orders to:
Kensington Publishing Corp.
C/O Penguin Group (USA) Inc.
Attention: Order Processing
405 Murray Hill Parkway
East Rutherford, NJ 07073-2316
Phone: 1-800-526-0275
Fax: 1-800-227-9604

Black Widow

by

Electa Rome Parks

Prologue

DAUGHTER: Mama, are you getting married again?

MAMA: Yes.

DAUGHTER: Why?

MAMA: I've met a man who can take care of us the way we deserve to be taken care of.

DAUGHTER: Do you love him?

MAMA: What do you know about love, little girl?

DAUGHTER: I know you are supposed to marry for love. Everyone knows that.

MAMA: Well, I tried marrying for love the first time and it didn't work out. So, this time I'm trying a new approach.

DAUGHTER: What happened?

MAMA: After the love wore off, he beat my butt like it was his own personal punching bag.

DAUGHTER: Oh. I'm sorry.

MAMA: Let me tell you something you will find out soon enough.

DAUGHTER: Okay, I'm listening, Mama.

MAMA: Love ain't shit. It can turn into something you don't even recognize. Something ugly. Marry for money; love can come later. And if it doesn't, then at least you are paid. And by the way, it's a myth that money can't buy you happiness. And, don't ever let a man put his hands on you. If he does, you get out of there. Leave. Run. Do you hear me, sweetie?

DAUGHTER: Yes, Mama. Of course I hear you, I'm sitting right here.

MAMA: That's my sweet girl.

DAUGHTER: Mama?

MAMA: What, sweetie?

DAUGHTER: I've thought about it. When I grow up I'm going to marry for love.

MAMA: Okay, sweetie. Good luck. You'll learn. There are some lessons you have to learn on your own.

DAUGHTER: If I don't get it right the first time, I'll keep getting married over and over and over again.

MAMA: Sounds like a plan, sweetie.

DAUGHTER: I'll keep doing it until I get it right. You'll see.

Big, Bold, and Beautiful, That's Me!

Chapter 1

A few years ago, when I was going through my self-discovery phase, I took a continuing education journal writing class for four weeks, two evenings per week, at the local community college. I was and am always searching for new and innovative ways to educate, improve, and entertainment myself. I admit I have a short attention span and get bored easily, so I'm always trying and experimenting with new ideas and concepts because I'm all about growth as a person. If we aren't elevating ourselves to the next level, what's the point?

But I digress . . . One of the first assignments from the thirty-something, sandy-haired, plain-Jane, anorexic-looking female instructor was to write down three words, three adjectives, that captured the true essence of who we were.

As I casually glanced around the drab classroom, with our desks situated in a semi-circle, I observed that many students had difficulty simply coming up with three adjectives. They were clueless as they sat at their desks, pens perched and ready to write, deep in thought, while I immediately wrote in bold, cursive letters on the first page of my lined, one-hundred-page pink journal: "big, bold, and beautiful." Those three words described me in a nutshell. Nothing more needed to be said. That was easy. Bam! Next!

By the way, I'm Erika Kane, named by my now deceased, high-spirited mother, for the heroine of her favorite soap opera, *All My Children*. At least she spelled the c in Erica with a k for a bit of distinction. Back in the day, I hated my name with a passion because I was always teased about it. Lucky for me, even then, I didn't suffer from any low self-esteem issues. In fact, I am and was probably the exact opposite, suffering from an overt high level of self-esteem.

I don't know what my mother was thinking, who knows. I am nowhere vaguely close in physical appearance to the Erica Kane on TV, or should I say the one who was on TV until the soap was cancelled after forty-one years on air. Erica Kane, the one who weighs ninety pounds soaking wet with her clothes on, with porcelain skin and barely towers over five feet, is my polar opposite.

I've accepted the fact that I'm a big girl, big boned and proud of every pound and every huggable, squeezable inch. There is simply more of me to love and go around. That's what my mama always told me, and I have come to terms with the fact that I love to eat. There is nothing wrong with that, nor is there anything like a hearty, delicious, fulfilling meal. I laughed at these skinny minis who starved themselves to remain a size four. For what? It should be a crime to have a 5.7.9 shop at the mall. Not me, honey; give me a twelve-inch well-done porterhouse steak with sautéed onions and a creamy, loaded baked potato with sour cream, extra butter, and chives any day, and I'll show you a happy lady.

My boldness, well I inherited that from my mama. I have always believed in giving credit where credit is due. My mother, bless her soul, was a damn fool, and I say that with nothing but love and respect. Mama didn't take anybody's shit, male or female. Plain and simple. That's probably why I had three different stepdads before I was eighteen and she was fatally stabbed by a lover the month before I turned twenty-five. I knew I carried her genes because I'm just as opinionated, feisty, and outspoken as she was.

No one has ever had a conversation with me and walked away without knowing my stance on issues ranging from religion and politics to sex. I don't scare easily and I rarely back down. My boldness and sassy mouth have gotten me into trouble on more than one occasion, but they have also gotten me the upper hand in situations as well. So, I consider them an asset.

Now, as for my beauty, I learned I possessed that early on. When some of my jealous teenage girlfriends, from back in the day, tried to make me feel bad about my weight by suggesting I try various diets, I ignored them. They thought they were so cute with their flat, deflated butts, tiny Barbie doll waists and 34B breasts. I had noticed how their so-called boyfriends couldn't keep their eyes off my ample bosom, plump thighs, or high-rise, juicy booty. I soon learned that the only thing that wanted, or needed, a bone was a dog. Men wanted a little cush in their push. And I had cush to spare, for days. No, I never had any problems attracting the opposite sex. Men flocked to me like bees to honey and my honey spot was sweet. Sweet enough to eat.

To top it all off, I had a great sense for fashion; I was definitely a fashionista. I could shop until I dropped, seven days a week if I could. I may have shopped at Macy's, Lane Bryant, or the big-girl racks at T.J. Maxx, but I rocked what I wore to perfection with full, sista attitude. I loved color and plenty of large accessories, big bags, and high heels.

Yes, big, bold, and beautiful, that was me.

A Helping Hand Goes a Long Way

Chapter 2

It was Friday. Friday the 13th to be exact. Bill day. Come rain or shine, I wrote out checks for my bills every Friday like clockwork. I got that from my mama. I was sitting behind closed doors in my chic new office at Last Chance, my newly remodeled hair salon, when there was a heavy knock at the door that pulled me out of my daydreaming reverie.

"Yes. Come in," I called out.

Nobia, my assistant/receptionist and best friend in the whole world for the last three and a half years, stuck her head in, smiling. That's what I adored about her: she always had a pleasant, peaceful demeanor about herself. If she was having a bad day, you would rarely be able to tell, unlike me. When I was having a bad day, everyone knew it. I made sure of that.

"She's here. Are you ready for me to send her in or do I need to give you a few minutes?"

I shook my head in confusion. "Who's here?" I asked. "Send who in?"

"Jasmine Bass," she said, raising her eyebrows in a quizzical expression. The last few days I had been absentminded.

"Oh yes, you mentioned she was on her way; send her right in." Jasmine was the young woman I had heard about through a long-time client. I had asked Nobia to contact her and ask the college student to come see me at the salon just the other day.

"Will do," Nobia said, stepping back out into the plush-carpeted hallway.

A few minutes later a pretty, young girl with bangs and a short bob entered my office dressed in dark denim jeans, a form-fitting multi-colored top, and red Van sneakers. She stood tall, lanky, and confident.

"Hi, Jasmine. Come on in. How are you?" I inquired. "Please, have a seat and make yourself comfortable. I'm Erika Kane, the owner of this shop," I stated, standing up and reaching out to shake her small hand.

To my surprise, she offered a firm, self-assured handshake and then proceeded to sit down in the chair in front of my massive Italian black lacquer desk. She looked at me as curiosity shone clearly in her bright, receptive eyes.

I cleared my throat. "I realize we have never met, so I guess you are wondering why I asked you to come to my salon/office?" I inquired, taking a seat back behind my desk in my black swivel chair.

"Actually, I was," she said, twisting slightly in the pink-cushioned black chair that accentuated my office. In fact, my entire salon was decorated in shades of pink and black, my favorite colors.

"Well, to be honest, I overheard one of my clients, one of your mother's friends, talking about your predicament a few days ago."

Jasmine remained silent, listening.

I continued. "I understand you are a junior at University of West Georgia, an education major and sociology minor. I understand you will not be able to go back fall semester, which begins in a couple of days, because you are short five hundred dollars."

She nodded and spoke. "Miss Erika, I worked two jobs this summer, as many as possible, but I'm still short by approximately five hundred because there were a few emergencies that came up that I had to help Mama out with. I'm a little short on my fees and I don't have any money at all for books. They get even more expensive once you start classes in your major," she said rapidly. "I guess I'll have to sit out this semester."

I didn't skip a beat. I reached into my open desk drawer and pulled out a check. "You aren't short now. I want you to have this," I said, walking around my desk, handing her a check with a beaming smile on my face.

She glanced at the amount. "Oh my God. Oh my God," she shouted, jumping up to retrieve it from my outstretched hand. "You didn't have to do this. You don't even know me," she said, staring at me in utter disbelief.

"Yes, I did. I didn't have to know you. I believe in you, Jasmine. There is no way in hell I could have slept at night if I knew of a young girl trying to make a better life for herself and couldn't finish college because of a five-hundred-dollar deficit. By the way, I wrote the check out for one thousand to give you an extra cushion to play with."

Jasmine jumped up again, hugging me tightly. "I don't know how I will ever repay you. Thank you. Thank you so much."

I pulled her back so I could see her face. "You already have. The smile on your face and the joy in your heart is enough. Paid in full."

"Really?"

"Really."

"Thank you so much, Miss Erika," she said with tears in her eyes. "You don't know how much this means to me. I can't wait to tell Mama."

"Just study hard and make us both proud, which I know you will," I said as I escorted her to the door. "And whenever you have the opportunity, lend a helping hand and pay it forward."

"I promise, I will," she said, walking away with a priceless smile.

As I closed my door to return to my bill paying and privacy, I felt giddy inside. Giving back always gave me a warm, euphoric feeling that I thrived on. That was another thing I had discovered about myself. If something made me feel good, then I was going to get mine, over and over and over.

"Ladies, we will be back in an hour or so. We are just down the block if you need me, at the Mexican restaurant," I called out to two of my stylists who were standing at their stations with clients. Loretta had been with me since the beginning of my new journey, over two years now, and the new kid on the block was Destiny. I had hired her about a month ago and was still getting to know her. As usual, Carla hadn't arrived yet, even though she had a client waiting impatiently in the sitting area, flipping through a magazine and checking her watch every few minutes. I never understood how Carla kept clients, but I guessed they were able to overlook her shortcomings because of the magic she performed on their hair. She was an excellent, sought-after stylist and the problem was that she knew it.

Nobia and I made our way a half block down to one of our favorite eateries. The service was good, the staff was friendly, the prices were reasonable, and the food was excellent. This restaurant, and many other retail storefronts just like it, was one of the main reasons I decided to open Last Chance in this particular neighborhood. I appreciated the entrepreneurial spirit of the small business owners and I relished how everyone looked out for one another in an ethnically diverse area.

"Erika, did I tell you that you were wearing that jumpsuit, girl?" Nobia asked, looking me up and down with no qualms, admiring my chic black outfit with gold accessories, including the open-toed high heels that gave a peek at my recent, weekly pedicure. I couldn't get enough of pampering myself. I deserved it.

I paused to model on the sidewalk, turning in a slow, deliberate rotation with my arms outstretched.

"You have, but you can tell me again." I laughed, tossing my long, straight, silky hair. Even though I owned a salon and had a cosmetology license, I adored wearing wigs and had many. Today I rocked my Naomi Campbell look, with bangs and straight black hair that hit right below my shoulder blades. I looked fierce, if I must say so myself.

Nobia and I walked farther, taking our time and enjoying the seasonal weather of September. "It's such a beautiful day. I wouldn't trade Georgia weather for anything or anyplace," Nobia shared. At forty, she had a round, chubby baby face that made her look younger. She had on a blue maxi dress with dark sandals, and usually wore her hair in a dark brown body wave that stopped right at the nape of her neck. She was also a big girl, but I still had to work with her on her sense of style because she would wear a maxi dress every day of the week. I think she thought they concealed her size.

"I'm waiting."

"On what?" she questioned, pausing in mid-step and looking at me curiously.

"I'm waiting for you to tell me again how gorgeous I look today."

Nobia burst into good-humored laughter. "Girl, you are too much."

"I know but you love me anyway."

As we opened the door to the restaurant and stepped inside, we were immediately greeted with "*buenos dias*" and cheerful smiles.

"Where do you want to sit?" Nobia asked, surveying the remaining open booths. At the moment, the place was only half full, but it was quickly filling up as customers filtered in for Tuesday's specials.

"Let's sit near the bay window, our usual spot, so that we can people watch and gossip," I shared, scooting into a wide booth near a large, open window that displayed all the activity up and down the busy intersection.

"Perfect," I said, exhaling as delicious aromas assaulted, tickled, and teased my nose from the nearby kitchen. I relaxed for the first time that day and admired my surroundings as I looked around. I simply loved the ambience of the restaurant; it was chock-full of vibrant color. There was original artwork displayed in every nook and cranny, along with handmade furniture. One-of-a-kind pottery vases and plants adorned high-perched shelves and there were hand painted details on the walls with countless suns, birds, frogs, and turtles everywhere the eye could behold.

There was no need for Nobia and me to study the colorful menus because we knew exactly what we wanted, so we were ready to order when the pretty Mexican waitress with the clipped English came over with pen and paper in hand. We placed our burrito orders and reclined, ready to enjoy each other's company and a good meal together.

"Are you pleased with the outcome of the remodeling project at the salon, Erika?" Nobia asked, dipping crunchy, hot tortilla chips into spicy-salsa-filled colorful ceramic bowls that had immediately been brought to our table.

"I can honestly say I am. I think the salon now has a chic, modern, sophisticated feel and that's exactly what I wanted. And you know my favorite colors are black and pink and the interior designer incorporated them perfectly."

"You don't say," she kidded. "Your favorite colors are black and pink?"

"Nobia, you are silly, but seriously I'm very pleased with how everything turned out. What do you think? Do you like it?"

"I think the salon looks great and I'm proud to work there. I must say, it was good to come back last week after the shop was closed for two weeks. I missed you guys."

"Oh, that is so sweet of you. You do wonderful work keeping me organized and sane. Hiring you was one of the best decisions I made."

"Thank you, girl. Did you notice the 'for lease' sign is gone from the window of the empty space next to us?"

"I'm glad you mentioned that because I noticed it was gone too, but I haven't seen anyone over there," I said, taking a sip of my diet Coke, which the waitress had placed in front of me. "I wonder what type of business is going to open. Hopefully, it won't be competition."

"I guess we will find out soon enough. Won't we? With the salon project out of the way, we need to focus on getting you a man."

I held up my hand. "Don't go there. I am just fine with me, myself, and I. I adore my own company. There's never a boring day in my world."

"Erika, I'm your best friend and I know it has been difficult getting over the death of Edward. Hell, you pretty much took to your bed the first year after he passed and shut down. I was so worried about you."

I nodded and sighed. "It has been difficult. Edward was the love of my live and, sometimes, I still can't believe he's gone. I still expect to hear his contagious laughter or hear him call me baby."

"You know I loved me some Edward, but it has been three years, girl."

"Three years next Tuesday," I whispered.

"Wow."

"Yep."

"Erika, he would want you to move on and live your life to the fullest. You deserve that. You are vibrant, full of life, beautiful, and you do so much for others. You are only forty years old and you need someone to share the rest of your life with."

"I'm doing just fine," I said. "I manage just fine without a man. Thank you very much."

"You are a hopeless romantic and have always been one from what I can tell. Regardless of what you say, I know you haven't given up on love. I know you, Erika. Stop kidding yourself."

"Now you are telling me what I need and what I feel?" I asked, staring her down, with a hint of annoyance in my tone.

"I just want you to be happy."

"I am. Again, I'm just fine. Don't worry about me. I'm a big girl."

Minutes later, our food was delivered to our table and we wasted no time digging in. Both Nobia and I didn't play when it came to our meals. Silence followed for the first time since we had sat down.

"Hmmm, this hits the spot; this is so good," I managed to say between bites. "I've been craving burritos since last week."

Nobia nodded in agreement.

"Girl, looks like you got you one," she said, grinning and looking directly over my shoulder.

"What?" I asked, turning in my seat to see what had captured her attention.

I spun around to see a fine, dark-skinned brother seated at the counter, but staring in our direction with no shame. He had a handsomely rugged, swagged-out look that used to appeal to me when I was younger. My first husband, Malik, fit the description.

I turned back around, uninterested, and continued eating.

"He's cute," Nobia gushed.

"He's okay."

"After we leave here I need to take you over to LensCrafters and have your eyes examined. I think you need glasses, Erika. No, I know you need glasses."

"Nobia, for the last time, I'm not looking for a man and definitely not a boy," I exclaimed.

"He does look kind of young, doesn't he?"

"You think?" I kidded, turning to take another look at him. He smiled. "Looks like he was recently weaned from his mama's tits. I think I see a milk moustache."

We laughed, enjoying the remainder of our lunch and knowing we had to return to the shop soon. Fridays were always busy. I rarely came in on Saturdays and we were closed on Sundays and Mondays, as most salons were.

"Uh huh, looks like he's coming this way with his sexy ass. Check out those arms and that six-pack beneath that black tee, girl," Nobia whispered under her breath.

I glanced back nonchalantly when I heard him clear his throat a couple of times.

"Yes?" I asked, in my most professional tone. "May we help you?"

"How are you lovely ladies today?"

"Fine now," Nobia volunteered, outright flirting. I didn't comment one way or the other. I took another sip of my diet soda.

"Before I left, I had to come over and introduce myself when I saw two beautiful sisters enjoying lunch and each other's company. I'm Jacob."

"Thank you," Nobia said, clearly taken in by his apparent charm and good looks. "I'm Nobia and this is my girlfriend—"

I interrupted before she could offer up my name. "Well, thanks for stopping by Jacob. Don't let us keep you," I said, without a smile to be seen. I noticed he had a tattoo with symbols on his right arm.

He extended his hand for a handshake and I left it hanging. "I'm sorry, I didn't catch your name."

"I didn't throw it."

Jacob paused, looked at me, and then chuckled. I was sure he wasn't used to this type of treatment from women, especially a big-boned girl.

"I like your spirit, but I do know you, well know of you. You own that salon . . . What is it called?"

"Last Chance," Nobia said.

I threw her a look that said, "shut up."

"Yeah, that's it. Catchy name by the way," he said, smiling at me again and revealing one dimple in his left cheek. "Ladies, enjoy the remainder of your day. "Hopefully, I see you around soon," he said and winked.

"You too," Nobia said.

"Don't count on it," I said under my breath.

As he was walking away, Nobia was all over me. "Erika, you didn't have to be so mean, girl. He was just talking. No harm in that."

"I'm not a cougar interested in chasing some young cub. I have enough whispering going on behind my back as it is."

"Well, he was sexy and seemed to be feeling you."

"Sorry, not interested. Next subject."

"Yes, please do."

I silently laughed. The reverend, in his mid-forties, was looking sharp in his stylish, very expensive blue suit with a gray pinstriped shirt, tie, and classic lace-up shoes. To me, there wasn't anything sexier than a man in a suit and tie, all dressed up and smelling good.

I had heard rumors over the years about extramarital affairs on the reverend's part, but I didn't get involved with nasty rumors because I knew how they worked. Once you told a lie or repeated it long enough, it became the truth to some people. Apparently, my three previous marriages didn't sit well with some. Especially since my marriages all ended in death for my husbands.

"What can I do for you today?" I asked, leaning back in my chair. "I know you didn't come all the way over here for me to cut your hair," I teased, tapping my Montblanc pen against my desktop.

It was Friday, the second one we had spent in the shop since it had been renovated, and I was once again in my office, behind closed doors. Mostly I managed the business aspect of my salon on a day-to-day basis. I only had a handful of clients whose hair I styled on a regular basis and they weren't due for another hour. I enjoyed being a stylist, but I found I preferred the business and marketing side of the industry. That was a challenge and I was always up for one.

"We have a new member, Sister Judith, who joined the congregation last Sunday and she's down on her luck."

"These are trying times for everyone," I volunteered. "We can only hope they get better and soon. That's why it's so important that we get out there and vote. President Obama needs us to make it happen again."

"Amen, sister."

"Amen."

"A few months ago, this sister moved here from Tennessee following behind a man. It didn't take long to discover the man was married when one plus one didn't add up. Classic tale."

I shook my head in disgust and sucked my teeth.

"She has uprooted herself and her young daughter, has no immediate family in the area, and has no source of income at the present time."

"I don't know when these women, young and old, are going to learn. I hear stories like this all the time at the salon from clients gossiping about themselves, family members, friends, and coworkers. It's sad. It's stupid. However, I'd be happy to make a donation to a fund. Hopefully, she has learned a life lesson from this experience. We all make mistakes and that's why Jesus Christ shed his blood on the cross. We're imperfect beings."

"Amen, sister, but that's not necessary. The church has put Sister Judith up for a month in a local hotel and given her money for expenses. You see, she's trying her hardest to gain employment, and she has an interview scheduled for Monday, but she wants to look her best. I was wondering if you could style her hair, free of charge of course?"

I laughed. "Is that all? I thought you were going to ask me something outrageous. Of course I can shampoo and style her hair. I'll have her looking like a million dollars."

"Bless you, sister. Bless you."

"Tell her to get here before I close and I'll fit her in."

"Sister Judith will be elated and you'll be blessed for your unselfish act."

"I need as many blessings as I can get. In fact, you have given me a wonderful idea, Reverend."

"God works in mysterious ways."

"I think I'm going to start setting aside a few hours on a certain day to wash and style homeless women's hair. Maybe I'll make arrangements with one or two of the local shelters to send over women, or maybe I'll go there. I'll work out the details later."

"Whew! They don't make them like you anymore, sister. Some man is going to be lucky to have you as a wife. Beautiful, smart, and you know your way around the kitchen based on dishes you've brought to the church," he gushed. "Can't beat that."

I produced a weak smile, but didn't offer a comment. For a quick second, surprisingly, images of Jacob from the restaurant popped into my mind. He did have the cutest dimple and those biceps were huge and bulging. I imagined he could throw down in the bedroom and I vividly pictured his head buried snugly between my open thighs. I shook my head to release my naughty thoughts.

I cleared my throat and coughed. "Before I forget, I have the salon's monthly box of donated food in the supply closet ready for pickup. My clients truly stepped up to the plate this month because the large box I always keep near the front door was overflowing with canned food and staples."

"I don't know what we would do without you at the church and in the community. You truly make a difference."

I nodded in appreciation. "I do what I can. To whom much is given, much is expected. However, Reverend, I would like to ask for your guidance and prayer regarding a personal manner."

"What is it? Is something worrying you?" he asked, suddenly sitting up with a serious scowl on his clean-shaven face.

I didn't hesitate. I blurted it out in one gush. "I can't seem to get past Edward's death and it has been almost three years. I think about him all the time, day and night. I'm beginning to think something is wrong with me."

"Everyone grieves differently, sister. Everyone goes through the various grieving stages at their own pace. It was tragic how Edward suddenly become ill and was gone shortly thereafter. It was unexpected. So sad," he said, shaking his head. "But God called him home and you will get past this in your own way and time. In the meantime, know that God has your back."

Reaching for my hand, he said, "Let's pray about it. Pray for strength and divine guidance during this trying time."

We did just that. Bowed our heads and prayed right there in my office, and after he left, I felt much better, more at peace.

Chapter 5

"Good night, Carla. I'll see you next week at my regular time."

"Okay, girl. You look gorgeous," I said, locking the door behind her as she click-clacked in her designer shoes up the sidewalk to the parking area.

Another Thursday night found me and Erika alone in the salon. She was in her office taking care of some paperwork and I had just walked my last client of the night to the front door. Of course, she was looking absolutely fabulous and was very pleased with her new hairstyle. Her ooohs and ahhhs and the fifty-dollar tip confirmed it.

I rarely brag—well, yes, I do—but I knew with certainty that I was one of the best stylists in the city and I had trophies from competitions all across the country to prove it. Based on my volatile history with Erika, I realized that was the only reason I worked in her salon; I had been with her for over a year now. I will give it to her though, Erika was smart. She was a savvy businesswoman. I realized she put up with my mess because she knew she had a star stylist who brought in clients, many of them high-profile and local celebrities.

I guess it was a tradeoff for me, too. I admit I reluctantly came to her asking for a job when a situation popped off at my old establishment and I had to leave, involuntarily. This time, my reputation preceded me—great stylist or not, no one at that time was interested in hiring Diva Carla. I was more trouble than I was worth with my diva-like ways. It took a lot out of me to put my tail between my legs, so to speak, and ask Erika for a job. So, here I was and we tolerated each other by keeping our distance and with minimal conversation.

After sweeping up piles of 100-percent human Brazilian hair weave and straightening up around my station, I was more than ready to call it a night. I was tired. Bone tired, as the old folks used to say. It had been a long day and the weekend was going to be even crazier. It always was and I relished it, adored the fast pace of the beauty industry. I could honestly say that my passion was making women beautiful. I lived for the times when a plain Jane shyly walked in, sat in my magical chair, and walked away with her head held high, totally glamorous. Total transformation. Magic happened.

I grabbed my new Coach handbag, compliments of a recent sponsor, and strutted down the hallway to let Erika know I was leaving. Today she had been extra nice to me. I swear she was Miss Jekyll and Miss Hyde. Some days she could be sweet as honey, but most days she was a bitch.

She had even gone out during lunchtime and brought back dessert for everyone, huge slices of red velvet cake with cream cheese frosting from the soul food joint a few blocks over from our salon. Even though I'm on a diet, I had to take a few bites, and before I knew it I had eaten the entire slice. It was absolutely delicious and I yearned for a second piece. I swear Erika was trying to make us all as big as she was. Nobia was quickly catching up and I dreamt of the day when I could sit her in my chair and give her a much-needed makeover. Nobia wouldn't recognize style if it was sitting in her lap.

I knocked lightly on the door, which now had a name plaque: ERIKA KANE, CEO. I shook my head and laughed. Some people thought they were way more important than they actually were. CEO. Ha.

"Erika, I'm leaving now," I called out.

At first there was no response.

I knocked again, harder. "Erika," I called out, cracking her door an inch or two.

She was on the phone and evidently having a great conversation based on the way she was cheesing. She looked up with a huge smile on her face and made eye contact.

"I'm gone. I'll lock you in on my way out. See you tomorrow."

She actually waved and smiled, then resumed talking. I did a double take. Jekyll and Hyde.

I made my way back to the front, turned off the lights, and made sure I locked the door as I stepped onto the sidewalk. Even though we were in a nice section of town, we had heard of an attempted burglary a few weeks earlier not far from us. The state of the economy was making people crazy.

Atlanta had had a recent string of burglaries where a gang of thugs targeted beauty supply stores that carried high-end hair weave. They would literally drive a truck or SUV vehicle right up to the front of the store and crash through. Then they would snatch and grab as much expensive human hair weave as they could and would be out of the store within minutes. They would make quite a profit reselling it on the street. Unbelievable.

I was single and lived alone. Never had children. So, my plans for the remainder of the night were to order take-out Chinese and chill for the rest of the night. I didn't have to be in the salon the next day until noon because I was doing a local reality-show celebrity's hair at her in-home salon. Yeah, I had it like that.

Thirty minutes later I had picked up my delicious-smelling meal and was ready to hit the interstate that would take me home when I realized I hadn't packed my favorite flat iron. I'd need it for work the next day and I wasn't about to come by the salon early morning.

"Damn."

"Damn."

"Damn."

I suddenly remembered that I still had the spare key to the salon that I hadn't returned to Erika when I worked really late the other night. I decided to stop back by the salon and pick up my much-needed equipment. I could be in and out in no time.

When I unlocked the front door, everything was just as I had left it. I had seen Erika's car still parked outside, so I knew she was still there. However, I thought she would be gone by then because she was not one for hanging around too late. She didn't even come in on Saturdays. Something didn't feel right.

Before I could call out, I heard strange sounds coming from the back that stopped me in my tracks. The hairs on the back of my neck stood up. I didn't hate Erika, just couldn't stand her, so I walked toward her office to make sure everything was okay.

I cautiously made my way, remaining alert. If I had to book, I wanted to be ready; and if a burglar was in the place, I didn't want to announce my arrival, too. I slowly crept my way to Erika's office and noticed the door was now cracked a few inches and the lights were dimmed.

"What is she up to?" I muttered to myself.

I inched closer when I heard a deep male voice. "That's it, baby. Back that ass up," the sexy voice commanded. Then I heard a sharp slap as flesh met flesh.

To my shock and amazement, I heard Erika's voice say, "You just keep giving me that good dick, baby boy."

He chuckled. "I got your baby boy."

"I don't break, sweetie. Give me that good dick. Make me feel it. Give me all you got," she commanded.

"You ain't ready for all this," he bragged.

I leaned against the wall like I was a cat burglar, with my heart pounding against my chest. I heard the sexy, raw exchange, but I couldn't believe it was coming from Erika's mouth. After getting up my nerve, I leaned forward to take a quick peak. All the noise they were making, I knew they wouldn't hear me; hopefully they wouldn't see me either. They were in their own lusty world.

"Hmmm, damn your pussy is tight and sweet. I knew it would be the day I saw you and your friend at the restaurant. You had my dick hard that day just from looking at you. Turn that sexy ass around."

I heard the palm of his hand make contact with her butt again. "Lord, you got ass for days. I can get lost up in there," he said. "Turn around."

I inhaled and took a quick peak. It was a sight to behold. Erika was buck-naked, stripped down to her birthday suit. Her young stud had her bent over her massive desk as he banged her like there was no tomorrow, showing her no mercy. He was rod stiff and I clearly saw each thrust as he steadily eased in and out of her. His tool glistened with her juices as she eagerly took him in, licking her shiny, pink, glossed lips.

They had their backs to the door and had no clue I was outside, playing voyeur. Erika had to feel each stroke because I heard as his balls made contact against her backside. The sound echoed inside the room. He stroked her long and hard as he palmed her ass with his large, skillful hands. Every now and then he would slap a butt cheek and rub it immediately afterward. Dude took his time.

Erika appeared to be enjoying every last inch of him—about eight inches from my estimation. She moaned seductively, then twisted and turned. Squirmed. Erika backed into him so she could take all he had to offer.

Don't ask me why I kept watching, frozen in place. I wasn't a pervert who liked to watch other people having sex, but for whatever reason I couldn't turn away. I couldn't rationalize what I was seeing; Holy Roller Erika was screaming obscenities and letting this young stud screw her senseless. Hell, I was getting wet and weak at the knees from his performance.

"Yeah, you love this dick. Don't you?" he asked between thrusts.

"Don't you?"

"Tried to act all high and mighty the other day like you didn't know what was up. Now look at you. You loving this dick. Slobbered all over it earlier."

"Let me hear you say it," he said, thrusting harder.

To my surprise I heard her scream out, "I love it, baby boy."

Dude stopped abruptly. "Back that ass up and get yours. Get you some," he said, guiding her ass backward.

"That's right. Get you some. Get your dick."

Erika grunted seductively.

"Yeah, you feeling that. I'm all up inside the pussy."

Dude started back up again and he was fine as wine. You could tell he worked out because of his obvious six-pack and bulging muscles, with a tattoo on his upper arm. With each stroke, I could see his thigh muscles expand, and he was packing and definitely knew how to work what God had so graciously blessed him with.

"So sweet. Own my pussy," Erika shouted. "Stamp your name all over it."

I could have walked up and joined them and she wouldn't have wanted him to stop. She had lost her mind.

Suddenly dude pulled out, reached around for her breasts, tweaked and squeezed them. Then he eased down and buried his face between her thighs from behind.

"Oh, Jacob, you do that so well. Eat it, baby."

"You like that don't you?"

"I love it."

"I knew you had a freak inside of you, just waiting to be released."

His tongue was going to town. Signing his name. In cursive. In print.

"Squeeze my breasts harder."

"You like it rough?"

"I'm not fragile. Pull my nipples. Yeah, like that. That's a good boy."

Dude did as commanded.

"Now, make mama come. And Jacob, I wanna come hard."

Just as he inserted three thick fingers inside her womanhood and continued to shower her with oral skills, I had seen enough. I hastily made my exit or I was going to start touching myself.

Just as I was grabbing my flat iron and running toward the door, I guess she got her request. She came.

All I heard was, "Awww, damn. Yesss, yesss, yesss."

I got the hell out of there and knew I would never mention what I had seen to anyone. It would be my secret ammunition if I ever had to use it against Erika. I knew our day was coming.

Oh, Denzie Baby!

Chapter 6

Friday night I entered my dream home in a lovely gated community, about a ten-mile drive from Last Chance. The first thing I did was kick off my four-inch cheetah-fur stilettos in the living room. I left them lying in the middle of the floor and my bare feet thanked me immediately. I swear I heard them purr like a baby kitten being stroked behind the ears. My toes felt wonderful as they sank into the deep, plush, thick carpet that was abundant throughout my home.

Next on my agenda was to pour myself a glass of red wine in my favorite wine glass, slip out of my designer black dress with the plunging neckline, and then take a relaxing bubble bath immersed up to my neck with my favorite products. Maybe I would even light some candles and play some baby-making music to relax my mind. I adored me some Trey Songz, Usher, and R.

Kelly. Maybe I would even take it old school with a bit of Marvin Gaye or Al Green. It had been a long week with a parade of clients, vendors, and finalizing marketing plans.

I was restless. Antsy. On the short ride home, my thoughts kept playing over and again the conversation Nobia and I had had earlier in the week when we had gone out for lunch. I realized she was absolutely right. I should think about dating again and moving on with my life. At times, it did feel like I was living my life in constant limbo. Waiting for something to happen and simply existing day by day, that was no way to live.

It had literally taken me a year to snap out of a deep depression when Edward passed away. I holed up in my previous home, didn't want to be bothered by anyone; I couldn't work, I couldn't sleep, and eventually lost my job at a Fortune 500 company. If it hadn't been for the insurance money my sweetie left me, over $450,000, I'm not sure how I would have recovered financially. The insurance money was a fresh lease on life. It's how I was able to rebuild my life, open Last Chance, and live out my dream as a business owner.

However, it was easier said than done to completely move on. I still had some of Edward's clothes in the rear of my walk-in closet. I had packed them when I moved from our previous house to my dream home. I simply couldn't make myself pack them up and donate them to the local Goodwill.

Nobia was right, I was a true romantic. I adored being in love and finding my black knight in shining armor. I could honestly say that I truly adored *all* my husbands. I married Malik when I was twenty-five, shortly after my mother died tragically. Brian and I jumped the broom when I turned thirty. My dear Edward, we said our vows when I was thirty-five. Now, here it was coming up on the three-year anniversary of his death and I was now forty years old.

I hadn't had sex in three years and I was horny as hell, all alone on a Friday night with no plans for the weekend. Welcome to my world. It wasn't like I hadn't been approached by men; I was all the time. I wasn't interested in just sex; I had to have a real connection before a man could partake of my creamy goodness. My body was my temple, not a Motel 6 to check in and out at a cheap rate.

I'm a woman, so I still had desires that I could take care of as long as the double-A batteries didn't go dead in my adult toy, but lately, that just wasn't enough. It wasn't hitting the spot, and seeing Jacob in the restaurant, with his hot and sexy body, had me thinking all types of naughty thoughts.

When I stepped out of my twenty-minute bath, and moisturized all over my body with this fabulous Bath and Body lotion, which had me smelling of ginger and oranges all day long, I walked into my bedroom refreshed, and had a big surprise awaiting me.

"Hey, sweetie. What a pleasure surprise," I cooed.

"Are you glad to see me?" he asked seductively, walking toward me. I loved his walk. He didn't walk; he strutted across the room with an air of confidence and masculinity that made you stop and say, "damn."

"Always. I never get enough of you." I literally mewed in his ear before our lips met for a tender, lingering kiss. I pulled away reluctantly after a few seconds.

"That's what I like to hear from my baby. Music to my ears."

His sensual lips found my neck and left a trail of hot, passionate kisses as they made their way around to my mouth. I moaned and took in his warm tongue, enjoying the taste, texture, and feel. I could never get enough of him.

"Hmmm, sweetie. I love what you do to me."

When I wrapped my arms around his neck, my powder blue towel fell to the floor, revealing me in all my divine glory.

"You are a sight to behold," he marveled as he took me in, his eyes never leaving my voluptuous body. Lust shone clearly.

I actually blushed and I never blushed. I was too old for all that.

"You get better with age, like a fine wine." It was hard to believe he was fifty-eight years old.

"Age is nothing but a number, baby," he said.

"You are so handsome, Denzie."

"I love when you call me Denzie." He smiled and stared through me, straight to my soul. I shivered.

"Say it."

"Say what?" he asked, in a deep, husky tone.

"You know. Say your line. You know how that turns me on."

As he reached for my right hand and slowly led me to the queen-sized bed, our eyes never leaving each other, he said it loud and clear, with such passion. I instantly became soft and wet. "'King Kong ain't got shit on me!'"

I swooned. My legs shook. My pussy quivered.

When Mr. Washington entered me a few minutes later, all I could say was, "Oh yesss, Private Trip. Glory. Glory hallelujah."

Carla's in the House

Chapter 7

"Good morning. Good morning. Good morning." I waved and greeted my coworkers as I sashayed into the salon with a lively spring to my step. I had experienced a fabulous Sunday and Monday off, during which I got in some much-needed sexual healing from an out-of-state friend and sponsor. So, I was feeling no pain like Marvin Gaye.

Nobia was at the receptionist counter, checking appointments for the day, and Loretta and Destiny were cleaning their stations, preparing for their first clients to arrive. It was a typical Tuesday morning.

I didn't see Erika.

"Is she here yet?" I questioned, nodding my head toward her office, but addressing no one in particular.

Nobia spoke up. "No, she hasn't arrived yet and I'm worried. I called her home and cell phone, but she didn't pick up."

I didn't comment. I didn't care that much.

"Erika is never late, unlike someone else I know."

I shot daggers her way. "Are you directing those comments toward me?"

Nobia simply smiled that fake-ass smile, the one I wanted to slap off that chubby face at times. I hated the way she constantly kissed Erika's fat ass. It was sickening. I seriously thought she wanted to be Erika.

"A hit dog will holler."

"I know you didn't just call me a dog."

"Ladies, ladies, it is too early for childish bickering," Loretta intervened. "Please, you two are gonna give me a headache before noon." Loretta was our resident mother hen and voice of reason.

"At least I beat her in." I smirked. "I don't have to hear that bitch's mouth going on about punctuality and professionalism."

Nobia didn't utter a word; she pretended to be busy at her desk. I'm sure she was taking notes to report word for word back to her best girlfriend. I didn't care. In fact, I wanted her to repeat it. If she wanted me to, I'd write it down for her in case she missed something.

Destiny looked astonished. "You talk that way about our boss?" she whispered, with her brown eyes as big as saucers.

"Speak for yourself, because Erika is not my boss. What is she going to do about it? I pay her a monthly booth rental, so I can come and go as I please as long as she gets paid. She is a bitch; thinking she's better than everybody else," I said, smacking my minty gum a little too loudly.

"Erika could ask you to leave," Destiny said quietly.

"Please, I wish she would. All the dirt I have on her," I halfway muttered to myself as I walked to the back. "I have enough to fill a sandbox. Wish she would."

In the tiny break room, I placed my lunch in the refrigerator. Mama had given me Sunday leftovers: smothered pork chops with green beans, dirty rice, and a slice of apple pie. I couldn't wait to heat up my plate later and dig in. I went to the bathroom, washed my hands, and mentally planned out my day in my head. I had seven clients, which meant I would probably walk out the door around six or a little after if there weren't any walk-in clients. Lately, Destiny had been taking many of the walk-ins though.

I returned to my station, which was decorated with photo after photo of celebrity clients, just as

Erika stormed through the door. I did a double take and stopped in mid-step. We all did. Girl-friend didn't say a word to anyone, simply threw up her hand as if to say, "Don't say a damn thing to me," and kept it moving straight to her office.

What made everyone stop and stare was what she had on. Girlfriend was dressed from head to toe in black. Now, we all knew black and pink were her favorite colors, but today she was totally rocking black, all the way from her fingernail polish, down to her toenail polish. She had her eyes made up in thick black makeup, which made for a ghostly, gothic appearance.

Erika had her hair pulled up in some kind of tight, matronly bun and, get this, she had a black lace veil covering half her face. Underneath the veil, her lips were outlined in black with black lipstick. When she was safely behind the closed door of her office, we finally picked our mouths up off the floor and breathed. We looked from one to the other, not sure what we had witnessed. Erika could be eccentric, but this was taking it to a new level of the Twilight Zone.

I was the first to speak and break the silence. "That chick cray."

Nobia gave me a mean mug as she started walking away to check on her best friend, but I heard the snickers escape from Destiny and Loretta as we looked at one another in disbelief.

Nobia tapped her forehead and stopped in mid-step. "Man, how could I forget? Today is the three-year anniversary of Edward's death," she said, looking back at us like that was supposed to explain everything.

"Poor baby," Loretta said. "She's going through it."

I clucked my tongue. "Whatever. That chick cray."

Destiny, who was new to the salon, asked, "What happened? Who is Edward?"

"That was her third husband," I said, holding up three fingers for emphasis. "One, two, three . . . husbands."

"Ohhh," she said. "I didn't even know Miss Erika had been married before."

"There's a lot you don't know. Let me bring you up to speed. Edward was the third one to kick the bucket after marrying her ass."

No one said anything for a few seconds.

"Black widow," I quietly spat. "Three dead husbands."

"Carla, why don't you stop telling all Erika's business and spreading rumors? Trying to start trouble. God don't like ugly," Loretta spat.

"I'm telling the truth, Loretta," I snapped. "It's not like I'm making up lies. The truth will set her free."

"What happened?" Destiny asked again, ignoring Loretta.

"According to your boss, Edward suddenly got extremely sick, had flu-like symptoms, and died over a weekend," I shared. "She was by his side the entire time; didn't think to take him to the hospital."

"Wow! I feel sorry for Miss Erika," Destiny said. "I see why she is tripping today."

"Don't," I said. "The half-a-million-dollar insurance policy she cashed in made her feel all better. Don't get it twisted. She's feeling just fine, sitting pretty in that mini-mansion of hers."

About fifteen minutes later, Nobia returned from the back, shaking her head and looking like she was about to burst into tears. Her eyes were red-rimmed and puffy.

"Are you okay?" Loretta asked. "How is she?"

"I don't want to talk about it," Nobia said, and quickly walked to the receptionist desk and buried her head in paperwork.

Destiny looked at me with questions on her face. I shook my head in disdain.

"Today's going to be a long day," I said as my first client walked through the door, carrying two bags of weave in her hand. "That chick cray."

That's What Friends Are For

Chapter 8

I wasn't sure what to expect when I had ventured toward Erika's closed office door. That was some dramatic entrance she had made into the salon. I was stunned, to say the least.

I knocked softly and opened the door. "Hey," I called out, entering her chic space. "Are you okay?"

"Do I look okay, Nobia?" she asked, softly crying as mascara ran down her face as she stared at her blank computer screen. She didn't turn to look at me.

"Well, actually you look like hell if you want to keep it real."

That stopped the sobs as she turned to glare at me. She actually laughed out loud.

"I guess I do look a sight," she volunteered, wiping tears away with the back of her hand.

"Erika, what's going on? This is over-the-top, even for you."

"Today is the three-year anniversary of Edward's death," she said solemnly. "I lost the love of my life."

"I know and I'm sorry, but—"

"But what?" she asked.

"The way you are acting isn't normal and it's not good for your well-being and your mental health."

In an instant, Erika turned and snapped at me with a malicious expression on her face that I had never encountered before.

"How would you know what's good for me? You wouldn't have a clue. You are always yapping, yapping, yapping about what's best for me. Mind your damn business and handle your own."

I was speechless. Erika could have a sassy mouth, but it had never been directed at me, not in this manner.

"I don't need you. I don't need anybody. I can take care of myself as I've been doing for as long as I can remember. My mother was always too busy with her various suitors to worry about what was going on in my life."

I started to turn away, not used to seeing this side of my friend. Maybe it was a mistake to address her regarding her dramatic entrance.

"I'm sorry, Erika. I didn't mean to pry. I was just concerned . . ."

"Fix your household. Start with doing something about your cheating boyfriend who will stick anything that moves. Handle that. Fix that."

Erika must have seen the hurt register on my face because she promptly stopped ranting and raving like a lunatic. She dropped her head in shame.

"Nobia, I'm so sorry. I'm so sorry. I'm not sure what came over me. I'm not in my right state of mind today."

I remained silent, stared at the floor.

"Please forgive me. You are the best friend I have ever had and I do appreciate you, even though I may not tell you often enough. I know you truly care about me," she moaned, pleading now.

Erika stopped talking when I wouldn't respond and she started to cry again. Quiet sobs.

"I can't lose you. I can't. I always lose people I love. I always drive away people. What's wrong with me?"

I sighed. "Girl, I'm not going anywhere." I moved swiftly to her side. "Now, stop all that damn crying. You don't look like the fabulous diva you are with snot running out of your nose."

She looked embarrassed. "Are they talking about me out there?" she asked, pointing to the front of the salon and reaching for a tissue. "They just don't understand."

"Well . . ."

"I knew they were," she said, with a sadness in her voice. "I guess I gave them every reason to."

"You think?" I laughed.

"I love you, Nobia."

"I love you too, girl. Listen, why don't I drive you home so you can change?" I offered.

"Okay. I guess I do look like a fool."

"You think?"

I finally got a smile out of her.

"I'll be up front." I started to walk out, still unsure as to what had just transpired.

"Nobia, I don't deserve you as a friend. You should know that. You are good and genuine and I'm just . . ."

"Girl, stop all that nonsense. Come get me when you are ready."

"I will."

"And, Erika?"

"Yes?"

"Take that damn veil and black lipstick off."

Lord Have Mercy on Me, It's Me, Loretta

Chapter 9

I wasn't one to talk and gossip about my employer because I didn't believe in biting the hand that fed me. My goal was to work for Miss Erika as long as I could. At sixty, I wasn't getting any younger and I knew my days in the beauty industry were limited. Don't get me wrong, I looked good for my age and could compete any day with any young'un. I had class and grace and maturity, older women loved me as well as their precious grandchildren.

I had learned from experience that the best thing to do was your job and keep your mouth closed, at least when it came to coworkers and gossip. I had seen too many employees come and go because of it over the years. Carla hadn't learned that lesson yet, or maybe she didn't care. That girl had a lot of mouth and attitude; she spoke many times without thinking. That was the problem with some of these young women, but the difference was that I knew Carla spoke the truth, at least partially anyway, with regard to Erika.

I may be older and Erika thought I didn't see things, but I did. I saw and heard quite a lot. I was more mature, but I wasn't an old fool. It took a lot to pull the wool over my eyes. The only one who had anything pulled over their eyes was Nobia. That child was sweet, but so naïve. Bless her heart.

I couldn't say that Erika didn't have me fooled in the beginning, though. She had. Up until recently, I overlooked snatches of conversation I had heard even though they didn't add up. I knew that one plus one didn't equal three, but I tried to come up with rational, logical explanations. Then one night, not too long ago, it all made sense. Actually, it was the week before the shop received the big makeover and we all received two weeks of paid vacation.

I finally understood why Reverend Hill was always at the salon. Evidently, he was picking up more than his monthly canned donations. I tried not to think about it because I didn't want to have a heart attack at just the mere imagery that came to mind.

It was late evening and, for once, I was the last to leave the salon. Destiny's boyfriend had picked her up with a stick up his ass and Carla had left over an hour ago, rushing off for a big date. I swear that child went through men like most of us went through stockings. Nobia typically left at five o'clock each day. As usual, Erika was behind closed doors, in her office.

I'm not a young bird anymore and I had quite a drive home each evening, so I always made a point to use the bathroom before I left. My bladder wasn't what it used to be and I didn't want to take any chances. Atlanta was known for its traffic and gridlock issues. Erika had a private bathroom, off from her office. It was adjacent to the public bathroom, the one we used, along with clients. The only thing separating the two bathrooms was adjoining doors. You could walk from our bathroom, and then come to another door, which was her bathroom. On her side was yet another door, which led into her office.

Typically, the door that led to her bathroom and office were kept locked with padlocks, but now that remodeling was going to start soon, everything was in disarray. I had done my duty, was washing my hands, preparing to leave when I heard it, loud and clear. Crying. Someone was clearly in dire distress.

I knew Reverend Hill had dropped by earlier to discuss important church matters with Erika. Seemed like he always had something to discuss. They were in her office, behind closed doors, but that didn't strike me as odd because he was our pastor, and growing up, I was taught to respect men of the cloth and their spiritual connection to God.

I knew Erika had strong spiritual ties because she was in church each and every Sunday, second pew, front and center, and she did so much for our church. She was highly respected and loved by most. There were some who whispered behind her back about the tragic endings to her marriages. People will gossip and they did. Erika was a favorite topic of conversation.

Then I heard it again. I found myself walking through to her bathroom. I couldn't help but feel sorry for her. *Poor baby, probably crying on the Reverend's shoulder or maybe he is praying with her again.* I knew she was going through some things; she had been, on and off, for the last few years. I ventured to the door, now unlocked, that led from her bathroom to her office, with every intention of knocking and saying good night. Perhaps joining in prayer and seeing if I could be of assistance. Something stopped me before I lifted my fist to knock.

Maybe it was divine intervention. I pressed my ear to the door when I heard loud moans, not cries. I was confused. Without thinking, I slowly eased the door ajar, just a few inches, not sure what I would see on the other side, and I got the shock of my life.

"Sister, let it go. Let it go. Release it in the name of Jesus," our pastor said from between her spread legs. His pants and boxers were pulled down around his knees. "Merciful God, hear her cries."

I gasped and quickly covered my mouth with my hand. My heartbeat sped up and beads of sweat broke out on my forehead.

"You know what I like," Erika called out as he pulled her red silk blouse open farther, and cast aside her red lacy bra; a few buttons tumbled to the floor. Her ample breasts came flopping out and he wasted no time burying his face and tongue within their confines. All I heard for a few seconds was sucking and groaning sounds.

Reverend suckled one breast as he caressed the other and stroked a nipple with his thumb. He alternated by gently stroking between her wide spread legs. Erika was naked from the waist down and I saw her skirt and panties strewn haphazardly across the floor.

Reverend took his time as he eased his thick fingers inside her. In and out. Out and in. Varying the speed. He was very familiar with her body. As she moaned, eyes closed, she held on to his private tool, firmly stroking it up and down.

They were a sight to see. I wanted to leave, but my feet wouldn't cooperate. I held on to the wall, willing myself not to slink to the floor below.

"You have such big, beautiful breasts," he said, touching and prodding.

"Hmmm," Erika said, moving around on the fingers still inside her.

"I want you to suck my dick like you did the last time, sister."

Erika nodded like a child would. I had never seen her submissive.

"God doesn't want you to be alone, sister. It's okay for a man of God, such as myself, to give you pleasure. Have faith that I'm here for as long as you need me. I'll take care of all your needs."

"Thank you, Reverend."

"You like that don't you?" he asked in a soothing, calm voice full of lust and desire. His voice was almost hypnotic.

"Hmmm."

"No, God doesn't want his children to be in pain. He wants you to be happy and fulfilled," he said, slowly pulling his fingers from her va-ja-ja and inserting them into her mouth.

"Yes, God spoke to me and he wants me to make that pussy feel good."

Erika licked his fingers clean as he bent once again to nibble on a nipple. He must have bit down a little too hard because she yelped in pain. I watched in disbelief as he twisted a nipple between his two fingers.

"Yeah, you like that." He cooed into her left ear. "It's all right if you enjoy a little pain, sister. Let God cleanse your soul."

Reverend twisted the other nipple, which immediately perked up like an overripe blackberry. He looked at her and grinned with lust-filled eyes.

"Oh, yes."

"Hmmm," was her response. Erika was still sucking his fingers and licking up the sides.

"Do you believe that God has blessed our union?" he asked, looking deep within her eyes as he stimulated her even more.

Erika nodded again.

"That's a good Christian woman," he purred, continuing to caress her breasts.

"Now, I'm going to make you come so you will feel better, but first I need you to get on your knees and suck my dick. Would you like that?"

Erika smacked her lips and reached for his tool.

Reverend helped her out of the chair, pulled her blouse completely off and slowly lowered her to her knees. Erika complied. The last thing I saw was her opening her mouth to receive his tool, which was now so erect that it was pointing straight at her.

"Take it all in. Praise God, sister."

"Suck it, sister. Awww, good Lord. Suck it."

"Awww, dear Jesus, bless this sister. Make her whole again. Let her know that she's not alone."

"Good God. Hear my voice. Hear my prayer. Ohhh, damn. I mean ohhhh, Lord."

"Open your legs wider, sister. Dear God, you are so wet," he said, stirring her with his thick fingers, two at a time. "You've got some sweet, sweet pussy. Lord, help me. Help me, Lord. I can't get enough of this sweet, sweet, tight pussy."

"Come here. Hurry, sister."

Erika, as directed, turned so that her butt was hoisted in the air. I had seen enough. I rushed out of there as fast as my feet would take me but not before I saw him bend down to lick her ass with his tongue, then bury his thick tool inside her.

"Dear merciful Lord. Merciful, glorious Jesus. Ohhh, God, yesss!"

Chapter 10

I encountered Carla in the break room later that day, finishing up her lunch. She had the room smelling like Sunday dinner and my stomach growled and my mouth watered up involuntarily. The morning had flown by super fast, especially after the earlier drama. That's what I liked best about working in the salon; there was never a dull moment. The clients kept it interesting and there was always juicy gossip to hear from them about people we didn't know and would probably never meet. However, I didn't appreciate the fact that Carla was sharing Erika's personal business to anyone who would listen.

Since we were alone, I figured now would be as good a time as any to speak with her privately.

"Carla, may I speak with you for a moment?"

She turned around, surprised, like she just realized I had walked in the room and was actually speaking to her.

"About what?" she asked with her usual attitude. "I'm on my lunch break."

I didn't waste words. "You need to tone it down with all the comments about Erika. It's neither appropriate nor professional."

She stared at me like I was speaking a foreign language.

"Excuse me?" Carla dropped her fork. "Nobia, I know you worship the ground Erika walks on, but I don't. If you'd take off those colored blinders, maybe you could see."

"See what?"

"You really just don't get it, do you?" she asked, shaking her head.

"I guess I don't," I said, frowning. "I certainly don't understand why you've been out to get Erika since you started working here. What's the deal?"

"I don't like fake-ass people."

"You can't possibly be talking about the Erika I know and love because she is the most caring, nurturing, and giving person I have ever met. We've been friends for over three and a half years now and I have never seen anything different."

"That's what she wants you to think."

"Are you really that malicious, Carla? Do you hear yourself? You sound crazy."

"Nobia, believe it or not, I like you and I don't want you to get hurt. From the outside looking in, I know you are impressed with Erika's designer clothes, purses, and shoes. I know you admire her elegant home and her expensive, shiny car. She does appear to have it all, but looks can be deceiving. That's all I'm saying."

I stared back at her in disbelief. "Are you really that bitter that she married your ex-boyfriend, Brian?"

Carla was very light-skinned and her face and neck immediately reddened at the mention of her ex. I guess the truth did hurt, still. I would have laughed out loud if it weren't for the expression that crossed her pretty face.

"Yeah, I know all about that."

For once, Carla didn't have anything to say.

"Erika told me that you used to date Brian before she came into the picture. Get over it. Accept the fact that he chose her and they became man and wife."

"And where did that get him?" she asked, finally getting her feisty voice back.

I remained silent.

"Six feet under. Besides you don't know the half of it, so butt out, Nobia. Mind your own business. You are not Erika's keeper."

"But that still doesn't negate the fact that Brian chose her. Over you. She stole your boyfriend and you never even saw it coming," I said as my final words as I walked out the door.

That shut her down for the rest of the day. I failed to mention that Erika had also told me to always keep your enemies close when I asked her why she had hired Carla to begin with.

Destiny's Last Chance

Chapter 11

Mid-October blew in with brilliant shades of orange and browns. I had been working at Last Chance for over three months now. I liked the salon. I liked the women who came in and my coworkers. At work, I was happy and content.

There was never a dull moment because the clients were entertaining all by themselves. People will say the darnedest things when they are relaxed, pampered, and have let their guard down. I always felt like a fly on the wall as they talked about their lives and careers. Even though I was only in my early twenties, sometimes I felt much older, like I was missing out on life.

Thanks to Carla, I had gotten the opportunity to meet local celebrities, mostly basketball wives and reality stars. I still couldn't believe I was standing next to Lil Scrappy a week ago when he dropped by to pick up his soon-to-be wife, Erica.

I tried not to act star struck. Loretta brought in the children, teenagers, and more mature women who fit to her skill set. I was still trying to figure out exactly where I fit in. Mostly, I received walk-in clients and a few of my former clients who had followed me from my last salon, where my boyfriend, Ray, had gotten me fired with his foolishness.

Loretta, with her elegance and class, reminded me of that actress from back in the day. I think her name was Diahann Carroll. My mama used to talk about her all the time. Carla reminded me of the celebrity LaLa a little bit. She was tall and light-skinned just like her, but Carla was off the chain. And Miss Erika, I simply adored her. I didn't pay any attention to the gossip mill or what Carla had to say. Erika reminded me of an older version of Toccara Jones from *America's Next Top Model*. She was always dressed to the tee and she had the flawless beauty of a model. That left me. If I had to place myself with a celebrity look-alike, I guess I'd say I was a young Meagan Good.

As I was saying, Miss Erika was cool with me. She was one of the sweetest, kindest people I had ever met. Take the other evening when I was at the bus stop; anyone else would have kept going, but she stopped.

"Destiny! Destiny!"

I turned.

"Hey, Miss Erika," I said shyly.

"What are you doing at the bus stop? Where's your car?"

"My boyfriend, Ray, has it and I couldn't reach him on his cell. I live off a bus route, so it's not a problem."

I saw her eyebrows arch up in disapproval, but she didn't offer a comment. I knew she wasn't fond of Ray. I had noticed how she reacted whenever he came into the salon.

"Get in the car. I'll drive you home, Destiny."

"I live all the way in Decatur. I can wait on the bus. I don't want you to go out of your way."

"Destiny, get in the car. Honestly, I don't mind. I don't care if you live all the way in Kennesaw; I'm not driving off and leaving you out here waiting on a bus."

My heart melted. I wasn't used to people doing nice things for me. My life hadn't exactly been rainbows and roses. I opened the passenger door and slid in, thankful. Her car was so nice and I sank into the soft leather seat; it still had a new-car smell. I imagined myself driving a car just like it one day.

"I don't like you riding the bus late at night. You never know if strangers are watching you as you wait for it, or following you when you get off. Next time—hopefully there won't be a next time—let me know. I'm happy to take you home, Destiny."

I remained silent.

"Okay?" she asked, looking over at me.

"Sure."

"Why does your boyfriend have your car anyway?" she asked, clearly annoyed.

I lied. "His is in the shop and he had some important business to take care of today."

"Uh huh," she replied. "I bet he did."

We drove a little farther in silence.

"Oh, I just remembered. Reach into my dashboard and pull out that black jewelry bag."

I did as instructed and pulled out a satin black pouch.

"It's yours if you want it."

"What is it?" I asked curiously.

"Look inside."

I pulled on the drawstring and inside were various pieces of costume jewelry, expensive costume jewelry. It contained everything from earrings, rings, to bracelets, chokers, and necklaces.

"I was cleaning out my armoire and I thought you might like these pieces. If not, I'll probably take them to a consignment shop."

"Yes, I do. Thank you," I said, clutching the pouch near my chest. "There are such pretty pieces in here. You have such good taste, Miss Erika. I always admire how you dress at the salon and you come in sharp every day."

"Thank you. By the way, you are doing a great job at the salon. Several clients have complimented you, and Nobia, Loretta, and Carla adore you."

"Thank you."

"Keep up the good work, Destiny. I knew I made a wise decision in hiring you."

"I love styling hair and I'd like to own my own shop someday. Like you. My mama always said I was a natural. I've been doing my own hair, my mama's, and family members' since I was twelve."

"Wow, you do have a natural ability. Let me know what I can do to help make your dream come true. I officially declare myself your mentor."

We laughed.

"And I officially accept," I said.

"Good, and I'm very serious. How long have you and Ray been dating?"

"About two years now," I said, glancing in her direction after she abruptly changed the subject.

"What does he do?"

"Well, huh, right now he is in between jobs."

"I see. What does he do when he is working?"

"Construction."

"You know, you remind me a lot of myself when I was your age. So, I'm going to give you a piece of advice. The same advice my mama gave me and it hasn't failed me yet. Don't ever let a man bring you down. You can do bad all by yourself. Do you understand?"

I nodded and, for some reason, I wasn't offended.

"If he can't be an asset, then you don't need him."

We rode along in more silence, almost at the exit ramp for I20-E.

"Are you getting enough walk-in clients?" Erika asked.

"It could be better."

"It will come. You've only been with us a few months. I'm going to ask Carla to let you go with her, as an assistant, to some of her hair shows. We need to get you out there. Visibility is key. Remember you want your own salon one day."

I beamed. Erika looked over at me and winked.

Right as we neared the exit ramp for the interstate, Erika said, "You know what? I'm starving and I don't like to dine alone. Let's go grab a bite to eat."

I hesitated. I knew I had less than five dollars to my name in my wallet and that had to get me through the next couple of days.

"It's on me. There's a fabulous Asian restaurant that serves all-you-can-eat crab legs and I have a taste for some. I have to warn you, I go absolutely crazy eating them. You in?"

"I'm in."

"They have these delicious mini eggrolls stuffed with shrimp that are to die for, and they have three or four different salads to choose from; I always have the Greek with feta cheese, cucumbers, and olives. Delicious."

I chuckled. "It sounds wonderful."

"Well, let's go do some damage."

The British Are Coming.
The British Are Coming.

Chapter 12

I was awakened in the wee morning hours with sweet kisses showered upon my sleepy face. At first I was confused and disoriented. I had no idea where I was or what was happening. Apparently, I had fallen asleep in the midst of watching *Criminal Minds,* one of my favorite shows on television. I enjoyed seeing that fine Derek Morgan, played by Shemar Moore, each and every week. Plus, I loved the quotes they started and ended the shows with. One of my favorites: "It was once said that love is giving someone the ability to destroy you, but trusting them not to."

And then, I saw him.

"Hello, baby."

"Hello," I whispered, enjoying the chocolate picture of delicious perfection before me. I couldn't get enough of dark-skinned men; I thought they were the most beautiful creatures on earth.

"You look gorgeous when you sleep. You know that?" he asked, crawling into bed beside me, completely nude. The slither of light that came through the venetian blinds from the outside street light cast him in a glowing silhouette. He looked like a god to me.

As I propped myself up on a pillow, I was suddenly wide awake. Every pore in my body was suddenly yearning for his touch.

"You are perfect. You know that. Absolutely perfect. I can't find one damn thing wrong with you. And I've tried."

"Erika, thank you, but I'm by no means perfect," he said in that smooth, sexy British accent. I could listen to him speak for days. His words caressed my ears and gave me eargasms.

"Lovely," he stated, releasing a breast from within the confines of my gown. My nipple instantly responded to his touch. I couldn't pull my eyes off him. He was such a manly man.

A deep, guttural moan escaped. "You make me so hot, Idris."

Pulling up my thin cotton gown and touching between my thighs, he asked, "Are you sure you aren't boiling, my love?"

I simply melted. I swooned over how it sounded when he called me "my love."

"You are probably right. I go from simmer to boil within milliseconds when I'm around you. All you have to do is glance in my direction and I'm wet."

"You're sweet," he seductively whispered, kissing along my neckline. I shivered. I trembled in anticipation when I felt the moist tip of his dick make contact with my rear end. He had exactly what I needed tonight and it was big, thick, and erect.

"Tell me why you like me so much." He placed a nipple in his warm mouth and gently sucked.

"That's easy, you're sexy chocolate, have a confident swagger, you're handsome and I quiver every time I hear that sexy accent, and you know how to put it down in the bedroom," I said, barely able to get it all out.

Idris smiled, pleased with my answer. Two fingers were inside now, working me to a slow frenzy.

"What character do you want me to be tonight?"

I didn't even have to think about it. I wanted Stringer. I needed some "down and dirty, let me fuck you until you can't walk in the morning. Let me fuck you so when you think about it, you'll come again. Let me fuck you so good that just the mention of my name makes you wet."

"Stringer," I said with a smile, like I was ordering a Super Size meal at McDonald's. Coming in a close second would have been Monty James from *Daddy's Little Girls*.

Ten minutes in, literally, I was speaking in tongues.

I'm About to Throw Some Bows

Chapter 13

Another Friday had rolled through like a spring rainstorm in Georgia. Suddenly, expected, but in the blink of an eye. Loretta, Carla, and I were working on clients' hair and Nobia was putting the finishing touches on advertising flyers we planned to hand out at the local malls and shopping centers as we did once a month.

Everyone was in a relatively good mood. I knew I couldn't complain because business had been excellent recently and our clientele continued to steadily grow. I was blessed. I realized I owed a lot of the growth to my staff, their expertise, skills, and entertaining personalities. I enjoyed doing something I loved and it was an added bonus that Last Chance was all mine. It was liberating and I could only thank my dear departed Edward for listing me as a beneficiary on his life insurance policy.

I could honestly say I eagerly arose for work each morning. Before Last Chance, I had done it all: retail manager, substitute teacher, marketing manager, and insurance claims adjuster. When I was younger, I had even worked briefly in an automotive repair shop. None of those jobs were as fulfilling as what I had now.

"Where's Destiny?" Carla asked. "When is she rolling up in here?"

"Destiny called in to say she was running a little late, but she'll be here," I said. Carla and I had an unspoken truce that we would be civil to each other at least 90 percent of the time.

"Her first client isn't due for another hour," Nobia volunteered.

"By the way, baby girl did an excellent job assisting me at the hair show the other day," Carla replied, taking tracks of strawberry-blond weave out of its plastic packaging. She was going to add highlights at her client's request.

I smiled like a proud mother. I may have even stuck my chest out a bit farther. "Destiny is working out well."

"She does good work, very conscientious for such a young woman," Loretta added.

Nobia came over, standing near my station. "Could y'all believe that Usher went on Oprah's OWN and admitted he sometimes makes love to his own songs?"

"I'll 'Dive' with him any day." Carla chuckled. "But can you say narcissism?"

Laughter erupted.

"Erika, did you hear that your boy DMX is coming out with a new CD?" Loretta asked, looking over at me.

"I heard and I'll be one of the first to purchase it. I love me some DMX with that bald head and raspy voice. I'm his number one fan."

Loretta and her matronly client chuckled knowingly.

"Erika, you never cease to surprise me. You can quote a biblical scripture on one hand and have a celebrity crush on a thug rapper on the other," Nobia noted.

"Back in the day, he was fine," I said. "Evidently, you never saw the movie *Belly*."

"She craves that dark chocolate," Carla said, looking at me like she was daring me to deny it. I didn't know what was up with her lately. More than once, I had caught her staring at me, but at least we weren't coming at each other with claws bared.

"He could still do me," Loretta's client, a mature, gray-haired woman said, nonchalantly flipping through a hair magazine.

We all broke into laughter.

"X gonna give it to ya," I chanted. "He gon' give it to ya."

"No, thank you, I'll pass, but if that fine-ass Michael Ealy ever walks through those doors, go ahead and call nine-one-one because I'm going to be arrested for multiple counts of rape," Carla said, cracking up everyone as usual. "Every time I hear 'Tonight (Best You Ever Had),' I start having flashbacks from the Steve Harvey movie."

"Loretta, who is your celebrity crush? You are always so composed and subdued. Who makes you hot?" Nobia asked. "It has to be someone."

I swear Loretta blushed bright as a red, ripe beet.

"I'd have to say the one and only Mr. Billy Dee Williams. Y'all wouldn't know nothing about that."

"Whew, she took it wayyyyy back, straight old school with that one," I said and we started snickering.

"Billy Dee Williams? Mr. Colt 45 beer, Billy Dee Williams?" Carla's client asked.

"Billy Dee Williams, 'You want my arm to fall off' from *Lady Sings the Blues*."

"Okay, I don't know about all that, but I'll give it to him, he was sexy in *Mahogany*," Carla said. "He and Diana Ross had great chemistry on screen."

About that time the front door opened and all eyes were averted in that direction. It was Destiny and she was a sight to behold. I instantly lost my laughter and it was replaced with outright anger.

"Oh my God, what happened?" Loretta asked, as we all saw the split lip and swollen puffy eye at the same time.

"Oh, it's nothing. Clumsy me. I tripped over my own feet and tumbled down the stairs at home," she shared, staring at the floor the entire time she explained what supposedly happened.

"Do you need us to take you to the hospital?" Carla asked, looking visibly shaken. "You look like you need medical attention, baby girl."

"No! No! I'm fine. I'll be okay. I'm going to finish up a few scheduled clients and then leave early for the day."

I placed my client under the dryer and watched Destiny struggle to walk to her station, obviously in pain. I swiftly rushed over to get a closer look at the damage.

"Destiny, who did this to you?" I asked a bit too loudly. Suddenly, all eyes were on us. It was so quiet you could hear a pin drop.

"What?" I asked, looking around. "You are all thinking it. I'm just saying it out loud for once. I'm sick of pretending we haven't seen the bruises before today. This has to stop. Who did this? Ray?"

"No, Miss Erika," she whispered, averting her eyes again. "I told you, I slipped and fell."

I snapped. "Fell my ass. His fist *fell* against your face. Destiny, don't let that motherfucker use your pretty face as a punching bag."

I realized I was making a spectacle of myself and clearly embarrassing Destiny, but I couldn't help myself. There was something about men putting their hands on a woman that set me off. I had grown up watching my mom and aunts go through changes at the fists of weak-ass men. I decided that would never be me. Never. Ever.

"You deserve so much better than Ray. He doesn't value you or respect you."

"Miss Erika, please," she called out weakly.

"That sick motherfucker. Did he drop you off in your own damn car again today?"

Destiny didn't respond. I could feel she wanted to slink under the floor and disappear, but I couldn't stop myself even if I wanted to. I had my mother's temper.

"You know he's fucking some skank while you are in here working? I would bet my life on it. He couldn't possibly love you and do this to you, Destiny," I said, throwing my hands up.

"Please, don't end up another statistic. I don't want to turn on the news one night and see your face staring back at me as a murder victim and, whatever you do, don't let him knock you up," I cried.

I realized I was making a complete fool of myself, but I couldn't control my rant. I was on a roll and, besides, I had my mother's sharp tongue.

"Ray's not worth it. Tonight, he'll try to be extra sweet, talking about what *you* made him do, how he loves you so much and can't live without you, and how it won't happen again. Bullshit. It will, Destiny. I promise you it will."

Carla, Loretta, and Nobia dropped their heads while clients looked on in astonishment.

"Tell her, Nobia." I was desperate for someone to back me up and make Destiny see that she needed to get away from Ray before it was too late.

"Come on, Erika," Nobia said. "Let's discuss it later. In private. When you have calmed down."

"Ray will cry on your shoulder and fuck you so good that you'll think his dick is a magic wand, but don't believe the hype. If he hits you once, he will do it again. And again, and again. And one day, you won't get up from it. Either you will be dead, or your broken spirit won't allow it."

"Come on, Erika. I'll let you know when your client is dry and ready to come from under the dryer," Nobia said, leading me away to my office by the elbow like I was a small child.

"Destiny, heed my words," I said, looking back as I was led away.

After Nobia led me to my office and closed the door, after pacing back and forth, back and forth, I finally calmed down to a mild simmer. I was able to finish up my client's hair and sent her on her way. I remained in my office for most of the morning after that, not because I was embarrassed, but because I couldn't stand to see Destiny bruised and battered. She had managed to put on sunglasses to cover the damage to her eye.

Around lunchtime I was trying to figure out what I would order from the Chinese restaurant down the street. I had a taste for shrimp fried rice, an egg roll, and some chicken chow mein; maybe even some egg drop soup. Suddenly I heard commotion in the front and I curiously ventured out to check out what was going on and causing the disturbance in my salon.

"Destiny, I've been sitting in that fucking car for thirty minutes. Bring your ass on," her boyfriend Ray screamed as he stood near the front door in a hoodie and black jeans that hung below his waist, showing his dingy boxers.

"Baby, I'm almost finished. Just wait in the car," Destiny said quietly and timidly, clearly frightened. "I'll be right out."

I swiftly walked to the front. Every step I took, I felt like one of those cartoon characters with smoke fuming out of my nose and ears. I had tunnel vision because everyone in the salon but Ray had disappeared. It was me and Ray and it was on.

"Ray? Oh hell no! You have the nerve to show your face. You are not going to walk up in my business ranting and raving like a lunatic. Get the hell out of here. Now."

The expression that crossed his face was one of utter surprise. He was clearly taken aback that a female was stepping to him like I was.

"I'll leave when I'm damn ready. And I'm not going anywhere without Destiny."

"You are going to leave, the easy way or the hard way, but you will leave."

"Bitch, shut the fuck up," he screamed, coming my way with balled fists at his sides. "Who in the hell do you think you are?"

"I'm not your bitch, bitch, and if you lay one finger on me, I'll have your pathetic, weak ass behind bars so quick you won't know what happened. Get it straight, don't get it twisted; I'm not Destiny."

"You'd better go sit your fat ass down before I knock you down if you know what's good for you."

"Try me, motherfucker. This fat ass has more punch than you might think," I said, walking the short distance right up to his face and making eye contact. We were so close that I could smell the beer on his smelly breath.

Ray hesitated, looking from one to the other of the scared faces that stared back at him.

"Erika, do you want me to call the police?" Nobia asked, finally snapping out of shock and picking up the phone, ready to hit 911.

"No, this motherfucker is going to walk away peacefully after he gives Destiny her car keys."

Ray laughed a bitter, cold laugh that chilled me to the bone.

"You are out of your mind, bitch. You evidently don't know who you are fucking with."

"No, obviously you don't know who you are fucking with."

Ray started walking toward the door, turning his back to me. Dismissing me. "You ladies have a good day. Destiny, your ass better be outside in five minutes; we'll finish this at home and you know what's coming."

"Patrick O'Bryan, 404-555-1212," I shouted.

Ray stopped dead in his tracks and slowly turned back around. If looks could kill, I would have been dead on the spot.

"Give Destiny her car keys, Ray. I know all about you. I've done my research and I know you wouldn't want me to call your probation officer, Mr. O'Bryan. That wouldn't be good for you," I said between clenched teeth.

The look he gave me was priceless. Even in his intoxicated state, he knew I had him by the balls and I was squeezing extra hard.

"This isn't over."

"Oh, but it is, Ray. You are going to crawl away quietly, like the snake that you are, without those keys. If you bother Destiny, or ever step foot in my salon again, I'm going to turn over to the authorities the video tape that just recorded your stupid ass," I said, pointing to the far corner of the ceiling. He looked up.

"Smile. You are on *Candid Camera*."

"Bitch."

"This bitch has you by the balls. Every client in here will testify against you, and I'll turn in the photos of what your fist did to her face," I stated, pointing in Destiny's direction.

She was frozen in place like a deer caught in the headlights of an oncoming car.

Ray threw the keys in my direction; tried to hit me in the face but missed.

"That's a good mutt. Now get the fuck out of my salon. Men like you make me sick to my stomach; weak-assed, bitch-ass punks who get off on hitting helpless women. How many times did you come, Ray? Once? Twice? You're a coward and a loser. Now get. Go back to the dark, slimy hole you crawled out of."

He took three steps and hesitated, glaring back at me. Anger wasn't even close to what I saw.

"Do something. I dare you. I double dare you. I have friends who will fuck your ass up so bad that your own mama wouldn't recognize your ugly face lying in your cheap coffin. Make me call them."

"Fuck you, bitch," he said as he finally exited the salon in a rage.

Every client in the place exhaled and excited chatter started at once.

"That's what I thought," I screamed out. I crossed the short distance to Destiny. "Are you okay?"

Destiny shook her head.

"Don't go home tonight. Do you have any-where you can stay? If not, you can crash with me."

Destiny didn't respond as she was visibly shaken. I placed my arms tightly around her, until the trembling stopped.

"Tomorrow, first thing, I want you to take out a restraining order on Ray. Now, let's go in my office so I can take photos of your face."

Destiny followed slowly beside me.

"I think it is over now. I have too much information that could send him back to jail."

"How did you know?"

"I make it my business to know everything about everyone," I said matter-of-factly. "We need to get you set up in another apartment ASAP—a gated community."

"I can't afford that."

I hushed her with my right hand. "Let me handle all that. Don't worry about a thing because everything is going to be fine. I'll make sure of it."

And I always kept my promises.

High Tea

Chapter 14

I was surprised and caught off-guard when Erika called me into her office. That office was her sacred spot and we, her staff, were seldom asked to enter its sanctuary, with the exception of Nobia.

"Loretta, have a seat. By the way, I love your hair that way," she said with a sweet smile.

"Thank you." Erika was wearing a chic short bob and a designer suit that hugged her curves. "I'm loving that suit, Erika."

"Thank you. Just a little something I found in the back of my closet this morning," she said smugly. "It still had the price tag and I had forgotten all about it and what a ridiculous amount I paid for it."

I nodded.

"I guess you are wondering why I asked to speak with you in private?"

"I am curious."

"I wanted to talk to you about an idea I'm considering."

"Okay," I said as flashbacks of her and Reverend Hill suddenly played before my eyes. I could barely look at Erika. All I could picture was her with the reverend's tool in her mouth and him sending praises up to heaven as he fondled her breasts.

"Are you all right?"

"Yes," I said, shaking my head to clear my thoughts. I offered a weak smile.

Erika looked at me curiously. "What do you think? I'd like to have a luncheon, an appreciation luncheon to be exact, for the ladies of the church." She paused for effect, clearly excited. "And I'd like for you to co-host it with me. Of course, I'd pick up all the incurred expenses."

I stared at her, still in flashback mode. I had had many restless, lost nights of sleep over the scene that I innocently walked into. I couldn't figure Erika out. On one hand, she was one of the most caring, giving people I knew. Yet, she'd willingly fall into the arms of a married man and a preacher, a man of the Lord, at that. And what about the other day when she flipped out and was going to beat Ray's ass, and she probably would have?

"I think it's a wonderful idea." And I really did.

"Me too," she said, clapping her hands together like an excited child about to start a great adventure.

"The women of our church do so much without much recognition in terms of outings or events catered just for them. I want them to feel special, even if it's for a few hours. We are literally superwomen. We work nine to five, volunteer in our community, cook dinner every night, own businesses, nurture and raise our kids, are lovers, friends, et cetera. We wear many hats."

"Very true. I couldn't agree more."

"I was thinking of calling it High Tea and we could rent out a fabulous venue, dress up in fancy hats and dresses mid-to-late afternoon, and have a real tea party with bite-sized sandwiches, scones and sweets and, of course, tea." She paused to catch her breath. "How does that sound?"

"I like it. Actually, I think it's an excellent idea."

"You are such a gracious, classy lady that I thought you would be perfect as a co-host. Are you interested?"

"Of course. Count me in," I said.

"Great. I can't wait."

"Me either. Sounds like fun."

Loretta's Conclusion

Chapter 15

A few days later, I literally heard Erika before I saw her approach the front. She had on four-inch red stilettos with a bow on the back of each shoe. Sharp. However, I never understood how she could strut around in those shoes all day long; I knew I'd break my neck if I even tried. Plus, I had long ago traded beauty for comfort. Erika had paired them with a black dress that flared out from the waist and she sported a medium-length black wig that had a body wave that looked really good on her.

"Anybody want anything?" she asked. "I'm walking to the corner convenience store for a cherry ICEE."

There were only myself and my client in the salon at the moment and she declined the offer. It was midday and Carla's clients weren't due for another hour or so. Destiny was out, and Nobia had stepped out for a few minutes to run an errand.

My client had brought in a photo of a celebrity thirty years her junior and she wanted the exact same hairstyle. She failed to notice she didn't have half the head of hair that the actress had, nor would the style do her any justice. I could only laugh inside, try to work with what I had, and convince her of a more age-appropriate, suitable style. Personally, I thought women of a certain age should mature gracefully and not try to look like a young'un.

"How is she?" she asked as soon as Erika cleared the threshold of the door.

I paused in curling a section of her hair. "What do you mean?"

"What is it like working with Erika?"

"I have no complaints. She's fair."

"I have heard so many interesting stories about her."

"Really?" I said, not willing to take it any further. I refused to gossip about my employer.

"What's she like?"

"Like everybody else. Surviving day-to-day."

That didn't deter my client. "I heard she has been married about five times and all of them died tragically," she said in a conspiratorial whisper, looking back at me. "Is it true that the police investigated her and seriously questioned the deaths?"

"Erika has been married three times," I said nonchalantly. "There are many actresses in Hollywood who have been married more times than that."

"And?"

"And, what?" I asked, knowing full well what she was fishing for.

"What happened to them?"

"I honestly don't know all the details." I really didn't. I had heard the rumors just like everybody else. Erika rarely discussed her deceased husbands and it was an unspoken rule not to bring them up around her.

"But they did die?"

"Yes. And she was investigated and cleared after the police didn't find evidence against her to support foul play in any death."

"Ump. Interesting. Why does she wear black all the damn time? Almost every time I come in here she is in black."

"I don't know. I guess it's her favorite color, just like blue is yours."

"She's a strange one to me, girl. You better watch your back and keep both eyes wide-open."

"Erika and I don't have any problems. There's a mutual respect. She's actually a great boss. Believe me, I've had much worse."

"Ump," she grunted, flipping through a glossy style magazine that showcased the newest trends in hairstyles across the country.

"Girl, I heard about what happened in here the other day."

I thought, *who hasn't?* "Really?" I asked again.

"Yes, girl, everyone is talking about it and what went down. I thought this was supposed to be a classy salon, not some ghetto shop that brought in thugs from the street."

"It was unfortunate that the incident occurred, but I personally admire Erika for standing her ground and taking up for Destiny. Someone needed to."

"If you say so. Does she really think she is that big and bad? Somebody is going to knock the shit out of her ass. She should have simply called the police and let them handle it."

"I think Erika did what she felt was right and she is very opinionated and will let you know exactly what she thinks."

"I heard she was cussing like a sailor and was right up in the man's face like she was a damn man."

I only murmured, "Did you hear what he was doing?"

My client didn't have too much to say for a few minutes after that.

Lately, I realized my opinion of Erika was slowly changing. No one was perfect and maybe I had seen and heard some things that weren't Christian-like, but Erika had a good heart. The way she took in Destiny and paid a deposit and three months of rent on her new apartment was very telling. She even drove her to court and was there with her from start to finish. So what if she was married three times and her husbands died? What did that prove? Absolutely nothing.

Erika wasn't lucky in love. Maybe God placed those men in her life knowing she was a nurturer. Who knows? People needed to quit talking like they just knew she did something to her husbands. We weren't there and she wasn't locked up in a prison for any crimes she committed. The police investigation cleared her. I also didn't agree with her and Reverend carrying on like that, but I guess a lonely woman could give into temptation and spread her legs based on the sweet words of a handsome, charismatic preacher.

"Carla was telling me—"

I laughed, cutting her off. "Now, I know you aren't listening to Carla like she is a reliable source of information. Something happened between her and Erika back in the day, and now the two of them don't really get along." I still hadn't heard the entire story, only bits and pieces, but lately they seemed to be getting along much better. That was a blessing.

"How is Destiny? Poor baby."

"She's doing okay and should be back some-time next week. Erika thought it was best if she didn't work until her bruised and battered face was healed and she was feeling better."

"What happened with the boyfriend?"

"It's my understanding that he is back in jail for at least a year. I'm not exactly sure what happened, but he violated his parole. So, he's off the streets. Thank God."

Of course, rumor had spread like wildfire that Erika had something to do with it; she snitched on him. If she did, good for her. The rest of the nonsense rumors I ignored. Personally, I didn't think Erika was capable of such vile acts. Just like Madea, from *Madea's Family Reunion,* said, "Honey, folks are gonna talk about you 'til the day you die. And ain't nothing you can do. *Let folks talk*. It ain't about what they call you, it's what you answer to."

Carla's Dilemma

Chapter 16

I typically didn't go out and splurge for lunch; I would bring in leftovers and heat them up in the microwave. I saved a lot of money on meals this way. Regardless of how people perceived me, I had great business acumen. I intended to retire by the time I was fifty-five. I was already on my way, too, with two rental properties. I had learned years ago that I loved, absolutely loved, loved, loved money.

Today, I found myself seated in a booth at the local deli, deep in thought. I couldn't for the life of me figure out why Erika popped into my head last night and at that particular moment. I was in the midst of a fuck-fest; I had one of my sponsors over. He had me bent over a chair, hitting it from behind. Hitting it real slow and easy and I was all into it, throwing it right back at him, when Erika's face, clear as day, popped into my mind.

That killed my entire mood, and to my lover's chagrin, I sent him on his way.

This was starting to happen frequently. Mostly, Erika showed up in my dreams, though; sometimes by herself and other times with my ex, Brian. I'd see her face and get chills because in the dreams she always came across as sinister and evil. I always felt threatened and I believed the dreams were trying to tell me something.

Erika and I had a history; we went way back and, yes, she did steal my boyfriend, Brian, and married him before I could say one-two-three. The worst part was that I never saw it coming. I wrongly assumed she was harmless. I'm a few years younger than Erika but, back in the day, she and my big sister, Jessica, were the best of friends. They were inseparable.

"Hey, what are you doing sitting in here all alone?" Nobia asked, walking up to my booth. I was so caught up in my thoughts that I hadn't seen her come in. Lately she and I were cool.

I smiled. "I'm just taking a break from the salon before my clients arrive."

"Same here. Well, I'm not waiting for clients, but I'm taking a break. You know what I meant."

I nodded and took a sip of my sweet tea. Nobia took it upon herself to sit down, without asking, and in the process interrupted my thoughts. She and I sat in silence for a few minutes. I absently watched her bite into her ham, turkey, and salami sub sandwich. I picked at my tuna salad and chips.

"Whew, the last few days have been something else haven't they?" I asked.

"You can say that again," she agreed between hearty chews. "I was terrified that Destiny's ex was going to be waiting for us one night in the parking lot. I literally had nightmares about him ambushing us."

"I admit I was glad to hear his ass was locked up and off the streets."

"You just never know what's going on behind closed doors at people's homes," Nobia said.

I remained silent.

"I never would have thought that Destiny was being abused. In the beginning, I actually believed she was simply clumsy when she'd have one bruise or another."

"Hmmm, huh," I said, shaking my head.

"What?" she asked, stopping mid-bite.

"I recall telling you not too long ago to pull off your rose-colored glasses. Remember?"

"I do."

"Nobia, people wear masks, we all do. Some are just better at hiding behind them than others."

Nobia frowned and placed her half-eaten sandwich down and wiped her mouth with her balled-up paper napkin. "What gives? What's the real deal between you and Erika? I've asked her but she hasn't really told me much more than she married your ex-boyfriend."

I shrugged my shoulders, not really interested in talking about it.

"There has to be more to it than that because that happened so long ago."

Suddenly my anger rose. "Yeah, you could say it's more than that. Much more. Did she also tell you that her mother slept with my dad when he was still married to my mother? "

"What?" she asked as her mouth dropped wide-open.

"Like mother like daughter."

Nobia remained silent, taking it all in.

I continued. "My sister and Erika used to be best friends back in middle and high school. Their senior year, my sister came home early from school one day and found Erika's mother screwing my dad in my mom and dad's bed."

"Wow."

"Yeah, wow is right. You think. Needless to say, the friendship ended, but as we became adults my sister and I realized we couldn't blame Erika for the sins of her mother. Erika was simply a child when this occurred, we all were, and this wasn't the first time my dad had stepped outside his marriage."

"True. Erika was just as innocent as you guys."

I rolled my eyes because she was always defending her. "We'd go out occasionally for drinks and hang out when we became adults. And then, then she did the exact same thing to me."

"What?"

"What do you think? She hooked up with my man. It started out innocent enough. Erika would ask me if Brian could drop by and fix this or that at her apartment because he was great as a handyman. I didn't have a problem with it if he didn't, because I thought I could trust her and him. After all, she was my friend and he was my man."

"What happened?"

"Brian started going by her apartment without my knowledge and she'd fix him home-cooked meals, and basically seduced him. Brian and I were already having problems, which Erika knew, and that was all he needed was for someone to stroke his ego. She lavished him with compliments, food, and sex."

Confusion was clearly etched on her face. "So why, after all that, why are you working with her? Wouldn't she be a constant reminder every day of their betrayal?"

"Number one: I needed a job and had enough sense to realize Erika would take her salon to the next level. I needed security. Number two: I had to forgive, maybe not forget. It was eating me up, and besides it's not like Erika and I are the best of friends. Basically, we stay out of each other's way. Number three: I think in the back of my head I thought I would find out what really happened in Brian's death. Maybe Erika would eventually share the details or let something slip."

"I thought he committed suicide; killed himself with his own pistol," Nobia said. "That's what I was told."

"That's what was officially reported after the dust settled. I never for two seconds believed that Brian would take his own life. That wasn't him. He was too strong to go out like that. Brian was vibrant and had a love for life."

"What do you think happened then? If he didn't shoot himself, then who did?"

I stared back at her. Silence spoke volumes.

"You can't possibly think Erika had anything to do with his death?"

I could almost see light bulbs going off in Nobia's head. "To be honest, I don't know what to think anymore. Like I said, Brian wouldn't have taken his own life; I'd bet my life on it."

"What happened?"

"That's a good question. One to which I am determined to get the answer."

Chapter 17

It had been an exhausting couple of weeks with Destiny's problems and ongoing activity at the salon. Friday night found me ecstatic about being in the comfort of my own home for the next few days. I walked in and collapsed on the sofa, flipping through channels on my flat-panel TV. I didn't have any major plans for the weekend and I preferred it exactly that way. Other than a passion for shopping, church, and hanging out from time to time with Nobia, I really wasn't what one would classify as a party animal. I enjoyed keeping to myself, indulging in pampering activities, and spending alone time.

I intended to drop a few household items such as plates and silverware, two lamps, and cleaning materials that I had packed a few days earlier by Destiny's new apartment. I was pretty sure she could use them and I was ecstatic that she was in a safe, secure environment now. Other than that, I wanted to catch up on my movies. I was a movie buff and would admit I was addicted to them. I wasn't picky, I enjoyed all genres: action and adventure, comedies, drama and thrillers. I simply enjoyed a good film, yet, I didn't go out to the movies that often. Redbox was one of the best things that happened in my opinion. New releases for one dollar, who could beat that? I had a list of about six I wanted to watch.

When I finally ascended the stairs to my bedroom, I had a pleasant surprise waiting. I must have shown all thirty-two teeth when I spotted my present positioned against two fluffy pillows.

"Hey, you. I thought you'd never arrive home. I've been waiting for you. Couldn't wait to see my baby," he said, looking just as fine and chocolate sexy as I remembered. A soft, involuntary moan escaped.

"Hey, yourself," I cooed, walking closer to the queen-sized bed. I wanted an up-close-and-personal view of the delicious, buck-naked specimen before me.

"Why don't you make yourself more comfortable? I wanna see that sexy birthday suit of yours. I've been waiting patiently all day."

"Sounds good to me. There's something I would like to see too," I said, reaching between his legs and firmly stroking. I couldn't resist. When he was around, I couldn't keep my hands off of him. I was like a crack addict feening for some dick.

"This is all for you," he said as his large hand slid seductively from the tip of his thick and swollen shaft to the bottom of his balls. I thought the big red bow he had tied around it was a nice touch. He was all wrapped up and throbbing.

"You sure I can handle all that?" I asked coyly, with my pinkie finger in my mouth.

"Why don't you climb on board, take a ride, and we'll find out? Won't we?"

"Why, Mr. Chestnut, are you propositioning me?" I asked in my best Southern drawl.

Morris grinned seductively and slowly stroked himself without breaking eye contact with those big brown seductive bedroom eyes. I was in heaven. There was a God.

"I've told you time and time again that Denzel and Idris are cool, but don't compare to this."

I smiled because he was always jealous that I saw my other two men on a regular basis. I couldn't choose. I couldn't give any of them up.

"I know, baby. You're right," I said, slipping out of my clothes as fast as I could, dropping them to the floor where I stood. I couldn't wait to feel him inside of me, expanding.

"Damn right. Come here," he said, reaching for me.

Morris helped me onto the bed and I squatted above him as he lay flat on his back with his tool reaching for the ceiling.

"Ready to slip on and take that ride?"

I nodded as I licked my dry lips in anticipation. I slowly eased myself down and enjoyed every delicious inch as it gradually entered and filled me up to the brim.

"Ahhh," he moaned as he lightly smacked my ass to get me moving. Morris tightly gripped the back of my buttocks as I lifted myself up and down, rotating my hips in the process. I had a delicious rhythm going that was already taking me to bliss.

"Your pussy molds to my dick. Damn."

"You are my best man, baby," I said, simply melting into what he was giving me.

Breakups, Construction, and New Neighbors

Chapter 18

"Somebody has leased the space next door," Nobia reported as soon as I walked in Tuesday morning wearing a pinstriped navy blue pant-suit.

"Really? It's about time. It's been vacant forever." I had thought about expanding Last Chance and leasing the space next door, too. Perhaps adding a spa with manicures/pedicures, massages, and eyelash extensions.

"I wonder what type of business it's going to be. I hope it's not another salon that becomes competition like before."

"I guess we will find out soon enough," I said, checking the mail and preparing to take it back to my office. Plus, I had to call Reverend Hill to discuss a church matter. He was on my calendar to stop by later that evening to brainstorm after hours.

"It will be good to have some new neighbors. Hope they are friendly." She smiled, but I noticed it didn't quite reach her eyes.

My instincts told me something was wrong as I shoved the pieces of mail into my oversized leather tote. It could wait for later. "You okay, Nobia?" I asked. "You seem a little down."

"I guess." We were the first to arrive at the salon, which was rare nowadays, but this meant we could talk in private.

"It's me, Nobia. I can tell something is bothering you. What's wrong? Spill it."

She blurted it out without further prompting. "Me and Billy broke up."

I didn't comment at first because I realized my mouth would get me into trouble if I said the first thing that came to mind.

"Erika, I know you never liked him, but I did. I may have even loved him. It's not like I get asked out all the time. I don't have men breaking down my door asking me out. I'm not you."

"It's hard dating in Atlanta," I said. "The women-to-men ratio is high, so the men in this city have lost their damn minds. They are spoiled."

"Yeah, whatever. I don't see you having any problems. You are always being hit on when we are out together. I become the invisible woman."

"I'm not looking, so they probably see me as a challenge. Men love a challenge. You know men love the thrill of the chase. I'm just fine with Denzel, Idris, and Morris. They never take me for granted."

Nobia giggled. I had told her about my celebrity fantasies that were getting out of control. Sometimes I thought the shit was real, and when I would see Denzel on TV with his wife, Pauletta, I would get jealous and feel like he was cheating on me.

"Last night, Morris Chestnut, aka Lance from *The Best Man*, rocked my world, a few times." I shivered at the mere thought.

"Girl, you are sick. Only you would be satisfied daydreaming about men you have never met and probably never will."

"You never know what the universe has planned for me or you." I winked at her. "You'll find someone when you least expect it. Someone who treats you right, like the Nubian queen you are. Mark my word."

"Remind me not to hold my breath. I wouldn't want to pass out, dead." She sighed. "I understand I'm a big girl and not every man is into my size."

"Not every man is into a twig either. Believe me when I say men want something to hold on to. Believe that. Don't buy into all that hype you see on TV and read in magazines. The only thing that wants a stick is a dog, and the dog is just playing with it."

"I realize you thought I was blind to what was happening right under my nose. I wasn't. I guess I was willing to share Billy as long as he was discreet and came home each night."

"You shouldn't have to share, Nobia. You can do better than that and you should have someone who is all yours. Yours and yours alone."

"Now I have no one. Last night Billy confided in me that we needed to spend some time away from each other for a while. He wasn't sure if he wanted to be in a serious relationship anymore."

I shook my head as I leaned against the counter and witnessed her distress.

"I have cooked, fed, washed, sexed, took out loans, opened credit card accounts, and the list goes on, for this ninja and now he isn't sure if he wants a relationship. What the fuck?"

"Good riddance. Walk away because he did you a huge favor. You may not see it now but you will. Like I said, when you least expect it, you'll find someone wonderful, your Mr. Right."

"Yeah, right."

"Seriously. It's the law of the universe."

"Again, I won't hold my breath."

"I see you are determined to be in a shitty mood all day until Prince Charming walks into your life and sweeps you off your feet," I said, kidding her.

"No, just give me a day to sulk and I'll move on," she said, bumping my shoulder with hers. "You know how I am. I don't have a pity party for too long. I'm like Scarlett O'Hara: 'tomorrow is another day.'"

"Deal. One day," I said, holding up one finger. "You get one day to sulk because I'm not used to seeing my friend without a smile on that pretty face. I'll even take you out to lunch if it will help."

"To my favorite restaurant?"

"Of course."

"Deal."

As I made my way to my office, I heard the beginnings of knocking, banging, and drilling sounds coming from next door. So, it began. I admit I was curious as to who our new neighbors were as well.

Surprise, Surprise, Surprise

Chapter 19

Thursday afternoon the salon was packed. Every chair was full and twice as many customers were waiting, some patiently, some not. Erika was running special walk-in deals, so we had more than our usual share of clientele, and there was a lot of activity in and around the shop since construction work was continuous next door. It had been for two days now. Even when I arrived home, I still heard the drilling and banging in my ears.

"Loretta, I saw that *Mahogany,* starring Diana Ross with Billy Dee Williams, comes on this weekend," Nobia shared, walking over near my station.

"You know where I'll be then. Front and center. That Denzel Washington, he's cute, but he doesn't have anything on my Billy."

"Your Billy, huh, Loretta?" Carla laughed.

"You damn right. I'd hit that," I said.

As they clutched their stomachs, they almost rolled on the floor in laughter. I realized they thought I was old and could be a stick in the mud, but I could have fun with the best of them.

Destiny was back and she looked healthy and content. No one mentioned what had taken place and we all went out of our way to make sure she felt comfortable. That child was good people, but just had had some bad breaks. No matter what people said about Erika, she was all right in my book, too, and she did right by Destiny.

Erika was sitting out front, installing a new software program on the PC that Nobia used every day. Today she had on a sharp red dress with matching shoes. Her hair was swept up with cascading soft curls, which framed her face, which, at the present moment, contained a pair of silver wire-rimmed glasses. She looked every bit a sexy yet sophisticated business woman. I was never one of those women who couldn't or wouldn't compliment another woman. Erika looked like a million dollars.

"Did you guys see the black version, all-star cast of *Steel Magnolias* the other night?" Erika asked, looking up.

"Damn, I missed it. I meant to set my DVD to record it," Carla said. "I got tied up, literally," she said with a mischievous smile on her face.

"I didn't see it either. How was it?" Nobia asked. "I loved the original. Made me cry."

"I have never sobbed so much in a long time. I just bawled like a baby. And that Ouiser, my favorite, was a mess; Alfre Woodard played that role and made it her own. Queen Latifah was good as well in her role as M'Lynn," Erika shared.

"Personally, I get sick and tired of Hollywood remaking movies with an all-black cast. Don't get me wrong; I enjoyed it the other night, too, but why can't the powers that be film and produce original works by black artists? What's next? A remake of *Beaches?*" I asked. "Or, *Urban Cowboy?*"

Everyone, clients included, nodded in agreement. Around that time, the newly installed bell on the front door chimed and all eyes instinctively went there to see who had come in. Even I did a double take over the young cub who had entered our establishment. I typically enjoyed a mature, salt-and-pepper, sophisticated, more polished look, but this young man had every female in the shop drooling, including me.

"Hello, ladies." He smiled, showing off a dimple in his cheek. I also noticed a deep cleft in his chin.

"Hi. Hello. Hey. Hey, yourself," rang out a chorus of womanly greetings.

He looked amused, standing before us in his jeans and white T-shirt with tan laced-up work boots.

"Just the person I was looking for," he said, staring directly at Erika.

For a second, she looked like a deer caught in the headlights of an oncoming car. *Did she blush?*

"You are Erika Kane, the owner of this salon?" he asked, extending his right hand.

Erika left him hanging. We were all pretending not to listen to their conversation, but my ears were wide open.

"That would be me," she said almost like she couldn't bear to speak, forcing each word out.

"I'm Jacob."

Nobia piped in. "I remember you. We met you awhile ago, at the Mexican restaurant up the block."

"You did." He smiled again. "I told you that I'd be seeing you around." He looked back to Erika. "Miss Kane, or is it Mrs.?"

"It's Mrs." She smiled stiffly. "I'm a widow."

"My uncle, the owner and operator of the barber shop, Regency, next door, asked that I come over and apologize for all the noise that we are keeping up over there."

"Oh, it's going to be a barber shop." Nobia smiled.

"Hopefully, with lots of fine men partaking of its services," Carla joined in. "There's nothing better than a little eye candy."

Destiny quietly observed Jacob. She had kept a low profile since her return.

Jacob laughed. "Our apologies for the disturbance. Me and my crew, we try to do the bulk of the work at night."

"You wouldn't know it," Erika murmured.

"If it's any consolation, we are almost finished with the project."

"Good."

"My uncle will probably drop by later to say hello."

"Okay," Erika said flatly. "Anything else?"

Jacob stared at her with an air of amusement and she boldly glared back, but it was clear that something was going on between the two of them. There was chemistry. Women can pick up on these things. Jacob and Erika were not strangers. There was something in the body language, the stares, and their entire demeanor that told the true story and gave it away.

"Jacob, are you a barber? Nobia asked.

"No. I'm in the construction field and I'm helping out my uncle in between jobs as I'm thinking about relocating to Georgia from Chicago."

"Damn. Too bad. I thought we would have the opportunity to see you every day," she said, clearly flirting now that she no longer had a boyfriend. We all were constantly reminded of that fact and she continually asked us to fix her up with any eligible men we might know.

"Mrs. Kane, by the way, you are looking lovely today," Jacob said, switching the subject again. "Red looks good on you."

I think Erika actually blushed again.

"Thank you," she said dryly.

"You're welcome," he said, licking his lips in an LL Cool J–type fashion. This was better than watching a soap opera.

"I'll be in the back working on paperwork if anyone needs me." Erika promptly walked away, leaving Jacob standing there. He watched her sashay away and shook his head in disbelief.

"She's something else. I guess that's my cue to leave."

"Yeah, a true piece of work," Carla said, catching my eye.

"It was nice meeting everyone. Take care, ladies," Jacob said as he made his exit. Nobia's eyes followed him out the door and up the sidewalk. She was almost drooling.

I had a feeling that things were about to get interesting. Real interesting with the arrival of Jacob.

Destiny's Shame

Chapter 20

After the incident with Ray, I tried my best to keep a low profile at the salon. I came to work, worked my ass off, and stayed even after everyone else had left with the exception of Erika. I was still embarrassed that my personal life had spilled over into my professional one. I didn't want my peers to see me as someone who couldn't pick a decent guy. Lately that appeared to be my mode of operation; losers flocked to me.

The women in the shop had been great. Basically, they pretended like the entire ordeal never took place. One evening Loretta and I found ourselves alone in the shop. We were cleaning up our stations and ordering supplies for the following week; the distributor was stopping by the next day. I saw her watching me out of the corner of my eye as I handled the task at hand.

"How are you doing, baby?" she asked, taking a seat in her chair.

I shrugged my shoulders. "All right," I answered with no real enthusiasm.

"Good. All right is still better than not good. If you ever need someone to talk to, I'm here for you, Destiny. Anytime."

"I appreciate that, Miss Loretta," I said sincerely.

"I'm glad to see that you are back on your feet and you didn't let your plight defeat you. You're a survivor, child."

"I've seen a lot in my lifetime and I guess you could say I've learned to be just that: a survivor."

"Amen. God's got you. Don't ever forget that."

"And it doesn't hurt that I have earthly angels in my life in the form of you, Miss Erika, Miss Carla, and Miss Nobia."

"That is so sweet, Destiny. I'm touched."

"I mean it. I've enjoyed working here and having you guys as coworkers and, most of all, friends and mentors."

"You keep holding your head up high and walking in God's grace, child. Soon, you'll be more than all right."

I nodded as I finished wiping down my chair.

I heard Miss Loretta sigh and take a deep breath. "I've been in your shoes before and I know what you are going through."

"You?" I asked in disbelief. "No."

"Yes, me. Years ago. I was in an abusive relationship and it took moving here, to Atlanta, to escape from my abuser."

"Wow." I took a seat in my chair as I became a captive audience.

"I loved that man so much and you couldn't tell me that he didn't love me. When he said jump, I asked how high. In my innocence, I thought he was extremely jealous and controlling because he loved me."

"What happened? How did you get away from him?" I asked with growing interest.

"You were lucky. It took me ending up in the hospital with broken bones and a concussion. When they discharged me, I left everything behind. I realized if I didn't, he would eventually kill me. My parents were already dead and I'm an only child, so I didn't have anything or anyone to miss me. I used my last few dollars to get on a Greyhound bus bound for Atlanta, Georgia, and never looked back."

"I never would have known."

"Why? Child, domestic abuse doesn't have a face. All races, ages, and ethnicities are affected. It doesn't discriminate."

"Very true."

"Not many people know my story; I don't share a lot of my personal life, but I thought you needed to hear it to know that you aren't alone. Just know that no one is judging you. We love you. What you went through was a life lesson you need to put behind you now, grow from it, and never repeat again."

"Thank you. I needed to hear your story, Miss Loretta."

"Are you about ready to get out of here? We can walk out together."

"I think so," I said, standing up and grabbing my purse as Miss Loretta turned off the lights.

"Just know that no one is perfect. From the outside looking in, it may appear that way, but don't be deceived. Okay?"

"Okay," I responded, not really sure who or what she was referring to.

"Erika is good people, but her life isn't perfect. Neither is she."

I walked out the door, wondering where that came from and why.

Bang, Bang, Bang

Chapter 21

Every single day, we endured hours of hammering, drilling, and unknown loud, annoying noises from next door. We couldn't wait until they finished whatever they were doing over there.

"Damn. I don't know if I can take another day of this shit," I said to no one in particular.

Nobia responded, "I know what you mean, Carla. At least the clients aren't complaining though."

I laughed. "Why would they? They are being treated like queens by being served champagne, grapes, cheese, and crackers for their discomfort and they are making a big party out of the commotion."

"Another plus is that we get to see Jacob nearly every day. He definitely isn't bad on the eyes. At all."

It was true; Jacob stopped by on a regular basis to say hello, get change, or just chat on his break, and I noticed Erika always disappeared during his short visits and never had much to say to him.

"I must admit he is fine," I shared.

"The word 'fine' doesn't even do him justice."

"What's the deal with him and Erika?"

"What do you mean?" Nobia asked, curiosity lighting up her face.

"Erika doesn't care for him and there appears to be history between them."

"You know how Erika can be. Her way of looking down on him is simply her way."

I looked on in disbelief because that was the first time I had ever heard Nobia say anything less than complimentary about Erika.

"Looks like there is chemistry between them that is familiar." I flashed back to the night I caught them together. It was still my secret.

"Erika and I met him at the same time, at the Mexican restaurant down the block."

"You sure about that?"

"Girl, Erika wouldn't give that young buck the time of day. He flirted with her that day but she didn't even bat an eyelash."

"Oh really." I thought, *Yeah, that's what you think, and that's what she wants you to think,*

but she gave him something or some all right.
He was tearing it up.

Nobia smiled a devious grin. "What's with all these questions? If I didn't know better, I'd think you were interested in Jacob."

"Let me set the record straight. Number one: I don't do babies. Number two: I don't do broke. Number three: I don't play sugar mama. If I got with Jacob, that's what I would be doing . . . one, two, and three."

"You and Erika must be blind."

"Now in one, two, and three, I never said that he wasn't fine, don't get me wrong. He is very easy on the eyes and he gets a sista hot thinking about what she could do with what's between his legs." I laughed. "But like I said before, I don't do broke. He's not that damn fine."

The Showdown

Chapter 22

I heard Jacob out front nearly every day. He would be flirting with the clients, as usual. What could I do? Not much without coming off looking bad in the eyes of my customers. They adored Jacob and he wasn't hurting anyone when he dropped by for a few minutes, most days now.

During those times, I would make up random excuses to head to the back to my office, if I was on the floor, until he left. I'm sure the ladies noticed, I'm sure he noticed, but I couldn't help myself. I didn't enjoy being in the same room as Jacob. I would definitely stay away after what happened last night. I almost gave into temptation, again.

I was alone in the shop, preparing to turn off the lights, turn on the alarm, and lock up, when a dark shadow appeared at the front door. It was Jacob. He knocked gently.

On my side of the glass, I asked, "Yes, Jacob?" with clear annoyance in my tone. I was ready to call it a night and go home and relax. I didn't have time to deal with him.

Jacob smiled and motioned for me to let him in. Against my better judgment, I unlocked the door.

"Erika," he said, walking in with his usual swagger. "What's up?"

"How can I help you?" I asked, stepping back a few feet because he was all up in my personal space. I hated that with a passion.

Jacob frowned. "What's up with you?" he asked. "I can't figure you out. You run hot and cold."

"There's nothing wrong with me. I could ask you the same thing." I frowned, already not liking the direction this conversation was suddenly taking.

"I come up in here almost every day and you act like I'm carrying the Black Plague or some other deadly disease."

"Exactly. Why are you in my place of business all the time? Are you stalking me? Was it that good?"

He laughed halfheartedly. "You are a trip, Erika. I'm still trying to figure out who told you your shit is the bomb. You ain't all that."

"I never said I was."

"You don't have to say a word. It is clearly written all over your smug face and how you carry yourself. You think you are better than me."

"Okay, I'm not going to argue with you," I said, holding up my hand.

"And who said I was stopping by to see you?"

I grunted as if in pain. "What do you want, Jacob? I was getting ready to lock up and go home."

"That's a good question. What do I want?"

I stood with my hands on my hips, waiting for him to finish so I could show him the door.

"Do you really want to know, Erika?"

"I asked didn't I? I'm not going to stand here all night playing silly games. I don't have time for this shit."

"That smart mouth is going to get you in trouble one day."

"It hasn't yet," I shot back. "Again, what do you want from me?"

"I want you to stop acting like some stuck-up, bourgeois bitch and acknowledge me. Be the woman from that night," he said, lowering his voice.

"Ha, acknowledge you how?" I laughed in his face.

"You don't have to announce to the world that we were intimate, but damn, at least act like I exist. You couldn't get enough that night, but now you don't know me?"

"Whatever. I don't care, Jacob. Get over it."

"I believe you were saying way more than that the night I hit it in your office."

"Again, I really don't care. I told you that night it was a one-time deal."

"I wanna fuck you again," he whispered, leaning in toward my ear like he hadn't heard a word I said. "Maybe I want seconds."

I had heard enough and I started walking toward the door. "This is going nowhere. I think you should leave."

"Why? Because I'm speaking the truth?" he asked, stepping in front of me, blocking my path.

"Move out of my way, Jacob."

"Or you will what? See, you are one of those women who like to control situations and their men. I'm not the one, baby."

"And you are one of those men who like his woman fawning over him and his dick. I'm not the one, either. Now go."

"I will. I'm not going to disrespect your spot, but first I simply want you to admit we had sex and you enjoyed it. That's all."

"Why? Why does it mean so much to you?"

He ignored my questions. "It's just you and me here. No one will hear you and your image will remain intact. Your secret will remain safe with me."

"I will say no such thing to stroke your inflated ego. You and I both know what we did."

"Admit you liked it, liked it a lot," he whispered, reaching for my left breast.

"Stop it!" I shouted, attempting to slap his large hand away.

Jacob squeezed harder. "You like that. You know you do, Erika. I had you figured out the minute I saw you walk into that restaurant. You are a woman who enjoys sex."

Jacob proceeded to slowly back me into the far back corner of the shop, to Destiny's station. He continued to expertly knead my breasts through the sheer fabric of my blouse as he turned and stood behind me with his erection pressing into my backside.

"Stop it. Someone may see us from the street," I said, barely above a whisper as I attempted to catch my breath as I moved and took a seat in Destiny's chair. I couldn't tell if I could not breathe because he excited me or because I was frightened of where the situation was headed.

"No one can see us in this corner and you locked the front door already," he said, aggressively pulling up my blouse and pushing my bra to the side. My breasts tumbled out. He bent to lick each nipple, one then the other. "You don't know how much you turn me on, Erika."

I think I purred as his thumb flicked a swollen nipple while he suckled the other like it was a delicate flower.

"Awww, that's what I'm talking about. Just let go."

"Stop," I said again, weakly trying to push him away with no success. He was built solid.

Jacob grabbed both hands and held them snugly to his chest. "You don't want me to stop, Erika. Don't you want to feel me filling you up again? Remember how you moaned and squirmed?"

I found myself nodding as he continued to touch and stroke relentlessly. The only sounds were our labored breathing, in sync.

Jacob planted kisses all over my face as he lifted me to a standing position and unzipped my jeans as he firmly palmed my butt. I felt helpless in his arms. I moaned as he pulled my pants down to my ankles and his hand dipped inside my panties and his finger found my sweet spot. I was hot and wet and about to burst.

He whispered in my ear. "You are about to come from my touch, aren't you?" He smiled knowingly. "I knew you loved being fucked."

I nodded and leaned into his thick fingers.

"Tell me," he whispered again. "I want to hear how I make you feel."

Jacob continued to stroke me and my body was ablaze and sizzling. Once again, he was working his magic. I was weak at the knees as he slid his slippery fingers slowly, ever so slowly, in and out as I held on to his shoulders for support.

"Do you want me to stop, Erika?"

I was just getting ready to say no when my cell phone rang inside my purse. I instantly jumped back like I had been shocked and immediately came to my senses.

"You have to go, Jacob."

He looked amused. "You're kidding."

"Please go. Like I told you, it was a one-time bang. It was good, you were one of the best I've ever had, but you'll never, ever get this pussy again. I hope that was clear enough."

"You are full of shit, Erika. You were ready to cream just now."

"Call me names and say foul things, but you still have to go," I said, hastily pulling up my jeans and adjusting my bra and blouse.

"You're right. I don't know why I'm acting like an immature schoolboy over some pussy, which is a dime a dozen."

"Good night," I said, walking to the door, unlocking, and opening it. I didn't bother to comment.

"Good night, Erika. Karma is a bitch. Sooner or later, sooner than you think, it's coming for you."

"Well, it won't be tonight."

I finally caught my breath as I watched him walk swiftly up the sidewalk with his head held low. I shivered as chills went up and down my spine.

Erika's Sixth Sense

Chapter 23

You know how you feel when you have a sense trouble is headed your way, full speed ahead with no brakes. You can't place your finger on it, but you have an unrelenting, nagging feeling that a darkness is about to descend upon you. That was my predicament the last few days and, as much as I tried, I couldn't shake my trepidation.

It all started when I had a mysterious phone call in my office and the caller simply breathed into the phone and then abruptly hung up. I probably should have forgotten about it because it was probably children playing a practical joke. Halloween was upon us and pranks increased during this time of the year, but my gut sensed the call was more sinister.

I had asked Nobia if she had experienced any hang-ups or unusual calls at the front desk, but she was adamant that she hadn't. Besides, the breather called my personal, private office line, which was different from the front desk. So, he or she wanted to reach me.

The ringing phone pulled me out of my deep reverie. I answered it reluctantly. "Last Chance, Erika Kane speaking. Beauty is our first priority."

"Hey."

"Nobia?"

"Yeah, it's me. I'm being lazy today. I didn't want to get up and walk to the back, it would take too much energy."

"That is pretty lazy." I laughed.

"Are we still on for lunch?"

"Sure."

"Usual time?"

"That will work."

"Where are we going?" she asked.

"We can figure that out later," I said, distracted.

"I meant to ask, are you okay? You appeared to be a bit frazzled when we spoke earlier."

I sighed and lied. "I'm fine. I'm just tired, physically and mentally. I need a vacation. You know I haven't been on one since I opened the shop. I didn't want to leave until it was operating in the black."

"I can't wait until we go on our cruise to Cozumel, Mexico and the Cayman Islands."

"It should be a lot of fun," I said. "Sun and fun. Perfect combination."

"I haven't seen Jacob the last few days. Has he been in?" she asked as I stiffened in my chair at the mention of his name. "Maybe when I walked out for a few minutes, he stopped by?"

"No, I haven't seen him." *Thank God*.

"Oh well. It has been pretty quiet next door. Maybe they finished up, but I can't believe Jacob didn't drop by to say good-bye."

I didn't comment one way or the other.

"A client just walked in," she whispered. "Let me get off the phone and handle business. I'll see you at one o'clock. Bye."

"Bye, girl."

As soon as Nobia hung up, the phone rang again on my private line.

"Girl, if you don't bring your lazy ass back here and stop blowing up my phone"—I laughed—"I don't know what I'm going to do with you."

There was silence. No answer.

"Nobia? Can you hear me?"

Heavy breathing filtered through the line.

"Nobia?"

"Okay, I'm getting ready to hang up."

Then I heard it, barely more than a whisper. "I know what you did."

"What?"

"You heard me, bitch. I know what you did."

"Who is this? Quit playing on my damn phone. This is a place of business."

"You aren't going to get away with it."

"Who is this?"

"Karma is a bitch, bitch."

Then I heard a click and the line went dead.

Could This Be Love?

Chapter 24

I hadn't experienced any more phone calls with heavy breathing or cryptic messages since the last occurrence and that had been a few days ago. During that same time frame no one had seen or heard from Jacob. That was absolutely fine with me, but I still hadn't figured out if he was behind the calls. It sorta didn't fit anything he would do. He was more in your face; from what I knew of Jacob, he didn't hide behind mysterious phone calls with threats. However, I wasn't 100 percent sure it wasn't him, so I couldn't count him out. He had recently told me that karma was a bitch and I was going to get mine. That's what the mysterious caller had said as well.

It was Tuesday evening and one client was still in the shop, asleep and softly snoring under a dryer. Destiny, Loretta, Carla, Nobia, and I were sitting around, chitchatting in the waiting area. It felt comfortable. Even though it was Loretta's client, no one appeared anxious to leave and I believed the group had finally gelled.

"Has anyone seen Jacob?" Nobia asked for the fifth time.

"No," we said in unison.

"How many times are you going to ask us that? You've been here just like the rest of us and we haven't seen him. Get over it," Carla chimed in.

"Well, I was just wondering," Nobia snapped back. "You don't have to get a stick up your ass."

"Sounds like someone was a little smitten with Jacob," Loretta said jokingly. "He was a cutie."

Destiny and I snickered. I noticed she was wearing one of the costume necklaces I had given her and it looked good on her. She had even added some highlights to her hair recently and she appeared happy; just like a twenty-something should be—happy, carefree, and enjoying life.

"If I didn't know better, I'd think they had knocked boots," Carla said, but was looking straight at me. "I bet baby boy brought it. He looked like he was packing."

I stared right back at her and didn't blink an eye.

"I wish, but he just made my day by being a friend. If I couldn't have him, at least I could look at him and fantasize. That's better than nothing," Nobia said dreamily.

"Nobia, you will find another man. Don't fret about it all the time," Loretta gently coaxed. "It's not a good look on you. You don't need to appear desperate."

It did appear that Nobia was on a manhunt lately. That was all she talked about.

"Dang, Miss Loretta. Hurt my feelings. Do I act desperate, y'all?" she asked, looking at the rest of us.

Carla answered for us. "Hell, yeah. Just chill."

"She will find someone. And he'll cherish her," I said, smiling Nobia's way.

"Miss Erika, how did you know when you had found the right mate?" Destiny asked out of the blue.

"You mean three, don't you?" Carla asked, leaning back in her chair, crossing her long legs at the ankles.

I rolled my eyes at her. This chick always knew what buttons to push to bring out the worst in me, but here we were, working together on a daily basis. We had learned to tolerate each other.

"How did I know I was in love?" I asked.

Destiny nodded.

"It's hard to explain, but I just knew. I realize that sounds corny but I did. There was a feeling that came over me that made me feel special and secure when I was in their company. I wanted to be around them all the time and when I did, I felt complete."

I paused, reflecting on the past. "It was almost as if I never knew I missed them until I met them." I smiled at the memory.

"Wow! That's so romantic," Destiny said.

"It's something," I heard Carla whisper to Loretta. I was beginning to open my mouth to say something that she wouldn't like when the bell above the door chimed and in walked a very attractive, forty-something, clean-cut gentleman. He instantly captured my attention with his confidence and my heartbeat sped up. That rarely happened with me.

"Hello, everyone. Good evening, ladies."

"Hi. May I help you?" I asked, standing up and walking the few feet to where he stood near the counter, eager to get a closer look.

"I sure hope so. I'm Lance Carter, Jacob's uncle," he said.

On hearing Jacob's name, Nobia's interest piqued and her face lit up like a Christmas tree with hundreds of lights.

"Jacob asked me to drop by and say good-bye to everyone. He finished up the work next door, did a fantastic job by the way, and was called away, back to Chicago for a family emergency."

"I hope everything's okay," I said, pretending I was concerned.

"It will be."

"By the way, I'm Erika Kane, the owner and proprietor of Last Chance."

"Good to meet you," he said, reaching to shake my hand. His hand swallowed mine. When we touched, I swear to you, I wouldn't lie, a warm surge spread throughout my body. It shot up and down my arms like an electric current gone awry. I couldn't tell if Lance felt it too because his expression remained unchanged, but I know what I experienced because I was still tingling.

"Well, Lance, welcome to the neighborhood. I'm sure you will enjoy it here."

"Thank you. I'm sure I will."

"By the way, this is Loretta, Nobia, Destiny, and Carla," I said, pointing to each in turn. He shook hands and offered a pleasant smile to every one of them. I took that opportunity to check him out from head to toe and I definitely liked what I saw. Clean-cut, masculine, muscular, toned, tall, and handsome always turned me on.

"Are you the owner of the barber shop?"

"Yes, this is my third location. I have other spots in Decatur and Conyers."

Financially stable, check.

The ladies talked to him a bit more and I held back to watch the interaction. There was something about him that made me simply revel in observing him. Lance finally said his good-byes and walked out the door with his head held high and a stride to his step. I turned to find the women staring at me.

"What?" I asked.

"Nothing. Nothing at all," Nobia said, smiling.

"Mr. Lance Carter, huh?" I walked back to my office with a renewed pep to my own step. He was worth getting to know a little better. Things were definitely looking up.

Doubts Playing With My Mind

Chapter 25

I loved Erika like she was family, as the sister I never had. Sure, she had her ways, the same as I had mine, but her positive qualities far outshined and outweighed the negatives.

Erika and I had been best friends a little over three and a half years now. I met her shortly before Edward passed away. So, I did get to witness her and Edward together as a married couple. They appeared like any average happily married man and wife from my vantage point. They were always together and enjoyed being in each other's company from what I could tell; they had fun together.

Now I was beginning to wonder how happy they truly were. I recognized I should be ashamed of myself for allowing Carla to speak doubts into my mind about my best friend in the world. Most of the time, I ignored Carla's comments, especially when they pertained to Erika. Everyone knew she was jealous of Erika; hell, she wanted to be Erika. She never quite got over the fact that Erika snatched up Brian and jumped the broom. At least that's how I saw it, or thought I did. Carla was very competitive and she thought she was drop-dead gorgeous, so she couldn't fathom the fact that Brian wanted Erika, the big-boned sister, over her. Carla could hold a grudge forever.

Doubts were creeping in to invade my brain, mostly because of Carla's little remarks placed here and there in my ear. She successfully started planting seeds of doubt that were starting to sprout roots, but also because of something Jacob shared with me before he was unexpectedly called away to Chicago.

Unknown to anyone at the salon, Jacob and I ate lunch together before he suddenly disappeared back to Chicago. It wasn't planned. I wished he had invited me out to lunch. I happened to be back at the Mexican restaurant, Jacob was already eating when I walked in, and he invited me to dine with him. Of course, I didn't decline. I'm no fool, I knew Jacob would never show any love interest in me, but I truly enjoyed his company and conversation, and adored being in his presence. We always laughed and I did harmless flirting, realizing it would go no further.

Jacob and I were seated in a booth across from one another, and I was feasting on my usual entree.

"You always have a smile on your face. I have never seen you upset," Jacob commented before talking a big bite out of his fish taco.

"People say that all the time. I'm a naturally happy person, I guess, and I try not to sweat the small stuff. My mother says I was a happy baby, too. I rarely cried unless I needed changing or needed to be fed."

Jacob paused and stared at me with a curious expression on his handsome face.

"What? Do I have sauce all over my face?" I asked, dabbing with my napkin.

"No. You're funny, Nobia."

"What then?"

"Can I ask you a question?"

"Of course you can, Jacob."

"Why is a nice girl like you best friends with Erika?"

I laughed. "Erika is cool. You have to get to know her first."

"How long have the two of you been friends?" he asked, leaning forward.

"Over three and a half years."

"That's a long time, and you are still friends?"

"I know the two of you didn't take to each other, but I love Erika. It's funny how people either see her kindness or buy into mean gossip, everyone is three-dimensional. I think she is a kind person, but she also isn't a push-over."

"Ump," he responded under his breath.

"Be fair. The two of you just met and you haven't had that much interaction. I know that you find her attractive and she *is* bourgeois, but you shouldn't be so hard on her. You'll like her once you get to know her better. Give it some time."

"I think you are a great friend and she's lucky to have you in her life."

"Why do I feel there is a big *but* on the tail end of that statement?" I asked cautiously.

"Be careful of people who wear masks."

"Stop talking in riddles. What does that mean?"

"I'm just saying that you don't know what Erika does behind closed doors, and don't believe everything she tells you."

"You are the second person who has told me that recently."

"Maybe you should listen," he said matter-of-factly.

It suddenly clicked. "Do you and Erika have a history that I'm not aware of?"

He paused. "Ask Erika."

"I'm asking you."

"I'd rather you ask your best friend. She's your best friend, right? She should tell you the truth. Right?"

I nodded.

Jacob and I talked some more and finished our meals. Twenty minutes later, I walked back to the salon more confused than ever. Doubt was playing with me.

Be Warned

Chapter 26

Nobia had left early because she had a dental appointment on the other side of town, so we were taking turns answering the salon phone. Thankfully, we had been lucky because it had remained relatively quiet. I had just placed a client under the dryer and handed her the newest copy of *Ebony* magazine when the second call of the evening since Nobia left came through.

I ran to pick it up and reached it by the fourth ring. Carla and Destiny had made no attempt to answer since they were busy with clients and Erika was in her office. I noticed she had been distant lately.

"Last Chance Salon. This is Loretta speaking. How may I help you? Beauty is our first priority."

Silence followed.

"Hello. Last Chance Salon. Is anyone there? Can you hear me?" I asked.

"Yes, I can hear you, but you need to hear this," a menacing, distorted voice responded. I couldn't tell if the caller was male or female.

"Excuse me."

"Something doesn't add up with your girl, Erika. Don't believe her lies."

"Excuse me. Who is this?"

"Don't concern yourself with who this is. If I were you, I'd worry about your boss lady. The Black Widow. They kill their male partners after mating."

"Don't call back here playing on this line. This is a place of business," I shouted into the receiver.

"Three husbands, three dead husband. What are the odds?"

"Did you hear me?"

"No, the question is: Did you hear me, Loretta? You've been warned."

Click and the line went dead. I was left standing holding the receiver, visibly shaken by the ominous message.

This is Love

Chapter 27

I'm not exactly sure what Lance had done to me because I couldn't get him off my mind. For the next couple of days, I thought of him often. Day and night. In my opinion, it didn't take all that posturing and boisterous words from a man to attract a woman. All it took, for me anyway, was a sense of confidence and manliness coupled with a sense of sincerity and kindness. From our brief encounter, I immediately gauged that Lance possessed those qualities and much more. He fascinated me and piqued my curiosity. I definitely wanted to get to know him better.

I was smitten and that was saying a lot. After Edward died, no man had captured my attention. It was like my spirit and the sense that I could love again died and were buried with him.

Okay, I admit, I had had a few indiscretions since Edward passed on; I'm only human. I had needs and desires every now and then just like anyone else. I intentionally gave Nobia and everyone the impression that I was celibate, and in my mind I was. Sex meant nothing to me, absolutely nothing, unless I made a love and intimate connection. Love was my high.

It was true and Nobia was correct. I was a die-hard romantic; I loved the entire concept of two souls coming together, through thick and thin, and living out the rest of their lives collectively. I needed and wanted a man in my life to share experiences with. Marriage and a spouse and family were when I felt most alive and complete. With love, I thought I could conquer the world and I was unstoppable. Without it, I felt incomplete, like I was missing a piece of myself.

The sex with Jacob had been hot, dirty, and some of the best I ever had. As soon as it was over, Jacob was forgotten, and now, he couldn't get past the fact that he meant absolutely nothing to me. He simply had something I needed at that time; it wasn't personal. My rendezvous with the reverend was wrong, but I needed someone and he was always there for me, praying and guiding my footsteps with the Lord. When I was feeling my lowest and loneliest, the good reverend always made me feel good and that's how I justified sleeping with a married man.

Did that make me a bad person?

As a child, I sensed I was different because I never had much remorse for bad things I did. As long as it benefited me, all was fine in my world. I was happy. I came to the conclusion long ago that I was selfish and thought only of myself. That wasn't a big secret anymore. What was the saying? "When you realized a truth, you were almost there, on the path to true enlightenment."

I grew up with a mother people talked, gossiped, and whispered about behind her back and smiled in her face, and that hurt her. She came across as in your face, take no prisoners, but she was really quite sensitive. My mother could curse like a sailor, smoked Ashton cigars with the best of them, and could drink any man under the table. She also loved men and living a life of luxury. Sure, she made some bad choices, exposed me to too much at such a young age, but I loved her with everything in me. She was a good example of not acting like a lady but thinking like a man.

I may be my mother's child, but I'll die having no regrets. That's what she always told me: "No regrets, Erika. Take responsibility for your actions, good or bad, and move on. Don't look back. Never look back."

I didn't want to be talked about behind my back either; I wanted to fit in and be liked. Maybe that was why I was always trying to help the less fortunate; the feeling and admiration afterward was exhilarating. During those moments, I was content.

Malik, Brian, and Edward all made me happy in the beginning. The initial stage of a relationship was always the best. I savored those moments—the courting, the dates, the wining and dining—more than I coveted the dick. Physical urges were great when they were satisfied, especially by a man who knew what he was doing in the bedroom, but the emotional and spiritual connection was powerful.

When the relationship turned sour, that was always the part I despised the most. I hated witnessing that special gleam in my man's eyes dim and realizing he didn't want me anymore. I'd do almost anything not to see that love dim. But again, I was my mother's child. Just as easily as I could stroke my man's ego and dick, I could cut him down and castrate him with my spewed words. I could be as sweet as honey and as deadly and furious as a lioness defending her cubs. Truth be told, I guess that's why I had been married three times. I was addicted to that first high. Now, Lance had caught my eye and I longed for him to hold me in his strong arms. Only problem was that he didn't appear interested in the least.

The Grand Tour

Chapter 28

Unseasonably mild weather for a November had invaded Georgia. Residents were still wearing sweaters and jackets but no coats, yet. That suited me perfectly. My favorite seasons were fall and the spring; the in-between seasons. Today, I was dressed in black True Religion designer jeans with a form-fitting pink sweater, paired with one of my favorite pair of black boots. I was hanging out in the receptionist area after placing an order with a national jewelry distributor. I was going to test out selling a few pieces of costume jewelry in the salon.

I was secretly hoping to get a glimpse of Lance as he passed by; I had discovered that he generally took a coffee break around this time of the day, as I had seen him several times walking back with a grande cup of mocha from Starbucks. During the last couple of weeks that his barber shop had been open, we had witnessed a steady male clientele coming and going. Lance had dropped by one or two times during that time frame, but basically didn't pay me any mind or special attention. He simply asked Nobia if he could place some flyers on our front counter and he would display ours in turn, or he asked about the best restaurants on the block.

"Nobia, do you want to take a walk with me?" I asked out of the blue.

She was finishing up the details on the specifications for holiday cards that we planned to mail to our clients with attached coupons for discounted services. That was my Christmas gift and token of appreciation to those who brought business my way.

"Sure, I could stretch my legs," she said, coming from around the counter to retrieve her jacket, which hung on the black coat rack near the front door.

"Where do you want to walk to? The convenience store?"

"Let's walk next door and visit. We can check out Regency and see how it all came together and say hello to Lance."

Nobia smiled mischievously. "Sure. We can do that."

I started walking toward the door.

"Aren't you going to grab your jacket?"

"I'm fine. It's not cold out, and besides we are only going one door down."

"Oh, you want to look cute for Lance?" Nobia kidded.

I couldn't help myself. I giggled, of all reactions. "I have no idea what you are talking about."

"Sure you don't."

A few minutes later, as we opened the door to Regency and stepped in, all eyes turned to observe us. The spot was nice, very sophisticated with an old-school flavor. I checked out eight barber chairs, four on each side of the room, and there were mirrors everywhere, from floor to ceiling.

One of the barbers, a short, stocky man, greeted us. "Are you looking for Lance?"

"We are. Is he here?" I asked.

At that moment, as if on cue, Lance stepped out of the back and my words were caught in my throat. Dressed in black slacks and a shirt, he looked much handsomer than I remembered. He made me breathless.

"Hi, ladies." He waved, strutting our way in that confident manner I admired. His walk was almost as sexy as Denzie's.

"Hello," Nobia said.

"Hi, Lance," I responded, trying to make eye contact.

"Good to see you again. Nobia, right?" he asked, looking directly at her.

"That's correct. Great memory."

"And Ellen."

"Erika," I said. "That's a first. No one has ever forgotten my name. I usually leave an impression," I joked.

Nobia glanced at me as Lance chuckled at my comment. I simply adored his laughter. It appeared to come straight from the gut.

"Well, there is a first for everything, but I promise you, it won't happen again, Erika."

"I hope not," I responded.

"What brings you ladies by? It's my pleasure of course."

"Nobia and I wanted to extend an official welcome and after enduring weeks of drilling, we wanted to check out your finished shop. So, here we are, the welcome wagon," I said.

"Thank you. That's sweet of you. Walk this way and I'll give you the grand tour."

I smiled sweetly and walked beside him, making sure our shoulders touched.

"You guys have seen the front," Lance said, pointing in that direction. "We have a full-service barber shop here at Regency, complete with eight barber chairs that are all currently full. I lucked out with some very talented and skilled barbers."

"I have to give you props on what you have done with the space. Before the walls were drab and boring and there was a lot of structural damage from the previous occupant."

"I have to give all thanks to my nephew, Jacob, for the final product. I'm very proud of him because he did an excellent job. Did you guys get to know him well? He's an interesting young man and has been through a lot over the years."

Nobia perked up. "I met him and he's a great guy."

"He is and I think of him as a son."

I remained silent until Lance turned to me for a response.

"And you, Erika? Did you have the opportunity to meet him?"

"Yes, I did."

"Good," he said, with his eyes not leaving my face. I smiled and for a second all I could picture was an image of Jacob as he moved inside my womanhood.

"If you step through the red double doors, you will see personal lockers, the bathroom to the right, and a small break room on the left."

"No office?" I asked, looking around.

"No. I prefer to work up front. Be a visible part of the ambience and customers. It's amazing how people will patronize your place of business when they get to know you. They'll remain loyal when they know you and what you stand for in the community."

Nobia responded, "Very true."

Lance smiled and I saw him look toward me from the corner of my eye. I didn't comment because I knew I would never give up my office and privacy.

"That's about it. My home away from home. Nothing grand, but it's mine."

"What does your wife or girlfriend feel about your new business endeavor?" I asked. I hadn't seen a wedding band on his finger, but nowadays you never knew. I had met many married men who simply didn't wear a band, or slipped it off when it was convenient.

I ignored the beginnings of a grin as it appeared on Nobia's face and focused my attention on Lance, which wasn't difficult.

"Nothing."

"Oh really?"

"I have neither. No wife or girlfriend. My business takes up much of my time and most women aren't that accommodating."

"The real women are."

"How so?" Lance asked.

"They appreciate what they have. What's that saying that behind every successful man is a strong woman?"

Lance opened his mouth to reply. At that moment, his cell phone rang and he looked down to view the caller ID.

"I apologize, but I'm going to have to take this. Sorry to cut the tour short, but it was nice seeing you again."

"Not a problem. Thanks again," I said.

Lance had already turned his back to us and was walking in the opposite direction, like he had forgotten us just that quickly. I couldn't believe he still hadn't asked for my number.

Chapter 29

Friday was once again upon us and I was hanging out in Erika's office before leaving for home. I wasn't in a rush; there wasn't anyone or anything waiting for me except four walls since I had been dumped by Billy. I didn't even have a dog waiting, tail wagging, delighted to see me.

"What's the word on Lance?" I asked Erika.

"The same as before. He is pleasant enough when he sees me. He waves, he smiles, he says hello, but hasn't made any attempt to ask me out."

"It's coming. He will. He likes you."

"How do you know? Because I'm not seeing it."

"I can just tell. Erika, you are used to men flattering you, complimenting you, but that's not his style. He's a doer."

"A doer?" she asked.

"Yeah, he likes doing things for his woman. Lance was in here for over an hour fixing the clogged sink the other day."

"He was being kind, that's all."

"Yeah, right. Give him some time; he'll bite."

"I hope so. I really do. Hopefully sooner than later because I'm not exactly the most patient person," she stated, all giggly. "I can't believe I'm all dreamy-eyed over a man. I never thought it would happen again. I really thought I would be alone for the rest of my life. Well, alone with Denzel, Idris, and Morris."

"I for one am very happy for you, girl. It's good to see you content."

"It has been awhile, but I feel I am finally ready to move on with my life and put the past behind me. And the past includes Edward."

"Just be patient, girl. Lance will ask you out and you guys will make a great couple, he's tall and handsome and you're gorgeous."

"Thank you. Thank you. Thank you," she had chanted, patting herself on the shoulder.

"It's not even too late for you to have babies."

"Whoa," she said, holding up her hand. "Slow your roll."

"I can be the godmother, of course, and maybe you two can have twins. Knock the girl and boy out with one pregnancy."

"First, I need to go out on an actual date with him. Do you think he has heard the rumors about me?"

"I'm sure he has. People will talk about you until the day you die. That's life, girl."

"Maybe that's why he hasn't asked me out," she said, deep in thought. "He thinks I'm a Black Widow."

I chuckled.

"What?"

"You must really like this guy because I have never seen you act this way, Erika."

"I do. I really, really like him and I have a feeling that we could be good together. We seem to have a lot in common."

"I don't think any rumors have turned him off. He seems like a man who has a mind of his own and makes his own decisions. So, please, girl, you are worrying about the wrong thing."

"Nobia, you always make me feel better. That's why I love you so."

"I love you back."

We smiled and sat in silence for a few seconds, comfortable with each other. I had come to terms with my doubts about Erika. I was her closest friend and I, of all people, would know if there was anything ratchet about her and I was ashamed of myself for even considering it.

"I can't believe Lance brought you fresh vegetables from his garden the other day. Now that is old-school courting."

Erika smiled, I guess at the memory of him sending over a full basket of onions, snap peas, and winter lettuce. "We had a delicious salad that day."

"So, no worries. It will all work out," I said. "Now, where are we going for dinner? Because I can't spend another Friday night all by myself."

"It doesn't matter," she said. "You choose."

"Okay, cool. Your treat?"

"My treat." She smiled.

Erika and Lance

Chapter 30

Nobia's prediction was on point, the relationship between Lance and me took an upward turn, much to my extreme satisfaction and pleasure.

The change occurred on a night when I was in the process of closing and Lance had just locked up and walked out his shop door, headed in my direction. I still say it was no coincidence. Much like Jacob had done, I heard a light knock at the door as I was straightening up magazines near the receptionist desk. When I glanced toward the source, there stood Lance with a smile on his handsome face.

My heart leapt in my chest as I walked the few steps, and unlocked and opened the door.

Just stay calm. Stay calm.

"To what do I owe the pleasure?"

"May I?" he asked, indicating if he could come in. I nodded and stepped back so that he could enter. When he passed, our shoulders accidently touched and a soft moan almost escaped my throat. He smelled wonderful and looked so sexy.

"I was leaving, headed to the parking lot, when I saw your light still on."

"I'm about ready to get out of here too."

"Long week?"

"Always, but I love every minute of it. Wouldn't trade it for the world."

"Same here. There's nothing that beats owning your own, even if it means working sixty-hour weeks. At the end of the day, it's all mine. The fruit of my labor."

I smiled as I sashayed to the sofa in the waiting area and took a seat. I felt him watching me, as he followed close behind.

"Am I keeping you?"

"No. What's on your mind?" He would never know I had dreamt of this moment for weeks. I could sit here all night and listen to him speak.

"Can you believe next week is Thanksgiving?" he asked, sitting down across from me.

"Nope, and I still have so much to do in preparation. This year flew by and I think I say that every year."

"Do you prepare a big, traditional meal?"

"No, but I always have a huge food drive at Last Chance, and a luncheon for my staff and clients. On Thanksgiving Day, I volunteer at one of the local homeless shelters, helping to feed the hungry."

"How noble," he said, looking at me oddly for just a second and then it faded just as quickly.

"It fulfills me. What about you? What are your plans?"

"I usually go home to the Windy City for a few days. Visit family and friends, eat myself to death, and try to relax for a few days."

"Chicago, huh?"

"Yep."

"Sounds like fun."

"It is. I look forward to it each year, especially since I moved down South."

"What are you trying to say? You don't like the South?" I kidded.

"I'm not saying that. I love y'all to death. Strangers speak on the streets, people wave when I drive by, and the civil rights history is rich with living legends. So, don't put words in my mouth," he kidded, winking at me.

"Don't forget the wonderful weather and the beautiful women," I said.

"The verdict is still out on that, the weather. Sometimes I want to feel the winter like I used to feel 'the hawk.' Plus, I miss steppin' on a Friday or Saturday night and listening to R. Kelly. Chicago has all that and much more."

"And Atlanta has *The Real Housewives of Atlanta* and *Love & Hip Hop*."

"How could I forget that?" he asked.

"And outside the city limits, we can't forget *Here Comes Honey Boo Boo*."

Lance and I chuckled together and it felt good. Felt right. I was relaxed and no defenses were up. I could be myself around him.

"Are you a genuine Georgia peach?"

"Proud and true," I said, reclining on the sofa, kicking off my heels.

"I didn't know they still existed. Everyone in Atlanta is a transplant from up North or the West Coast."

"Oh, we are very real. You are looking at one, sir."

"That I am. There's nothing like a Georgia peach. All sweet, ripe, and juicy. Nothing beats that first taste when the rich juices drip down your chin."

For a few seconds, I wasn't sure if he was talking about peaches or something sexual.

I cleared my throat and looked away.

"I have an aunt who makes the best peach cobbler," he shared.

"Really?"

"Maybe you can try a slice one day soon. The crust is crisp and flaky and the peaches are just so."

I grinned. "I'd like that."

"Listen to me." He laughed. "Having flash-backs over food."

"Don't stop on my account. I enjoy hearing you talk."

"Well, I've kept you long enough. Let's blow this joint. May I walk you to your car?"

"Of course. Just like a Southern gentleman. See, you are picking up some Southern traits."

"Lady, that was already in me. I treat my woman right," he said, staring into my eyes. I looked away, afraid of what he might see staring back.

"I thought you said you didn't have a girl-friend."

"I don't at the present time, but I have my eye on a woman who I think is beautiful, sexy, and a joy to be around."

"Do you now?"

"I do, but I'm not sure if she's into me," Lance said, walking behind me. "I'm still trying to feel her out."

"For some reason, I think she is."

I turned off the lights and locked up. Lance and I took our time walking to the parking area, not ready to part ways. We were content to enjoy the chill air, the stillness on the block, and each other's company. When we got to my car, Lance took the keys, and unlocked and opened my door. I eased into the driver's seat.

"Good night, Ms. Erika."

"Good night, Mr. Lance."

"We have to continue this conversation very soon."

"I would like that."

"Then, it's a date."

"Yes. Soon. A date."

I backed out of my spot with Lance watching me. As I glanced in the rearview mirror, he waved and smiled.

I was smitten.

We Give Thanks

Chapter 31

The next few days went by in a complete flurry. The holidays are always bustling in the beauty industry. Clients want to look their best before a holiday and it all starts with the hair. Ask any woman. So, we always had frantic customers trying to get their hair hooked up before the family gathering or trip out of town.

Last Chance was buried in canned goods of every imaginable kind and size, much to Revered Hill's pleasure and delight. The ladies and I also each contributed beautiful gift baskets, which contained hair products and pampering items such as nail polish, lotions, makeup, et cetera. We even made a contest out of it, to see who had the best basket, and the customers participated by placing their vote in a fish bowl that sat on the counter. We were going to announce the winning basket the day before Thanksgiving, the day of our luncheon. We would only be open until noon and then we would sit down to our feast. I always provided the ham and turkey and the ladies brought the side items.

I hadn't seen Lance since our interesting encounter and it was a bit disappointing, that is until the UPS man came around 11:30 a.m. with a lovely display of fall flowers, in lively hues of reds, oranges, and yellows.

"Happy Thanksgiving," I shouted as the driver hurriedly walked out.

"Somebody has an admirer," Nobia announced, trying to read the attached card over my shoulder.

"Who are they from?" Loretta asked, walking to my side, carrying a white-and-black casserole dish that she had warmed up in the microwave. We had started to set up our Thanksgiving luncheon and the delicious aromas were making my mouth water.

"You guys are so nosey." I laughed. I reached for the card, and I was pretty sure I already knew who it was from. It read:

Sorry I couldn't say good-bye before I left for Chicago, but I had to leave earlier than expected. Thinking of you and your beautiful smile, GA peach. Truly, Lance.

I think I blushed as I attempted to turn away so no one could witness it.

"It's from Lance," I whispered tenderly.

"He has excellent taste, those are nice *and* expensive," Carla said. "My kind of man."

"How romantic," Destiny said, bending down to take a sniff of the bouquet. "Hmmm, they smell good. This was sweet of him."

"The flowers are lovely. We can use them as our centerpiece," I said, carefully picking them up and placing them on the table with the burnt orange tablecloth that was set up in the center of the room.

I think I walked on clouds for the remainder of the day—at least it felt that way. I was on cloud nine.

Around lunchtime, just as we began to sit down and feast on the various goodies everyone had brought in, including my turkey from HoneyBaked Ham, another delivery arrived.

"Erika Kane, sign here please," another delivery person said as he handed me his handheld computer to scribble my signature. I did and he hurriedly left with Thanksgiving greetings to everyone.

"What is it?" Nobia asked. "Damn, two deliveries in one day. You have that man sprung already."

"Give me a few minutes to open it and we'll find out."

When I finally managed to open the medium-sized white box with the red bow, inside was a pie. A peach cobbler to be exact, with an attached note card.

> Sweets for the sweet. Thought you might like this. It's not my aunt's peach cobbler, but it's a close second. Enjoy and I can't wait to see you again. Best, Lance.

If I was on cloud nine before, I was now on cloud eighteen. Two times the joy.

After our main meal, I bit into the first slice of pie after I had shared with everyone. All I could think about was how sweet, ripe, and juicy it was. It simply melted in my mouth. It reminded me of something else that I hoped Lance would experience soon.

Reconciliation

Chapter 32

I was seated in the break room checking e-mails on my iPhone when Erika strolled in to grab bottled water out of the refrigerator. It was a few days after Thanksgiving and we were slowly returning to our normal routines. I couldn't believe Christmas was around the corner and it was time for me to get my lists ready for my current sponsors. There was no shame in my game. My motto: you have to pay to play.

My previous nightmares, with Erika being the big, bad boogey woman, had finally ceased. Thank God. I still hadn't made heads or tails of why she had invaded my night dreams to begin with, but at least it was over. I was in church Sunday, after a long absence, and it was as if the preacher was speaking directly to my soul. He spoke of forgiveness and moving forward. *For if you forgive men when they sin against you,*

*your Heavenly Father will also forgive you. But
if you do not forgive men their sins, your Father
will not forgive your sins.* His sermon made me
think of Erika's and my situation. I realized I had
to offer forgiveness even if it was solely for the
purpose of moving on with my life. Grudges and
bitterness were toxins that corroded the spirit
and blocked blessings from coming your way.

Life was looking up; in fact, in another year
I could picture myself with my own salon and
a line of hair products. I had learned to never
underestimate the power of networking with the
right people, the connected ones, and Atlanta
had its share. So, I decided I had to let go of
negativity so that I received the right energy in
my life and the right blessings.

If you looked at it in black and white, my ex,
Brian, made his decision years ago and I had to
live with that. Evidently he saw something in
Erika that was pleasing. I don't know for sure if
she seduced him, but if she did, he didn't have
to take the bait and I also realized Erika had to
take responsibility for her actions, too. However,
that was on her. She had to reconcile that guilt,
if there was any.

Brian didn't ask me to marry him; he asked
Erika. He dropped down on one knee, offered up
an engagement ring, and proposed to her. Not

me. I needed to lick my salty wounds and move on, like I should have years ago. However, a deep jealousy and resentment stood in my way.

The bullshit that happened between our parents, it was just that, between our parents. Erika and I couldn't control what two consenting adults did, no matter how wrong or hurtful it was, no better than we could control the sun's rotation. All the horrible things and thoughts I had said and felt about Erika, I was ashamed about now.

Evidently, I didn't know Brian as well as I thought I did. I never in a million years thought he would betray me, our love, and marry Erika, so how could I say he could not have committed suicide? When it came down to it, I wasn't sure what he would do. After all, the investigation, the police report, and coroner's report said he killed himself. It was time for me to pull up my big-girl panties and practice kindness and forgiveness.

"Hey, girl," I said.

Erika looked startled that I was speaking to her. Usually I ignored her.

"Hey, Carla."

"I love your hair that way. It looks good on you."

"Thanks. You know me, always switching it up." She kind of chuckled, walking toward the exit. Today she was wearing a short jet-black bob as opposed to the long hair she usually sported.

"Do you have a minute?" I asked, searching her face for an answer.

"Sure," she said hesitantly. I could see the uncertainty in her eyes and body language. Erika walked over and sat at the small table, in front of me.

I put away my phone and for a few seconds the only sounds were my frantic heartbeat and the clock that hung on the far wall. We were alone. "I wanted to say that I'm happy for you and Lance. Since he has come into your life, you are glowing."

Erika displayed the first genuine smile since coming into the break room. "Thank you."

"He's good for you."

"I think so," she replied, visibly relaxing. "Since Lance has returned from Chicago, we have talked on the phone nearly every night, for hours. We have our very first date this weekend."

"Really? Are you excited?" I asked, genuinely curious.

"Nervous is more like it."

I laughed in spite of myself. When Lance came around, Erika acted like a teenager with a serious crush. I was truly delighted for her; Erika really wasn't that bad. She hired my crazy ass in spite of our differences. She realized I was in dire straits and now opportunity was coming my way because of connections I had made at Last Chance.

"Listen, I just wanted to say . . ." I paused. "I'm not very good at this."

Erika remained silent.

"All our drama in the past . . ."

I assumed she finally figured out what I was trying to say without much success.

"You don't have to go there, Carla."

I held up my hand to stop further comments.

"I know I'm not good at this, but I have to get it off my chest. What I'm trying to say is let's let bygones be bygones. This is something I should have said years ago."

"I would like that. I feel the same."

"Erika, I'm sorry about how I've treated you over the years. Brian made his choice and I have to finally accept it."

"Apology accepted, girl."

Just like that, we had come to a truce and who knew where our friendship would go from there. Life was always full of surprises.

At Last My Love Has Come Along

Chapter 33

Lance and I were seated at a table at one of my favorite restaurants, Fogo de Chao, in Buckhead on Piedmont Road. I loved this authentic Brazilian restaurant and the select choices of never-ending hearty meats roasted over an open pit. As we walked in, a beautiful bar was directly to the right and a large salad bar sat in the middle of the dining room. A large wine wall covered an entire section and Brazilian-style murals were featured on the walls. We had a semi-private corner, at a dark wood table covered with a white tablecloth and napkins.

"Have I told you how beautiful you look this evening?" Lance asked as his eyes tenderly admired me.

"Yes, but you can always tell me again." I giggled.

"Sure. You are simply breathtaking tonight, Ms. Kane. I can't keep my eyes off you."

"I know." And I did. I had on a stunning royal blue designer dress that hugged every curve and left very little to the imagination. It also complemented my deep brown complexion. I looked like a million dollars.

"No one should ever say you are modest. You are too much, Erika, and there is never a dull moment with you."

"I know but you can handle it." I laughed as I reached out to casually stroke his hand.

"I'm sure I can," he stated with confidence.

He looked around as a large group was seated at a nearby table.

"This is my first time here. It's nice, thanks for suggesting it," Lance said as he looked around appreciatively.

"You are very welcome, Lance. I figured you for a meat-and-potatoes kind of man."

He nodded. "Can you believe we are finally on an actual date?"

"Miracles do happen, but better late than never," I cited.

"With your schedule and mine, I was beginning to think it was almost impossible."

"We made it happen and here we are, enjoying each other's company without any distractions."

"I hear you, princess. Hopefully, this is just the beginning of many more dinners *and* breakfasts."

"I like the sound of that," I said, looking deep into his eyes and wondering what the future held for us.

"I would ask you to tell me about yourself, but we have talked so much over the last couple of weeks that I feel like I know you already."

"Actually, mostly you talked and I listened." I shifted in my chair.

"Are you trying to say I talk too much?" Lance laughed.

"No, never." I giggled, taking a sip of my drink and starting to dig into my gourmet salad before I got to the real meal of the evening.

"Well, tell me about yourself," Lance suggested. He was looking handsome in his tailored black slacks and black sweater. It hadn't gone unnoticed by me that he favored black in his wardrobe, too.

"What do you want to know?" I questioned. "Ask me anything."

Lance's mood suddenly shifted. "Let's get the topic of previous relationships out of the way. You mentioned you had been married three times before and you have to know I've heard nasty rumors."

I remained silent, listening.

"In fact, one of my barbers, when he heard we were going out tonight, he joked that he hoped to see me alive next week."

"Ouch."

"I'm just being honest, I'm not trying to hurt you with what I've heard because some people have been brutal with their opinion. I want to get it all out in the open."

"I have been married three times and they did die. Does that scare you?"

"I'm here aren't I, Elizabeth Taylor? Next question."

With those words, I started laughing and probably didn't quit for another three minutes. Every time I would stop, I would look at Lance and start all over again. I'm sure the people at the table near us thought I was crazy or on something. The seriousness of the situation was suddenly diminished with Lance making light of it.

"Do you find it strange that I've been married three times and all three husbands passed?" I asked after finally getting my composure back. I took a sip of water and awaited his response.

"No. Life and death happen, but I do find it telling that you found love not once, but three times in your lifetime. That's very rare. Three men fell in love with you and I can understand why."

I thought about his comments. "No one has ever stated it that way before. I'm usually judged and deemed the big, bad Black Widow."

"Are you?" Lance asked, his eyes not leaving mine.

"No, of course not. I'm not a monster. When I'm really in love, I love deeply."

"You lose yourself."

"I wouldn't say that. I would say love completes me."

"Then, that's all that matters. You know your heart and that those men loved you. You were there during their last moments on earth and that's a beautiful thing. Don't you agree?"

I cleared my throat several times, attempting to get rid of the lump that had suddenly formed. I couldn't speak.

Lance understood and simply reached for my hand and held it gently across the table. It was our moment. Words weren't necessary. The remainder of the night was enjoyable as well. We ate, we drank, we laughed; and then we laughed some more. I realized I could definitely love this man. That realization made my heart and spirit leap with joy. I never thought I would experience this feeling again.

After a lovely evening, almost perfect actually, Lance dropped me off at my house. Like a gentlemen, he walked me to the door, kissed me lightly on the lips, and simply left after seeing that I was safely in. He didn't invite himself in, but said there would be plenty of times for that later. I melted as my love came down.

Much like the other times I experienced love connections, I tossed and turned for most of the night in my queen-sized bed, longing to have Lance beside me, holding me in his arms. Images and dark scenes from my exes came back to haunt and tease me.

Malik, Brian, and Edward all invaded my dreams, one at a time, patiently waiting their turn. All men I had loved and married at some point in my life. However, they all taught me a valuable lesson that I never forgot: love can quickly turn into hate without warning. There really was a thin line between love and hate.

Malik

Chapter 34

He was dressed in his usual attire of dark denim baggie jeans, a navy hoodie, and expensive Jordan sneakers. And to think when I first met him, I thought that attire was sexy and super swagged out. I attributed it to being young and dumb.

"Where do you think you're going?" I asked, with my arms crossed stiffly against my bosom as I stood in the doorway of our tiny bedroom.

"Out."

"No, you're not," I said boldly.

"Who's going to stop me? Not you," he said, looking over at me from across the bedroom with a hint of anger as he sat on the edge of our bed.

I glared at Malik with almost as much hatred as I'd once had love for him.

"You can scowl at me, pout, do the holy dance, the Hokey Pokey, but I am still going out for drinks with the fellows tonight."

"What about me?"

"What about you? You're a big girl, entertain yourself until I come home. Damn."

"I'm sick of this, Malik. We never spend any time together anymore. What happened to us?"

As he stared at me, for a moment I glimpsed the man I used to love with all my heart. Malik literally saved me after Mama was killed by a lover. After we hooked up, Malik was my reason to live and go on with my life and not give up. He was strong and street confident. I thought that was powerful, that I could lean on him for strength, but I soon learned that swagger and skills in the bedroom didn't pay bills or keep a roof over your head. We were barely getting by and this was not the life I dreamt of, or desired. I had much bigger dreams and goals.

"How is your job search going?"

"Don't start with that again, Erika. I told you I'm looking and that's the best I can do. You know the white man don't wanna give a brotha a break."

"Evidently, you aren't looking hard enough and that bullshit you are spewing is just an excuse."

For a few seconds, Malik gave me a look that said I had gone far enough. I was a bit nervous of what he would do, but I knew I could hold my own. Two weeks earlier, he had hit me for the first time. Out of nowhere, he slapped me with the back of his hand over something I had said.

"You'd better watch that smart mouth of yours. I have told you about that shit, Erika. Don't make me go there again."

"Baby, don't leave. Stay home tonight. I need you." I instantly hated myself for begging him to stay with me, but I couldn't help myself.

Briefly, I thought I saw a short-lived glimmer of love reflected in his eyes.

"When you lose some weight, I'll start staying home."

I had gained a few pounds, twenty, since we married, but I wasn't exactly slim before. Malik used to tell me that he loved a woman with some meat on her bones; he wasn't looking for a twig. He loved having something to hold on to as he eased himself inside. All the stress Malik was putting me through had gotten to me and I coped by eating. A lot.

"You used to love it."

"That's the operative word, used to. Look at you. You look like a fat, lazy slob. You wear my sweats and T-shirts all the fucking time.

You don't fix your hair. Get yourself together, Erika.

I murmured, *"I will when you do."*

"What? What did you say?" he asked, looking up again from completing the task of lacing his sneakers.

"Nothing," I whispered, taking a step or two backward to let him pass as he walked by. *"You are making me crazy with your shit, Malik."*

I followed Malik into the living room. He reached for his keys on the coffee table; or, rather, my keys to my car. His vehicle had been repossessed a few weeks earlier, so now we only had one car. He dropped me off at work each morning and supposedly went job searching. I was no fool.

"I'm only having a couple of drinks and then I'll come home," he said, like that made everything all right.

"Don't do me any favors."

"Okay, I won't then. No problem."

I walked to the sofa and plopped down on it.

"By the way, I took a twenty out of your wallet earlier."

"Malik, I needed that for lunch for the rest of the workweek."

"It won't hurt you to skip a few meals." He laughed. *"I'll make you a salad."*

The man standing in front of me was a shell of the man I loved and married. There was a time when he could do no wrong in my eyes and I worshipped the ground he walked on. He was my savior after Mama passed. Not now. He hurt me, ridiculed me, hit me, and wasn't changing. I realized I hated him as he walked out the front door without a backward glance or good-bye.

Malik stumbled into bed around three o'clock that next morning, smelling like liquor and cheap perfume. I stared at him through the darkness and shadows as he slept, snored, and called out in his sleep a few times. I thought of the man who used to made sweet love to me like no other and whispered sweet words that made me feel like I was special. Now, all I felt was contempt and disdain that he was a part of my life. Ruining it.

The next morning, Sunday, I got up bright and early and fixed Malik his favorite breakfast. Scrambled eggs, hot, runny grits, crisp bacon with thick skin, raisin toast, strawberry jam, the works. If I do say so myself, I threw down, put my foot in it, and Malik ate every single bite. He didn't leave a crumb and didn't utter a "thank you, baby," either.

Later, I was patient as he lounged around our rented two-bedroom house in his underwear, no worries to be seen. Not an apology to be said. Unknown to him, he could have stopped it at any time with two simple words: I'm sorry. But he never did. So, he paid.

"I'm going to drive over to Mike's for a few hours and catch the first half of the game," Malik offered.

"Okay." I smiled. "Drive carefully."

He looked at me curiously.

"What's up with you?"

"Nothing. Nothing at all. Why do you ask?"

"You've been acting sweet all day today. Most of the time you are running your fucking mouth a mile a minute, griping about something or another."

"Things change. What's the point?"

"Yeah, I'll see you later. I'm running late."

"See ya." I whispered, wouldn't wanna be ya, to myself.

I watched Malik walk out the door for the last time as I munched on an ice-cold Snickers candy bar that I had just taken out of the freezer. My favorite. I wondered how far he would get before it happened. I wondered if it would be sudden and what his last thoughts would be. Maybe his life would flash before his eyes and he would regret how he had treated me.

My mother always told me, "don't get mad, get even." Last night, really early morning, I made my decision and quietly slipped to our garage and cut the hose to the brake line. I knew my way around cars from back in the day when Mama dated a mechanic and he taught me a thing or two about cars, among other things. I even briefly worked in his automotive repair shop after school.

The call came later. Tragic accident. Lost control. Crashed. Hit the wall. Instantly killed. So young. Catastrophic.

All the words ran together in a jumble and I sank to my knees and cried. Cried for days. Cried for what could have been before it went bad.

Brian

Chapter 35

With his boyish good looks, Brian was my second chance at love. I placed the past behind me, almost like it never happened, and looked toward the future with new enthusiasm. Everyone told me I was still young, I could get past my grief and rebuild my life. And I did.

I started a new life with new friends, well actually old ones who I simply hadn't seen for a while. Carla and her sister, Jessica, my best friend from back in the day, were back in my life and we partied together. That's how I met Brian, through Carla. It was love at first sight even though I knew he was dating Carla, but we couldn't help who we loved. My heart fluttered each time I saw him. We ended up sleeping together a few months later and before I knew what was happening, we were man and wife. Carla was out of the picture, bitter as hell.

Love hung around for a brief period of time before it, too, turned bitter cold and betrayed me. In the beginning, I was very happy with Brian. I doted on him, we had a strong sexual attraction, and we were inseparable. He proved to me that I could love again, but then things suddenly took a turn for the worse.

"I heard you were talking with Carla the other day," I said as we reclined on the sofa. Brian was watching the game and I was flipping through a celebrity magazine. I loved to read about how the stars lived.

"If I did, what's your point?"

I looked at him in disbelief. "She is your ex-girlfriend and you of all people know that she can't stand me. That's my point."

Brian didn't comment. Didn't even look in my direction. I was invisible.

"Brian," I screamed, throwing a small pillow at him. "Answer me."

"What? What, Erika? Damn!"

"Did you see her?"

"Yes, I did. I ran into her at the convenience store up the street. As I was walking out, she was walking in."

"Don't you think that's too much of a coincidence? Carla doesn't even live on this side of town."

"So, she's stalking me now?" he asked, shaking his head in disbelief. "Is that really what you are suggesting?"

"That's all you did, simply talked?"

"No, I took her home and fucked the shit out of her. Two times."

I stared at him and rolled my eyes.

"Brian?"

"Erika, what? I'm trying to watch the game of the season and you are making it very difficult."

"Answer my question."

"There's nothing to answer. I saw Carla and we spoke for a few minutes, asked her how she was doing, caught up, and that was basically it. You are going to believe what you want to believe, so what's the point in explaining?"

"Ummm," I said and sucked my teeth.

"What is that supposed to mean?" he asked, glancing in my direction, finally.

"You figure it out."

"I don't know what your problem is, Erika. It's almost like you are obsessed with Carla. You won, okay? I'm here with you. Don't that count for something?"

"It's no secret that she'd get you back if she could, in a heartbeat. I hear the talk around town."

"I'm not going anywhere, Erika. I'm exactly where I want to be. Married to you."

"You promise?"

"I do, but you have to promise me that you'll go back to the way you were. I miss the way we used to be before Carla moved back to town and you lost your damn mind. I can't take much more of this."

"I haven't changed."

"You definitely have. Stop trying to control me, Erika. I'm not the one. Never have been and never will be. I wear the pants in my household. I understand how you grew up, what you witnessed and what your mama taught you about men and relationships, but I'm not going to hurt you, nor am I going to let you dominate me."

At that moment I believed him, needed to. I had heard rumors that he had hooked up with Carla since she returned to Atlanta. After Brian and I married, I thought she had moved out to California for a stylish gig with a local celebrity. For now, I let it be. Took Brian's word as gospel. A couple of weeks later, I discovered the real answer when I picked up Brian's phone as a text came through. He was passed out in our bed. When we made love, he always slept like the dead afterward.

The text read:

I miss you, baby. When can you slip back over and give me some more of that good loving? I didn't realize how much I missed that dick. LOL. Don't worry about that fat cow of a wife of yours. She is too stupid to suspect anything and is probably too busy eating everything in sight to notice. Hugs and kisses, Carla.

Something inside of me snapped, just like the last time. I couldn't see clearly, I felt like I would vomit as I threw the phone down on the bed. I gave Brian everything he needed and asked for and he repaid me by betraying me by having an affair, not with just anyone, but with Carla.

I snapped. Snapped hard.

I can't remember much that happened afterward. I remember talking to the 911 operator, don't remember calling, to let her know that my husband had committed suicide with a gun he kept in the nightstand while I slept on the sofa after falling asleep downstairs.

I was in a daze.

I remembered the mess. The blood. So much blood. The gore. It was everywhere. Brains. Later, I was told that this was how scenes looked when a person shot himself in the head at close range. My husband didn't leave a suicide note and I never realized he was depressed until then. Brian always kept everything bottled up tightly inside. That was his way. Later, I discovered we were heavily in debt and he had kept that from me as well since he took care of the bills. People speculated that may have been the reason he was extremely depressed. I never knew. I just knew he was gone. Then came the vicious rumors that I had something to do with Brian's death. The police investigated and also discovered my first husband had died from a tragic accident. Eventually, the investigation was dropped after they couldn't find any evidence against me.

Life slowly returned to normal, as normal as it would ever be, and my grief subsided to a manageable level. That's the way with life. It goes on. I saw Carla out and about eventually and I went up to her and hugged her. No hard feelings. I whispered in her ear, "Brian's in a better place. God has him now and we both lose." I walked away with her staring at me strangely.

Edward

Chapter 36

What's the old adage? Strike three and you are out? When I met Edward, I was determined to make our budding relationship work, always and forever. Failure was not an option. I had learned from my other mistakes and this time around, I was older and wiser. I looked at the first two marriages as trial runs. Trial and error.

Edward was the real deal, as my Mama would say, but everybody she met was the real deal, so I started to wonder at a young age how you could tell who really was a keeper. Edward came with the total package: tall, dark, handsome, and charming. He was a gentleman and a professional man. I later learned that he had a checkered past as a young man that almost led him down the wrong path and so he had to get out of Chicago. Quick. He never talked much about that time in his life and I had met very few of his family members over the years. It's funny how life throws different paths our way and depending on the one we choose, it can make all the difference in the world. I met Edward when we both worked at a national insurance company; I was a claims adjuster and he was a manager. We simply clicked and it seemed right. We were meant to be together and he was the love of my life.

In the beginning, we were very much in love and extremely blissful. Joy shone all over my face. I glowed. I couldn't believe I could love someone as much as I loved Edward. I kept expecting to wake up and find it was all a dream, just a figment of my imagination. I knew I shouldn't say it, but Edward completed me.

Edward and I were your all-American couple until we realized I couldn't have a baby. We had tried and tried and tried unsuccessfully for years. When we finally tested, it was determined that I was the sterile one. I couldn't conceive. I cried for days and Edward tried his best to console me, telling me everything would be okay. We could adopt. I wanted to believe him, but soon the small, subtle changes started and I noticed. I saw the resentment in his eyes that displayed he was stuck with a woman who couldn't give him children.

***

I had rushed home to prepare all of Edward's favorite dishes: well-done New York strip steak with sautéed onions, baked potato with sour cream and chives, a light Caesar salad and a nice merlot wine. Just as I finished setting the table, the phone rang.

"Hello."

"Hey, baby."

"Hey, yourself. Where are you? Are you almost home?"

"That's why I'm calling."

I sighed. "No, Edward. Don't tell me . . ."

"I'm sorry, baby. I'm working late again. I can't help it. Since I've gotten this promotion, I have more responsibility, which translates into longer hours spent at the office, at least for right now."

"It seems like we are never under the same roof anymore, except when we are sleeping, and we haven't made love in ages."

"Stop exaggerating, Erika. You are always overdramatic. I promise I'll make it up to you. Our anniversary is coming up in a few weeks, maybe we could leave town for a few days and stay at that bed and breakfast you love so much in Savannah."

"I would like that."

Edward took good care of me. I was never lacking in new clothes, expensive jewelry, designer purses and shoes. Edward spoiled his wife and I loved every minute of it.

"It's a plan then, baby."

I listened closely to his words and tried to determine if he was telling me the truth or trying to pacify me for the moment.

"Are you there? Erika?"

"Yeah, I'm here."

"I love you, baby, but I have to run. This won't last forever. Be patient."

"I made you dinner, all your favorites. Steak, baked potato, salad."

"It sounds wonderful. Put a plate in the microwave and I'll eat when I get home."

I knew he wouldn't. Edward would be so tired that all he would manage to do was take a hot shower and crash. He wouldn't have the energy to ask about my day or spend any time with me.

"What time do you think you'll get in?" *I asked.*

The line was silent.

"Hello. Hello, Edward."

All I heard was the dial tone. He had hung up; had dismissed me. I was so angry that I jumped up and dumped the entire meal in the trash can and sulked on the sofa, staring at the

TV but not really watching the reality show that was on. This was the third time this had happened within the last two weeks.

Edward's hours appeared to get longer after a new employee started working in his office. Bella was his new assistant and I didn't trust her with those short skirts and low-cut blouses she wore. She couldn't fool me. She wanted my man, and who wouldn't? Edward had it all. He was the perfect catch.

I picked up the phone and quickly dialed my husband's direct line and just as I thought, Bella answered with her disgustingly sweet voice. I quickly hung up the phone and threw it back down on the sofa. They were working late, together.

I was so mad that I didn't know what to do. Tonight I had planned to bring up the possibility of us adopting a baby. He had mentioned it before, but I wasn't open to adoption until now. I realized if I could give him a baby boy, our marriage could get back on track and I wanted that more than anything. Edward and I had simply hit a detour in the road called life. It happened. As weeks flew by, we never really had the opportunity to discuss adoption. We came and went as strangers. Edward was always at the office; he might as well have taken *his bed down there, and Bella was always at the office. My peers started to whisper and look at me with sad, pitying eyes.*

When we were together, Edward was distant. I realized it was only a matter of time before he left me for her. Edward couldn't love two women. Believe it or not, he was loyal and noble. I couldn't allow him to leave me. I just couldn't. It wasn't fair. I calculated a plan in my head and prepared to carry it out with clarity.

I gave myself a weekend to accomplish my mission. Let's just say it all started and ended with food. Meals laced with arsenic, basically undetectable.

Edward did suffer, but I comforted him and nursed him through the entire ordeal. If I couldn't have him, no one could or would. I never figured out if he realized what was happening to him, probably not. He was in too much pain, in and out of consciousness. I nursed him, played the good wife, told him how much I loved him and how happy I was with him, until recently. I believed he knew. I apologized for sometimes being nagging, controlling, and clingy. I explained how that still wasn't a reason to run into another woman's arms while you were married.

As he took his last torturous breath, I realized I was finished with love and men and relationships. They were too much trouble and too much work. After I managed to cremate his body so that the coroner couldn't examine it and discover the poison, life went on. It was curious that a few weeks after Edward's death, Bella came into the office with a huge diamond ring and announced her engagement to a long-time boyfriend. A month later, I also received a check, the payout to the life insurance policy that Edward had taken out with me as the beneficiary. Even in death, my man was looking out for me. I was able to start over. Yet again. I was safe. I was undiscovered. My luck hadn't run out; I had the luck of the Irish because I always seemed to land on my feet when bad circumstances occurred. Eventually, I started over with Last Chance.

Now, I had the chance to prove to myself that I could find true and lasting love. Lance was different, I was different now and I was sure we could make it work. I was giddy with the possibilities.

Lance Anthony

Chapter 37

"Man, I can't believe you are going through with this," my nephew, Jacob, shared.

I stared at the phone for a few seconds as if I could see him through it.

"Believe it," I said firmly. "There's no turning back now. That bitch won't know what hit her when I'm through with her."

"She's pretty sharp. I'm surprised she hasn't suspected anything yet."

"Why would she? We never met before now and even if Edward mentioned me in the past, he would have referred to me as Anthony. That's what everyone from the old neighborhood knows me by, not Lance."

"True dat."

"She's going to get a dose of her own medicine, literally."

Jacob chuckled. "She has some sweet pussy though, Unc. You sure I can't hit it one more time?"

"You just stay put until I need you. You have plenty of jump-offs who can satisfy your needs in Chicago."

"You know I got your back. That's what family and blood does. Just call and I'm there."

"Ms. Ericka Kane won't know what hit her when I'm finished with her. She mistakenly thought she could murder my half brother, Edward, and get away with it."

"She did get away with it. Some people did believe her bogus story that he was sick with flu-like symptoms and simply passed away a few days later," Jacob shared.

"Yeah, she pulled the wool over a lot of people's eyes and she's good, too. She covered her tracks well with the cremation because she should be sitting in federal prison, but she's going to discover that I'm smarter and much more ruthless. I'm going to enjoy this."

"Do you think she really offed the other two husbands because the authorities couldn't prove it? That's a bad bitch if she did."

"Who knows, and I really don't care. I just want street justice for *my* brother. He didn't deserve what she served up to him. Edward was always too weak, that's why he had to leave Chicago and distance himself from us. He wanted to go legit. He didn't have the stomach or the heart for our criminal lifestyle of drug trafficking and illegal gambling, but I loved him nevertheless. He was blood and I am my brother's keeper."

"Erika comes across as a do-gooder, everyone says she does a lot of charitable work in the community and her local church. You would never suspect she's a black widow, Unc."

"That's her cover and she wears it well," I said. "Living large off the blood of my brother in that big house and thriving salon with no shame. I honestly believe, in her mind, she has talked herself into believing that Edward did die from an illness. In some ways, I can't figure her out. Psychopathic bitch."

"To be honest, Unc, I wasn't so sure she would take the bait. She was cold as ice in the restaurant that first day I introduced myself to her. You should have seen how she acted like she didn't need a man and I was beneath her. I thought maybe you had gotten it wrong, pegged her wrong, but then I stopped by a few nights later and she literally jumped my dick. Rode me like a pro. It was like she was a different person away from the prying eyes of her friends."

"You did well, son."

"I was able to find out a little more personal info from talking with her friend, Nobia. That was a good idea to get to know her better. I guess it's also good to know people in high places who can be paid off, because the copy of the file from the police investigation pretty much confirmed that they believed Erika had something to do with Edward's death, but didn't have any evidence which would stick."

"I know she did it and don't need a police report to confirm it. I told you that a few months before he died, Edward reached out to me. We talked for hours, like the old days, and he told me that he was starting to wonder if there was some truth to the rumors about her previous husbands' deaths. Evidently, Erika had been displaying irrational behavior; he felt like he didn't know her anymore. And then he was gone."

"Like you said, we'll dish out our own brand of justice," Jacob said.

"That we will, and as much as you've talked about that ass, you best believe I'm going to sample it several times before it's all over. Don't think I won't have my fun, too. In fact, I'm looking forward to it. I'm going to enjoy taking my time and you know I've always been a very patient man."

"You are cold-blooded." Jacob laughed.

"My family is not to be played with. Vengeance is mine."

"Well, I'm here when you need me. I'm getting the house ready now. I'm on schedule and it's almost secure."

"I know I can depend on you, Jacob. The family was disappointed when Edward decided to go in another direction because he was definitely the brain behind the family business, but I'm still my brother's keeper. I swear to you, every time I look at that bitch I think about what she did to my brother, I want to kill her with my bare hands, but that's too good for her. Erika has to suffer and suffer she will."

"Erika's day is coming. It always does sooner or later," Jacob said. "I can't wait to see the expression on her face when she figures out the connection between you and Edward."

"Maybe I'll reveal it to her as she is coming," I said.

I hung up with a smile on my face. I was looking forward to dispensing my own brand of justice on Ms. Erika Kane. She had finally met her match. Let the game begin.

Oops! I Did It Again

by

Eric Pete

Chapter 1

Artemis

I let my negligee straps fall lazily off my shoulders as I gazed down into his lustful eyes. Placing my hands on his muscled chest, I rose and plummeted with him as if he were the majestic ocean upon which I sailed. Along every inch of his I took, I made my ass clap like I'd seen in them videos, shuddering with more orgasms than a sister could count. I was enjoying myself so much that I almost had to remember to breathe.

"Baby, are you all right?" I asked, acknowledging the sudden grimace that had crept onto Carlos's face.

It wasn't a "fuck face." I knew those all too well.

"Yeah, Artie," he said, using his pet name for me with just a hint of a gasp. "A little gas, s'all. Can't eat spicy food like I used to," he admitted with a grin lingering on his lovely full lips.

I could kiss them all night long, but preferred when he was placing them on me.

Crawfish were in season and earlier tonight, we'd had our fill of several pounds of the seasoned mudbugs along with corn and potatoes at Ragin Cajun on Westheimer. Our stomachs satisfied, we took our party just up the Sam Houston Tollway to City Centre to work on other cravings and desires.

"All right. As long as you're okay," I said, resuming my grind atop him after his assurance. Carlos worked for HPD, particularly the division that patrolled this area of Houston. And that gave him the hookup here at Hotel Sorella, which we were enjoying tonight. With the lit candles filling our penthouse suite with traces of sweet vanilla, and Elle Varner's melodic voice requesting a "Refillllllll," I wasn't about to let my nerves ruin the mood.

Nah. Tonight was right. And here, having exquisite sex with my man, I was so right that I was wrong. Don't make sense, huh? Well, just go with it.

Carlos grunted, pumping me deliberately as he gripped my ample hips with his powerful fingers.

"Mmm. More," I ordered as firm, calloused hands felt over my body. Without warning,

Carlos flipped me onto my back, startling me by his suddenness. That experience with taking down perps was paying off for me. Carlos loved a woman with some thickness and he was gladly showing me just how much, too. I was a plus-size woman, and not easy to handle, but he certainly showed and proved tonight.

"Baby, you're gonna make me not wanna leave. Ever," he admitted in my ear as he smoothly worked about my middle, stemming my sweet honey tide with his dick's steadfast hardness. As he stroked me right, I sang his name. For he gave me the refill the singer Elle Varner had been asking for again and again.

Hate on, Elle. Hate on.

Before long, Carlos had me begging him to stop as his pelvis bore down with steady, firm strokes.

But when he really did stop, I wasn't exactly thrilled with him.

"Carlos? Wha . . .? What's wrong, baby?" I panted as I opened my eyes.

"My . . . my chest," my chocolate god replied, suspended over me as he struggled to catch his breath.

I frantically slid out from under him, then had Carlos sit up on the bed. He tried to stand while pounding his fist against his chest, but almost fell over. I caught him though and sat his ass right back down as I felt panic rising inside me.

"Oh God! Oh God! What do you want me to do, baby? Do you need some water? Or fresh air? I knew we shouldn't have ordered that last pound of crawfish!" I screamed more to myself while standing over him.

His strength quickly fading, he managed to point toward the room phone on the other side of the bed and mouthed, "Call nine-one-one."

Before I could even grasp what Carlos was telling me, he gasped, then collapsed back onto the bed, motionless.

"Oh shit! Oh shit! Oh shit!" I rambled as I scurried over him and got to the phone. I reached out and touched his sweaty forehead as I placed the receiver to my ear and pushed the button for the front desk. "Baby, it's gonna be okay," I said as calmly as I could just as somebody answered.

"Front desk, how may I help you this evening?" the hotel operator cheerfully chimed like she'd been waiting all night for my call.

"Please! Get an ambulance!" I pled while sobbing. "We need help! I . . . I think my boyfriend's having a heart attack!"

Chapter 2

A Week Later

"Whooo. You can do this, girl," I said aloud as I checked myself in the rearview mirror. I'd gone shopping at Ross in Meyerland Plaza yesterday and bought this black outfit. It wasn't snug by any means. I think it complemented my shape. But as I fidgeted in my seat, imagining flaws in my makeup, it suddenly felt tight and confining. Even though I'd done nothing wrong, all these police cars in the parking lot had me feeling like I'd stolen something. But in their eyes, maybe I had stolen something from them—their brother-in-arms.

Y'see—Carlos suffered a massive heart attack that night we were together.

He made it to the hospital that night, but only lasted 'til morning.

Now, the viewing of his body was here on Reed Road in the Sunnyside neighborhood of

Houston from which he hailed. I guess I was in mourning of some sort. But like everything in my life these days, this too was complicated.

What had been sunny skies was now an overcast patchwork of gray clouds taunting me with the raindrops just beginning to pepper my windshield. I'd never live myself down if I punked out though. And if I ever had any feelings for Carlos, I had to show up and pay my respects. Debate and hand-wringing over, I got out my car and walked into the funeral home on Reed Road.

Besides his fellow officers, other people who were obviously like family to Carlos paid their respects as well. Soft, comforting gospel music played in the background as I signed the guestbook in the lobby, trying my best to tune out the private conversations and low wails escaping the mouths of family members I never got a chance to meet or know. It had only been a month since I first met Carlos, when he let me slide on a speeding ticket in exchange for my number. And with how my past marriage ended, we were kinda winging it, just being noncommittal and enjoying one another's company. So much was left undiscovered between the two of us. In fact, one unknown turned out to be so much bigger than I expected.

It was torture coming here under these circumstances. And I still didn't know how I'd react when I saw him. Lord knows, the large framed portrait of Carlos in full dress uniform on display outside the viewing room had me choking up.

Maybe if we hadn't had sex that night. Maybe if I'd noticed his symptoms earlier. Maybe if I'd reacted quicker. But enough with beating myself up; what was done was done.

As I took my first cautious steps inside the viewing room, two women, a mother and daughter, sprang to their feet from off a bench to my right and stormed over. Even to a complete stranger, their resemblance was uncanny. And I'd been expecting them.

"You have some nerve coming here," the older woman hissed as she stepped in front of me, looking ready to spit in my face.

"I had to pay my respects," I solemnly commented, not making eye contact so as to not go off on the mother for whom I still had respect.

"By disrespecting me?" her daughter asked as she intentionally bumped against me. Her hands were trembling like she was thinking about doing something.

Now her, I had no qualms about laying my hands on. "This ain't about you, Anitra. Now excuse me," I said, moving to gently push her aside.

But she wasn't having it. Despite being about forty pounds lighter, she bowed up. "But it is when that's my man lying dead in that coffin! And you put him there, Artemis!" she growled a little too loudly, drawing everybody's attention to us.

Just great.

I knew these two all too well; for they weren't Carlos's family.

They were mine.

My sister Anitra took after our mother while I resembled my father's side of the family, a glaring reminder of the man who left her, probably why she favored my sister over me. And in this awkward, unfortunate situation, it was no different.

I stayed out of Anitra's business and she, living clear over in Summerwood with her bougie ass, stayed out of mine. How was I to know her business *was* Carlos?

Yes. We were sleeping with the same man, an awful coincidence in a city of over four million people.

Except, Anitra had the privilege of knowing Carlos's family.

She was engaged to him.

"Sis," I said as I took a deep breath. "I already told you. I did not know you were seeing Carlos.

And, to be honest, he didn't strike me as your type, what with him being a 'civil servant' 'n' all."

"I'll have you know, Carlos was due for a promotion. You see all these officers here. They loved him! Bitch, you should have some class and civility about you. Carlos's family is probably wondering what's going on. Lord knows I already have to deal with the embarrassment and whispers of my . . . my fiancé sleeping with another woman. But for them to find out it's my own sister . . . well . . . I just will not stand for it," she huffed with that indignant face I'd seen way too many times in life.

I honestly did not know we were seeing the same man until after Carlos died. Y'see, my sister and I weren't the type to trade stories over coffee and such. I found out from my mother that Anitra was in mourning for her fiancé, a man who'd died in the midst of cheating on her with another woman. Had almost chalked it up to some fluky coincidence until my mother let it slip that Anitra's fiancé was a police officer. Let's just say my first conversation with my sister in months was less than civil.

"It's always about you, huh, Anitra?" I cracked. "Maybe that's what made him seek someone a little less selfish."

"And obviously a lot more desperate," my sister spat, her voice dripping with bitterness and contempt. "I don't know what he was doing with you. Must've gotten him drunk," Anitra remarked as she looked me up and down before turning that nose up that probably sniffed the Ross on my outfit. Not everybody in this town was earning six figures working for Chevron like she was.

"Isn't it obvious? He liked what he saw," I chimed, throwing back Anitra's remarks about my body. Just because she was slender like our mother, she somehow thought that made her better than me. But she was ugly on the inside, something which drove a bigger wedge between us than any man ever could.

"Artemis, you're not welcome here. I told you that before you decided not to listen. You should go now before you upset your sister anymore," our mother, Ruth, begged.

It turned my stomach to hear her so steadfast in her support for Anitra over me.

"We can talk about this later, but right now Anitra needs to be in there with Carlos's family."

"Excuse me? Who the hell are y'all? And why are y'all yellin' in here?" a Hispanic woman with a little boy at her side asked as she tried to pass. We were blocking the entrance to the viewing, but she seemed kinda bossy for just another person paying their respects. She was a thick, curvy woman like me and, upon my doing a double take, her little boy didn't appear to be quite . . . fully Hispanic. With those puffy cheeks, one could swear he looked like a tiny, lighter-skinned version of . . .

I blinked, stunned by thoughts assaulting my mind; didn't even hear what my mother and sister were saying to her just then except that they hadn't a clue. As I opened my mouth to ask the obvious, a woman I presumed was Carlos's mother peered from the viewing room before my words could form. She saw the accusation crystallizing in my eyes as I stood beside Anitra.

The elderly woman in black with silver hair nervously smiled, then cast her gaze on the woman and child. "Luz, where have you and Carlos Jr. been? Come on in here, girl," she urged, giving the two of them a hug as she ushered them to view Carlos's body.

Then, almost as if we were an afterthought, she doubled back and addressed us. "Luz and my Carlos have been sweethearts since high school. Of course, my baby did love the ladies," she admitted, grinning sheepishly as she turned to leave us looking like fools. The non-invite to join the family was all too evident and totally understood.

My mother and Anitra were caught flat-footed, no longer feeling so special right now as Carlos's real girlfriend and son took their seats in the front row of the chapel with his relatives and family.

"That bitch," Anitra cursed. "Who does she think she is?"

"His *number one* to your *number two*," I mumbled, knowing she really didn't want me to answer. But I did anyway. "You know what, Anitra? You are right," I admitted with a smart-ass smile. "Carlos was all yours. So I'm gonna 'respect your wishes' and leave you and Mama so I can go return this outfit to Ross before I sweat in it. Deuces, y'all."

Then I smartly took my leave while they debated whether to start a fight in the funeral home over a dead man.

A damn shame.

Chapter 3

"How was your weekend, baby?" my coworker Miss Nancy asked, as I trudged in Monday morning looking like death on two weary legs. I guessed my being here was a testament to my being among the living though.

"Meh," I replied, not even bothering with an eye roll as I plopped in my cubicle chair opposite her. I hadn't slept well since Carlos died on me and this weekend, after the fallout at the funeral home, was no different. Hadn't taken any calls from my mother as that shit she pulled with my sister was inexcusable. Besides, I could hear her mouth; but not just about the deal with Carlos. It must be some bizarre kind of record, but Carlos wasn't the first man to die on me. My husband— my late husband, Maurice—died in the act too. Two men, two heart attacks. Yeah. Having done it again, I was a regular black widow. *Maybe I should just shut the coochie down.*

"When I'm looking forward to coming into work, you know the weekend was pretty bad," I offered as I turned my computer on to begin my dreaded day of collections here at our company, Bram-Lect on Briarpark Drive in the Westchase area of town. If my debt hadn't spiraled out of control after Maurice died over a year ago, I'd have quit by now. But with the lack of two incomes, my student loan debt, and no life insurance, I was pushed into a corner from which I'd found no escape. Funny how my job was hounding people in similar situations as mine. I guessed that made me an expert, and why I was so good at what I did. Didn't make me any happier doing it though. If my coworkers knew about my recent dating history and how it ended, the office scuttlebutt would've been off the charts. And, child, this place could gossip with the best of 'em.

"Damn. Furreal?" Miss Nancy said as she took a sip from her coffee mug then grimaced. "Girl, you need to get out. Have some fun. Maurice would want you to."

"Uh huh," I commented as the big Windows symbol sprang to life on my monitor. "I just wanna bury my nose in these accounts and try to bring in some money. For somebody at least."

"Not so fast, girlfriend," she chimed. "You forgot about the dog and pony show today?"

"Huh?" I balked with a big frown. "Oooh. That's right. Damn. Big boss comin'?"

"Yep. Already here. You didn't put it on your Outlook calendar?" she asked before moving on without waiting for confirmation. "Karyn picked him up from Hobby last night. Took him out to dinner at Perry's by Memorial City from what I hear. And probably had her *own* meeting with him, too, back at the hotel," she joked, making a motion as if sucking a dick. We all talked about how overly flirtatious our office manager, Karyn, was in his presence.

"You nasty," I teased while allowing a smile to form for the first time in days. "No. I didn't put the meeting on my calendar. Too much stuff on my mind. Other stuff," I answered.

"Well, get yourself together. We got at least an hour of bullshit ahead of us. And if it goes through lunch, you know it's gonna be cheap. Karyn always gets those sandwich platters from Walmart. Now she know she could come through with some catfish or somethin'."

The seven members of our collection team were summoned to the large conference room on the fifth floor of our twelve-story building. Already seated along one side of the large cherry wood table were: Rhonda, our immediate supervisor; Karyn, the officer manager; and the "big

kahuna," Roy Bramlett, our company president
and owner of Bram-Lect Collections. Roy was
wrapping up a phone conversation as we entered. The tall, redheaded fiftyish man smiled
and motioned for us to be seated, whispering
that it would be only a moment longer.

I slid into a seat opposite the big three while
Miss Nancy plunked down her coffee mug to my
right. While we all waited for "Our Boy Roy" to
finish his talk so we could begin, Karyn distributed the agenda around the table. Like me, most
of us just wanted to hear about the bonus we'd
earned for our hard work this quarter.

"No. No, Marie. I already told you, I'm in
a meeting and a Porsche is out the question,"
Roy said into his phone to somebody who was
probably either his daughter or wife; maybe his
mistress. "Did you see your tuition bill for this
year at Duke? Well, then you know a Porsche
isn't going to happen."

Okay. Definitely, not his wife. Still could've
been a mistress if he liked 'em young . . . and on
a meal plan.

Roy continued his personal call on our time,
his monogrammed cufflinks visible as he instructed, "Marie, tell your mother to take you
by the BMW dealership and pick out what you
want. But make sure it's reasonable. I'll call

Larry and tell him to be expecting you. Uh huh. Uh huh. I love you too. Bye."

The room was uncomfortably silent after listening to this bullshit. Miss Nancy bumped her knee against mine beneath the table, to which I subtly nodded.

"Tell you what; I'll take a Chevy Silverado," Matthew, one of the other collectors, mumbled under his breath in his lazy East Texas drawl.

I stifled a giggle.

"So sorry about that," Roy offered as he stowed his phone and nodded at Karyn. "Kids. We all know how they can be."

I knew what most of us were thinking, but we held our tongues while waiting to get to the good part of this meeting. Our team brought in the most money, and the percentage bonus I'd calculated based on that was going to take care of my most urgent bills.

"And with that out of the way, I'm sure all of you know Roy," Karyn said with a brief introduction and acknowledgment of the man in the tailored gray suit beside her. "Roy has been meeting with all the collection teams around the country and has saved the best for last. Roy?"

"Thank you, Karyn," he said with a wink that made me think of Miss Nancy's inappropriate joke. "I have to say that it's always good to make it back down to Texas. Good steak and darn good barbecue. Even if it gets too hot here for this Illinois farm boy," he said, yukking it up with an implied "aww shucks" at the end that only made Karyn laugh.

Get to the good part, Roy, I thought.

"And as you know, I wanted to thank each of you teams personally for the job you've been doing. Despite the tough economic times and trying workloads, you've persevered." Roy stood up from the table and applauded all of us in his goofy Midwestern way.

Karyn quickly followed suit, but our supervisor Rhonda remained seated.

"We're just glad to contribute toward the company surpassing its goals, Mr. Bramlett," Rhonda said, echoing what we were all kinda thinking as the big boss and Karyn sat back down.

"And you certainly have. Especially the Houston office. That's why that makes this visit so much harder," Roy commented as he cleared his throat and fiddled with the papers before him.

Noticing the sudden somber turn, all of our ears perked up, including our supervisor who appeared blindsided. Karyn sat nervously at Roy's side probably wishing she was somewhere blowing him instead.

"I'm sorry," Roy said as he cleared his throat. "But the current economic climate has led us to temporarily suspend our bonus program."

"I . . . I don't understand," I said before realizing it was spoken aloud. On my phone display was a missed call from one of my creditors. After this meeting, I planned on having an answer for them.

Now, thanks to Roy's announcement, I wouldn't.

"Excuse me? What does that mean for us?" one of our teammates, Marisol, asked, knowing damn well what he said, but daring him to break it down again.

"It means we ain't gettin' paid our bonuses we earned," Miss Nancy said as she tapped her coffee mug on the table.

"Exactly," Karyn chimed in. "But is it our sincere hope that this belt tightening is just a temporary setback. So with that said, we managed to come up with something to show our appreciation for what you do day in and day out in such a thankless environment."

"*Gift cards?* Motherfuckin' gift cards?" I spewed unapologetically as me and Miss Nancy shuffled back to our cubicles along with the rest of our stunned collection team. "A Chili's gift card ain't gonna pay my bills."

"Well, if they thought this was gonna make me bust my ass, then they're crazy. This sumbitch on the phone talkin' 'bout BMWs and Porsches then turns around and says 'I can't pay y'all, but here's a fuckin' gift card'," Miss Nancy cursed while imitating Roy in a most unflattering way.

The grumbling subsided and everybody got back to work, harassing and threatening for the company's money, yet, I couldn't move. I came to work thinking it might be an escape, but it just made my mood that much worse. I stared at my monitor, fingers refusing to respond to my commands. *Fuck it. Fuck it all.* If Rhonda was monitoring our time on the phones, my graph was going to be a flat line.

"Artemis, you okay?" Miss Nancy asked as she reached over and tapped me on the shoulder.

"No, I'm not. Haven't been in a while," I replied as I looked over at her. I was drowning beneath a wave of frustration with no life preserver in sight.

And sometimes one needs to breathe.

I reached beneath my desk and grabbed my purse. Ignoring whatever was running on my computer, I depressed the power button until it all disappeared, not bothering to properly shut down a single program. After locking up and turning off my lamp, I rose from my seat.

"Where you goin'?" Miss Nancy asked, looking

at the clock. We weren't due a break for several more hours.

"Use my gift card," I answered flatly. "I'm suddenly hungry."

"You coming back today?"

"Girl, I really don't know," I replied as I left my job, not sure if I was ever returning or whether I'd be welcomed back.

Chapter 4

I was barefoot and humming to myself, my heels dangling off my finger in one hand, as I turned the key in the lock.

I came home with my to-go bag full of leftovers from Chili's, a mingled smell of Southwestern fried mediocrity escaping it. Walking out on my job like that was never so wrong while feeling so damn right. But most of my generous gift card balance had gone on margaritas anyway, leaving me feeling pretty much indifferent at the moment.

I put my purse down and laid my car keys along with cell phone on the counter. I'd smartly silenced it, but I knew there were a ton of missed calls from people at work worrying about me. If I still had my job, I'd deal with it later. For now, I wanted nothing more than to catch up on crazy Kenya Moore from *The Real Housewives of Atlanta*'s shenanigans, which I'd DVRed last night. She knew good 'n' damn well that guy didn't want to marry her.

"Hmm," I mused as I turned on the TV and read the message across the screen telling me to call my provider. It spurred me to get up off the couch and walk over to a pile of mail I'd been intentionally avoiding. There, in the third envelope from the top of the stack, was my final notice from Comcast. No need for warnings anymore. My cable was officially turned off so there would be no Kenya, no NeNe, no Phaedra nor any fine-ass Apollo either.

"Ain't this some shit," I grumbled just as the house phone on the wall next to me chirped.

Since I wasn't going to be able to watch my show right now, I decided to entertain whoever might be looking for me. Besides, if it rang any longer, I'd have a headache.

"Hello?" I answered, already annoyed.

"Artemis, what are you doing at home?"

"Besides talking to you, Mama? Trying to have a stress-free day. Guess I failed," I replied to Ruth with a heavy sigh. *I should've checked the caller ID first.*

"Oh. I tried reaching you at work first and when you didn't answer your cell phone, I thought I might get lucky."

"Why? Want to yell at me over a dead man who ain't even Anitra's anyway?" I taunted. "I'm so over the two of you ganging up on me and treating me like I'm a redheaded stepchild. No . . . that's not fair to redheaded stepchildren. Y'all treat me worse. Matter of fact, I'm so over everything right now."

"What are you saying? I hope you're not talking suicidal. Lawd, I knew something was wrong when you weren't at work. Especially the way they work y'all. I should've put you on my prayer list sooner." She tsked.

"No, Mama. I'm not thinking about ending my life," I said wearily. "Just ending the bullshit. That's why I'm not at a fuckin' job right now that takes me for granted and doesn't pay me shit!"

"Artemis!" Ruth howled.

"What, Mama? Ain't like you haven't heard me curse before. Damn," I grumbled.

"Have you been drinking?" she asked.

"Save your false concern for the public eye. I ain't Anitra, remember?"

"What does your bad behavior have to do with your sister? You can't blame everything on her," she said.

"You mean like you do with me? Even before this stuff with Carlos, you were always comparing us, Mama. And not in a good way. Always telling me what I'm doing wrong or what I need to do to take better care of myself. I'm sorry I'm not Anitra, but I can only be me. And I'm sorry

Daddy left you, but I had nothing to do with that."

"Artemis . . ." she said as her voice cracked. Had my pleas finally not fallen on deaf ears? "You're . . . you're not my daughter," Ruth mouthed softly.

"What do you mean? I . . . I'm adopted?" I spat, my buzz totally gone. "Or are you saying you're disowning me?"

"No, neither. I'm not saying that. But I can't keep this up any longer," my mother replied. "Artemis, you're Henry's daughter . . . just not mine."

"Mama, stop. This ain't funny," I begged.

"It sure ain't, baby," she agreed, her voice dripping with a hint of softness I hadn't heard since I was a child. "I accepted you and took you into my home despite my reservations. But it's always been hard living with a reminder of Henry's infidelity all these years. Then when he left us all . . . for another one of his . . ." Ruth muttered, and she paused. "Lawd," she said, unable to complete her statement.

"I don't understand. Who's . . . my real mother then?" I begged to know, still struggling to process it.

"Some trifling woman he met on one of those trail rides," she replied, referring to the horse-back-riding groups my father used to hang with out in the country. "Don't know much about her except that she was unfit. She just showed up at our doorstep. With you. Said she couldn't raise you. You were barely a year old at the time. I wanted to shoot Henry and her both. But then . . . I saw you. And everything changed in my heart."

"Why didn't you tell me?"

"What good would that have done?" she offered.

"It would've explained why you despise me so much. Would've finally made sense," I proclaimed.

"I don't despise you. It's just—"

"Daddy," I answered, cutting her off. "And my resemblance to him. I see it in your eyes sometimes. It reminds you of all the shit he's done to you over the years. Isn't that right?"

"Yes, baby. And I'm sorry if I've played favorites with Anitra over you. It wasn't intentional. I'm so sorry. I've always just wanted to do right by you. Even if your father didn't."

"Mama," I said, the word sticking in my throat as I said it. "This . . . this is too much for me to deal with right now. I'ma have to call you back. Later."

"All right. But just promise me you won't do anything rash. I can go over there if you'd like."

"No, no. Don't," I said as I suddenly felt like throwing up. And, maybe breaking something. "I won't do anything crazy."

My father, Henry Clay, was a jolly soul. The bear of a man was outgoing to a fault and way too charming for his own damn good. Thing is, his charm was always wasted on the next young thang to come along. I remember the day the woman I'd considered my mother finally kicked him out the house.

And kept me with her despite what she'd just told me.

None of us had either seen or heard from him since.

Word from my Aunt Freda, his sister, was that he'd moved to Midlothian and started another family.

With a sudden sense of purpose, I went to my bedroom, where I opened my laptop and went online. With the two windows I opened in Internet Explorer, I used one to check my Bank of America account balance while searching travel sites with the other. My mouth curled as I confirmed what I already knew.

I had a little less than $3,000 to my name. Certainly nothing to sneeze at in today's economy.

Except I had about $4,000 worth of bills due.

It was hardly the most liquid of situations, especially with news no bonus would be coming. And it was not like me to do anything random and reckless either.

Until today, that is.

Armed with all I needed to know, I focused on the other Web site. The one that was more pleasurable than the reality of a bank balance on borrowed time.

Turns out I didn't know who I was. And didn't want to be who I thought I was. Maybe it was time to live a life other than my own for a change. And to be someone I wasn't.

To do that, I moved the mouse over what I'd been searching for.

And clicked.

Chapter 5

"Well. Viva Las Vegas to me," I mouthed under my breath after saying "buh-bye" to the ever-smiling flight attendants. I'd safely arrived here at McCarran International. The four-inch heels to die for I was wearing were doing just that: killing me. Since people were being so nice, I should've asked for a foot massage on the way over.

I'd narrowed my foolish choices down to Ocho Rios or Sin City. But with my nonexistent budget, I figured it best to keep my slightly irrational ass stateside rather than wind up in a Jamaican jail with no money to get home. Besides, I'd never been this far west, nor flown first class in my life, so it was still all so lovely. Sure, I felt some guilt over the price of my seat on the United flight out here, but being able to sit without feeling like I was wearing Spanx was oh so worth it. *A sister could really get used to this,* I remember thinking as I wiggled about in my seat with ample leg and hip room. But as the people in general boarding filed past me to their rows, it was as if they could sense my empty bank account and that I was simply fronting. I just buried my face in one of those SkyMall catalogs and waited for that separating curtain to shield me from their knowing, accusatory eyes all the way from Houston here. When given the warm towel by the flight attendant, who politely called me by name, I had to wait for the other passengers in my row to see whether to put it on my face or use on my hands. It probably startled them how many "free" Bloody Marys I'd downed while in the air, but I was making the most out of every step of this trip. And with my killer shoes and best outfit on, those steps were gonna be memorable.

Finite funds didn't mean finite fun, right?

Lord knows I was gonna pay for it when I returned to a home back in Katy without electricity.

"Business or pleasure?" a voice called out to me as I daydreamed about that which was more like a nightmare for me.

"I'm sorry?" I said to the man who had shared the seat beside me in first class.

"Are you a gambler?" he asked, still bothering to converse while hastily stowing his iPad in his satchel. Looked like some idealized western businessman with his chiseled features, suede blazer, crisply ironed jeans, and denim button-down shirt.

"You might say that," I replied sheepishly. Of course, there was no risk in what I was doing because I didn't even know what I was doing. When I booked this trip with the last of my money and credit, I just wanted—no—*needed* to get away. To be free is all. Because sometimes in life you gotta say, "Fuck it."

"I figured you were. You got a serious face yet dress like you're here for fun, little lady. You look very lovely," he commented with a smile.

Was he actually checking me out? Guess he had no qualms with my being thicker than a Snickers, or my milk-chocolaty goodness.

"When you hit it big, just be careful with them winnings. And don't forget to tip your dealer. Everybody counts when good things happen," he offered.

"I will definitely take your advice, sir," I answered, wishing I really were a gambler. As bad as my luck was, I'd probably wind up owing the casinos money.

Just past the TSA security, we went our separate ways as he had bags to retrieve. Not wanting to spend a dime more, I rolled strictly carry-on. Just beyond the luggage carousels, finely dressed limo drivers held signs with their fares' names displayed in black marker or even pre-printed for the higher-end folk.

The third one of those drivers I saw caught my curiosity and held it. In his black suit, he was a smooth peanut-butter complexion with dazzling green eyes. And he held me in his manicured fingertips.

Well, actually he held a sign with my name in his hands. Close enough. Details, details.

"Miss Clay?" he asked as I stopped before him.

"Please. Call me Artemis." I gushed over having a man like him in my service, even if only as my driver from the airport. He was such a cutie.

"Oh. I thought you were Jill Scott for a second," he said, smiling widely. "Welcome to Las Vegas."

And I did my best to outdo his smile.

Chapter 6

I told my driver that it was my first time in Vegas, so he volunteered to drive slowly, providing me a mini-tour of the Strip before dropping me at my hotel. From my limo, I marveled at all the places I recognized from television such as the MGM Grand, that pyramid-shaped Hotel Luxor, Caesars Palace, and the fountains outside the Bellagio from that movie with George Clooney's sexy-old ass, *Ocean's Eleven*. At one point, I couldn't contain myself and briefly stood out the sunroof to yell at the top of my lungs. I think that was just the last of the Bloody Mary in my system kicking in though.

My driver just laughed as I'm sure he'd seen it all. "Treating yourself, ma'am?" he asked.

"Why, yes, I am," I replied as I flopped back onto the long leather bench seat, kicking my feet about with excitement like some kid on Christmas morning. "And stop with the 'ma'am' stuff. I ain't that old," I playfully chided him.

"No. You most certainly aren't," he commented as our eyes met in his rearview mirror. We probably were within a few years of one another in age. My sister—half sister—Anitra would look down on him even though he was obviously a hard worker. But, with those irresistible looks of his, she might make an exception. Of course, I wasn't about to play matchmaker for her siddity ass. Just thinking to myself, s'all.

"Where ya from?" he questioned, the formality tapering off this time.

"Houston," I replied. "You ever been?" I asked, a little too concerned with his answer. Who was I kidding? I wasn't interested in him for Anitra, but I wasn't ready for a relationship for me either. Even though he turned out to be nothing like I thought he was, maybe Carlos's death was my tipping point to get me to this moment.

"Yeah," he answered, pausing to check an incoming message on his phone. It was probably his instructions for his next fare, if I had to guess. "Have some cousins in Texas. They live west of Houston. Small town called Sealy, I think."

"I know where Sealy is. Actually, I live in Katy," I admitted, intrigued. "Sealy's not too far from me."

"Oh? We've been to that mall in Katy before. Katy Mills, right?"

"Yes, that's the place. You and your wife went there?" I asked, having picked up on the "we" in his comment.

"Nah. I'm divorced," he replied. "I went to your mall with my moms. That was when she could travel. How about you? You married? No worries, no matter what you tell me," he offered. "Because whatever happens in Vegas—"

"Stays in Vegas!" I completed with a soft chuckle. "Yeah, I've seen the commercials. But, no. I'm a widow," I offered, surprised to be sharing that much with a stranger. Don't think he could handle not one, but two, grown-ass men dying on me.

"Oh. I'm so sorry." He gasped as he watched a couple crossing the street in front of us while arguing with one another. When the woman cocked back and slapped the man, we both winced.

"Don't be. It was awhile ago. I've since moved on," I admitted. Yep, right into the arms of the next man to die on me. With my track record, I sooo wasn't in Vegas looking for a match. It being the wrong city for that anyway, this was just an escape from myself. Or maybe I was seeking the real me before it was suffocated, never to be found.

"Good to hear you've moved on," he said, a little too cheery, before catching himself and clearing his throat. "Oookay. Well, we're almost to your hotel, ma'am. Just up ahead at the end of the Strip," he said, directing me where to look.

But I couldn't miss it anyway. It looked just like the online pictures, only more beautiful. I'd booked myself four nights' luxury accommodations at Aquos, the second addition to what was, in the end, going to be a set of four towers and casinos themed on the elements: earth, wind, fire, and water. Aquos had been open for only a month, joining its sister hotel, Stratus, the older, air-themed one on the grounds. From what I'd read, people like Mariah Carey, Samuel L. Jackson, Kim Kardashian, and the ginger Brit, Prince Harry, had already stayed there.

"You're gonna like it there," he stated.

"Oh?"

"Beautiful inside. I had a hookup and got to take a walk-through before the grand opening. Its water theme is bananas, like something outta Hollywood. Any plans on seeing some shows 'n' stuff while you're gracing us with your lovely presence?" he asked, blatantly flirtatious now.

"Let me stop you right there. Thanks, but no thanks," I blurted out before he tried to steer me to one of those seedy places where he got commissions for referrals. Just because I'd never been to Vegas didn't mean I was stupid. I wasn't trying to get bogged down in some tourist trap.

"Got it. Just shut up and drive," he remarked, taking a professional tone once again. "My apologies, ma'am."

"I . . . I didn't mean it like that. And I apologize if I came across as rude," I stated. "This whole trip was impromptu and I don't want anything planned because I don't even know what the next hour holds, so . . ."

"Got it. No pressure. I try too hard to help sometimes. My bad," he said with a sweet grin as the black limo pulled up to the Aquos hotel. My driver popped the trunk then exited to retrieve my bag.

On my phone, I received a notification that someone had posted on my Facebook page. I should've ignored it, but checked nevertheless. It was from a few of my coworkers back in Houston. With the time difference, over half the workday had elapsed back home. And I hadn't bothered to call in or anything. I read the two most recent posts on my timeline:

Girl, they said you're sick. Hope you get well soon.

Call and let us know you're okay. Praying for you in Jesus' name.

As I considered replying and what I would say, the driver opened my door. Looking at him made me draw a blank as to what I would say anyway, so I instead tossed my phone back in my purse. And admired him.

"Got a call you need to take?" he questioned.

"Nah. Just mindlessly checking my Facebook page. You busted me," I admitted, grinning way too much to where my damn cheeks were hurting.

He chuckled. "The Internet's a good thing, don't get me wrong. But sometimes it connects us too much in ways that aren't so healthy."

"And it's lacking that personal connection?" I asked with a raised eyebrow over his voluntary observations about the Internet and social media.

"Right! Right!" he agreed wholeheartedly. "It distracts you from the *here and now* with junk like friend requests, tweets, 'retweets,' 'catfishing,' 'Likes,' and other petty stuff. That's not how the world got along back in the 'stone ages' before that. That kind of stuff shifts priorities from what's really important."

"The world's changing though. And we can't do much about that," I said with a sigh. Boy had my world changed.

"Ahhh, but we can control that which we can control. Like maximizing the important up-close encounters," he dropped all philosophical on me as he took my hand to help me exit the limo. "My name's Lowell, by the way. And here's my card," he offered as he plopped a business card in my purse before I could object or politely decline. Then he smiled as if daring me to remove and discard it in front of him. When I didn't, he continued. "In case you need anything during your stay, I am volunteering to be your personal driver. Or even for just a ride back to the airport once your business has concluded. I hope that you will consider me and my humble car service."

"Thank you, Lowell."

"No. Thank you, Artemis," he said in a way that made me feel all good inside.

Good. Not gooey. Get your mind out the gutter.

"Oh. And I have one simple request," he said.

"What's that, Lowell?" I asked, curious and intrigued.

"Could you go to my Facebook page and 'Like' my car service? It's listed on my card," he said comically.

As the doorman held the door open for me, I just shook my head and turned to enter the gleaming building, surrounded on both sides by backlit glass holding coral and fish.

Chapter 7

"Welcome to your adventure," the doorman said as he refused to let me carry my own bag. "Do you already have a reservation with us, ma'am?" he humbly asked.

"Of course. Don't leave home without one," I replied, trying to play that indignant role. I know I looked like a baller because I'd dusted off my best, least-used clothes for this trip. I guess playing "dress up" suited me.

"Well, allow me to show you to your reservation host, ma'am. Right this way," the young man with honest, old eyes ushered. The exterior wall of the entire first floor was one large aquarium, its projected lights bathing me in an otherworldly glow as if we were entering a tunnel of light. When we emerged out the other side, I stared wildly at my new surroundings.

People snapped away with their cell phones, taking countless pictures as I was led to whatever a "reservation host" was. Made me feel special 'n' shit. Of course, they weren't snapping them of me exactly. Rather, they were capturing images of the hotel and I was just part of the background, a perfect blend of the contemporary with traces of the ancient.

"Ms. Clay?" the desk clerk asked as my reservation was retrieved from the transparent computer screen she tapped with her perfect French tip. My girl's weave was one of the best I'd ever seen and she carried herself with the poise of an actress. Hell, things in just the hotel lobby alone looked like something from off a movie set. Even the group huddled at the desk next to me, Lake Scott, rising star with the Brooklyn Nets, and his big-ass entourage were gawking at the neon-colored women swimming beneath our feet. Visible through the illuminated glass floor, they swam about like new-age mermaids, waiving at stunned guests like us then disappearing, probably to come up for air somewhere out of view. How much were they paying these bitches, anyway? The whole thing made me feel like I was in the middle of one of those Cirque du Soleil productions, an adult Disney World, or something.

"Y . . . yes," I answered, not sounding too confident in who I was. Maybe I needed an entourage like an NBA baller to stay here. *Lawd, they're gonna decline my credit card and throw my broke ass outta here,* I nervously thought, while grinning to hide it. *Maybe I should've told the limo driver Lowell to stick around in case a Holiday Inn or something was more in the cards. I guess his business card he forced on me wasn't a waste after all.*

"Here we are. It's our pleasure to have you, Ms. Clay," she said instead as we made eye contact again with her smiling warmly at me.

I was safe for the moment and breathed easier.

"Welcome to Aquos."

"Wow. This is so nice!" I gushed, letting my true feelings escape. The only people grinning around here more than me were the eager-to-help hotel staff. They appeared to be everywhere while surprisingly appearing out of nowhere in their crisp black uniforms with these unusual gold serpentine bracelets around their wrists.

"How many keys to your suite will you be need-ing, Ms. Clay?" she asked, gaining my attention again.

"Um . . . just one," I replied, thinking how nice it would be to have someone with whom to share this experience.

She handed me a standard key card adorned with the hotel logo, then also presented me with a golden bracelet that looked identical to those worn on the staff's wrists. "Allow me to explain," she announced, probably used to puzzled guests. "This is the Aquos royal bracelet. Just place it on your wrist like so and it automatically grants you access to our day club at poolside Tidal, gyms on all floors, the VIP level of our casino, the business center, express seating in our theatre, where Mary J. Blige will be performing three nights this week, and admittance to our underground nightclub, Trident. Oh, and it's waterproof, of course, so feel free to get wet here at Aquos."

"Well, I ain't gonna be getting my hair wet, but the rest of me don't mind," I joked with a wink at the sister. She nodded and gave me one of those "I know that's right!" looks before resuming her corporate facade. That weave of hers hadn't seen a bead of sweat let alone a drop of pool water.

"Your suite is located on the thirtieth floor with a view of the Strip as requested. And those are your private elevators," she said with a gesture over my left shoulder.

I turned to follow her outstretched hand and watched an elevator that looked like a floating glass bubble descending from above. I marveled at the globe as it came to rest atop a small pond in the center of the lobby as if it had levitated down.

The same young man who led me to check-in followed me with my bag to board the elevator, beckoning me to enter first. If he hadn't been with me, I would've snapped a few pictures. But I could always do it later.

As the elevator rose to take me to my floor, water flowed down on both sides, hiding the elevator shaft and giving the impression that we were floating up on a column of water.

While amazing, it only served to remind me my water bill was due.

Too sad, huh?

When we exited on my floor, we trailed behind a man in dark blue slacks and a crisp white shirt wearing sunglasses indoors. As he argued way too loud on his phone, he was oblivious to us.

"Tell them we can get the job done just as easy with someone else! And probably for less money, too. So they need to get their heads out their collective asses and finish the project before I fire them all!" he snarled at whatever poor soul was listening on the other end.

In the middle of his next sentence, our footsteps alerted him and he spun around, catching me staring dead into his mouth.

"Can you believe this?" he had the nerve to ask me. I guess he knew he was busted and figured I was sympathetic and had rich-people problems like him. Oh, he was soooo wrong.

"That someone would want to work for you with that attitude?" I replied snappily. "No, I can't believe it." The young man carrying my bag took a step back, worried about where this was heading or what he should be hearing.

"Oh? Okay. Well tell me, what do you recommend? What are your thoughts about motivating underperforming employees?" he asked, giving me a full view of his broad shoulders.

"That they don't like being taken for granted. Or talked down to. They like to feel their opinions matter," I snapped, perhaps thinking more of my situation back home. "Even if their bosses really don't care."

Then with a snap of my finger, I got my bellman in check and we sidestepped the stunned asshole en route to my suite.

Chapter 8

"You sure told him back there," my bellman said gleefully as he opened my door for me.

"Yeah. I guess," I replied, trying to play it down as I stole a final glance at the man looking back at me as well. Don't think he was too happy with me despite the smile he flashed before retreating inside his suite—the one that had three floors and its own bowling alley. Yeah, I'd researched the hotel. Even though I was frontin', I couldn't even fake being on his level for a minute.

"I can tell that you would be a good person to work for. It's obvious you care about your people," the bellman added, thinking I really owned something other than my name. If he was buttering me up for a job then he was sadly mistaken, for we both would be in the unemployment line together.

"Uh . . . thanks," I replied as I tentatively fished a twenty from my purse, now feeling kinda cheap after his praise. "Is this enough?"

I asked, hoping that it was. Back home, I could stretch that for lunch the entire week. Out here, it probably wasn't even dessert. *Damn. Why did I ask him?* Now he was gonna know I was either a tightwad or just out of touch.

"Whatever you wish to give me is fine," he replied, keeping with his training while not revealing whether he meant it. "You packed light for your trip, huh?" he commented further as he placed my bag on the floor just inside the entryway.

"Yeah. Lets me shop. A ton of baggage would be like bringing sand to the beach," I lied, knowing I'd only be window shopping and salivating like a dog at The Forum Shops at Caesars Palace before I left. But for now, I was good just enjoying my junior suite. "Junior" seemed funny when I could fit more than eight people comfortably in here. Made me think of my senior trip back when I was at Stephen F. Austin University. Ten of us shared a room with just a single bed at La Quinta in Panama City back then. Sad as it is, I had more net worth then, too. Gawd, I missed those days.

"Well, you will enjoy the shopping out here. Most fashionable women, such as yourself, do," he said, clearing his throat. "But let me explain to you all you need to know about your suite, then I'll get out of your hair."

"There's more than meets the eye?" I asked as I tried to resist the dopey-ass smile plastered across my mug. The suite came with a kitchenette, complete with one of those gourmet single-serving coffee machines that I love. And, as promised by my "reservation host," from the glass balcony doors I could see the Strip beyond them. And I hadn't even laid eyes on the bedroom.

"Yes, ma'am. With this right here," he said as he tapped a clear glass screen on the half wall I'd just walked by. Whatever he did caused it to light up, colors suddenly forming into the image of a woman wearing the same uniform as the rest of them.

"Hello, Ms. Clay. Welcome to your adventure," the woman said just like the doorman had downstairs, making me a little uncertain as to whether she was real or some kind of Pixar animation. I leaned in for a closer look while he went about touching it again, bringing up a menu beside her—its—face.

"This here controls room temperature, room service, as well as reservations for our spa, restaurants, and poolside cabanas at Tidal downstairs. Whatever you need is right at your fingertips and your virtual assistant can guide and recommend things for you. But if you prefer the more traditional methods, just call us on the room phone. We make it easy for you either way at Aquos. And as our first-time guest in one of our suites, we have complimentary credits for you downstairs at the casino, and the first stocking of the minibar is on us."

"You've got me ready to book my return trip already," I said honestly. I was definitely dreaming, so pinching myself didn't matter.

"That's the idea. And bring your friends next time," he said before presumably wondering what I was gonna do all by my lonesome in Vegas. *Get into some fuckin' trouble is what.*

"Oh. My girls will be arriving later," I offered, knowing I ain't had many real girlfriends for quite some time. Too much grinding at work, trying to manage my debt, while letting the old me get lost in the shuffle. "Since I'm the one who *made good,* they look to me to pay for these trips. Last year, it was Dubai," I said, way too comfortable with my lies. Fuck it. Wasn't like he was gonna see me again. And, besides, wasn't Las Vegas about reinvention anyway?

"Oh? Well, you are certainly a very good friend, Ms. Clay. If you need more room keys just let us know," he said with a nod as he went to leave.

"Will do," I said as I slipped him another of my hard-earned twenties. Ain't that some shit? I'd guilted myself into tipping like the person I was pretending to be. Yep. If not for my return ticket, I probably would be Greyhounding it home. *Those chips down in the casino had better be lucky.*

As soon as I was left alone, I couldn't wait to give my feet a rest. I kicked my heels off, popping them into the air with a flick of my foot one at a time. I was overzealous with one, it landing on an end table where it almost knocked over a vase probably worth more than one of my paychecks. Disaster averted, I ran barefoot through the lavish suite, laughing like somebody had told me the funniest joke ever.

Stop me if you've heard this one. A girl without a penny to her name and a credit rating in the low 300s walks into a hotel . . .

Ba-da-bump!

I was starving and eager to play around with the touch screen, but first I turned on some music then raided the bar. With some generic Flo Rida pop concoction playing, I pulled out a bottle of Roederer champagne and swiftly popped the top. After launching the cork, I took a drink directly from the flowing bottle at first before finding me a flute hanging upside down from its stem just beneath the cabinet.

By the time I slid the balcony door open, I was already pouring my second glass. From my view, I could make out cars and people walking about on the Strip, but directly below me were hotel guests partying down to some poolside DJ. *Must be that day club, Tidal.* I smiled, imagining them without a care in the world except to get laid or be seen as they danced and strutted around. *Maybe I should take my lone, free bottle of bubbly down there and join them.* But I couldn't forget my lucky bracelet. As I leaned over the railing on my tippy toes, a voice cried out.

"Don't jump, girl. There's a lot of white linen down there," it said. "A lot of white people, too. They'll send your estate a bill for the dry cleaning even if you die."

"Huh?" I said as I noticed a woman lazily lounging by herself in a blue bikini on the adjacent balcony. She was slender with a pretty, medium-brown complexion like Jennifer Hudson's, holding a tall mixed drink in one hand while resting an iPad in her lap. I strained to recognize her in case she was somebody famous.

"Relax. I'm fuckin' with ya," she said with a grating cackle while swirling the brown liquor around in her glass. "Name's Ladonna."

"Artemis," I yelled across, replying in kind while briefly considering renaming myself during my time here. Some Sasha Fierce shit. "Naomi Reckless" or somethin'.

"You just got here?" she asked more like a statement than a question.

"Yes. How did you know?" I asked in kind, thinking that maybe she saw me checking in downstairs or something.

"Because you're still working on that free bottle of cheap shit they give each suite," she joked while pointing at the bottle in my hand. "Giiirl, we're gonna have to get you right."

Since when did Roederer become "cheap shit"?

Chapter 9

Suddenly feeling my remaining champagne wasn't good enough in my neighbor Ladonna's eyes, and that maybe I wasn't either, I excused myself from her. She smiled, making me promise I'd continue our chat later, but minus the shouting over balconies part.

Knowing I should've eaten more on the flight, I decided to give the virtual assistant a try. I always liked tech anyway, so why not. My mother Ruth called just as I tapped the screen, pulling up a virtual menu that was making my mouth water. The gourmet Chilean sea bass tacos looked tantalizing and, with a plink of my nail, I added them and a fresh garden salad to my room service request. Had to order it quick before the prices would've made me flinch.

"Hello?" I answered, sick of people hounding me. Especially when they had a lack of sympathy for my plight mere days ago.

"Artemis, where are you? I've been worried sick since you haven't been answering your phone. I went by your place and when I didn't see your car, I lost it," she stated tentatively as I tried to unsuccessfully tune her out. She hadn't displayed this much concern for me ever. I guess the guilt over her revelation was hard for her to live with.

"I just had to get out of town for a minute. Clear my head," I replied. "I'm not out somewhere trying to hurt myself, if that's what you're getting at."

"Good. I just want to let you know that I'm sorry about what I said."

"Why? It's the truth, right? You're not my mom. And my real one didn't give a shit about me," I pronounced, my intoxicated voice doing little to hide my pain.

"I may not be your mother by blood, but I might as well be. I love you, Artemis," Ruth said as if pleading with me to come in from off a ledge.

"Thanks," I said with a sigh, torn about whether I had any reason to blame her. In a more reasonable state of mind, I might admit she was just doing the best she could all these years. I ordered some tea with my meal to maybe help me sober up a little, then turned off the display just as it promised a delivery time of fifteen minutes. If only life were as easy as a set of choices on a video screen.

"So are you going to tell me where you are?" she pushed after my pause, not knowing I was distracted by my new toy. "And is that music I hear? Lord, where are you, child?" she asked.

Damn. I'd left the patio door open. She could hear the music from the pool downstairs?

"Yeah, it's music," I answered, almost calling her "Mom" out of habit. "I'm in Las Vegas."

"Artemis, it's the middle of the week." She gasped. "Does your job know where you are? I hope I didn't set you down this road."

"Look . . . I'll talk to you later. Just know I'm doing fine," was my answer. "Be happy for me. I just need a little fun in my life after all this recent mess."

After that call, I figured maybe a lie down might be needed. The king-sized bed looked very inviting with its soft down comforter, to the point where I feared not waking up. I'd just sat on it and bounced in place while imagining how it would feel beneath the sheets before a knock came at the door.

Room service in less than fifteen minutes? Damn, these people were good.

I scurried to the door and opened it, but neither my fish tacos nor my salad were here.

And "room service" wore dark blue slacks and a white shirt, not the standard black.

At least he'd put up his sunglasses.

"My name is Julian Jackson," the asshole with the broad shoulders announced. "And you are?"

I almost slammed the door in his face. But instead, I answered him. "Artemis. Artemis Clay," I said all formal-like while my mind unintentionally wandered to casual things. Couldn't help it. For an older man, he was fine. Plus, he had no wedding ring . . . or tan line. Yeah. I was feeling down, not dead. "What can I do you for, Mr. Jackson?"

"Besides making me look like a fool, how do you really manage your people? I'm always open to new ways of doing things and improving. You could almost say I'm obsessive about it."

"You knocked on my door to talk shop? *Really?*" I asked, incredulous. What kind of odd people were they out here? Maybe Texas was more my speed.

"Well . . . yes. That is part of it. How about we discuss it? Over dinner, tonight?" he asked before dialing back on his enthusiasm. But I'd caught on to his game. "That is . . . if your schedule will allow me to give you a proper apology for my rude behavior."

I didn't have any plans. And a high-end dinner with a handsome man, a dinner that I assumed he was paying for, would be something I could tell my kids about one day. Maybe.

"I shouldn't. But yes. I accept, Mr. Jackson," I said with a hard stare.

"Please. Call me Julian," he said.

"And you can still call me Ms. Clay," I commented. "For now."

And if a third man happened to die on me, at least this one kinda deserved it.

Not to say he was gonna wind up in my bed.

Or my panties.

Jus' sayin.

And shouldn't my fish tacos be here by now?

Chapter 10

After lunch and a quick nap, I went downstairs to the hotel's pool area . . . *ahem* . . . day club Tidal, proud of my all-access bracelet, which was getting more attention than the white linen wrap I was wearing. Sure, it was about looks around here, but it was also about status. And I guess I may have been a tad more voluptuous than these bitches, but I had the golden ticket. I don't know what was funnier: these young'uns wildin' out after waiting in line for hours just to get in here or the people my age eager to feed off the youth of the desperate. All of them were blowing through more money than I collected in a month back home. Me? I was just a tourist in this social experiment, wondering what I'd done wrong in life.

I'd gone touch-screen crazy upstairs and reserved myself a cabana in the midst of this madness, so I was gonna experience it, dammit. Some R&B like Alicia Keys and mixed in with a little house music made a sister wanna two-step for a minute. But I figured I'd spare unworthy folk my killer moves, and kept it minimal. As I found my way past size-negative-two stick figures with boobs as big as mine, I got my shimmy and shake on just a tad.

A white boy, his long, scraggly blond hair slicked back in a ponytail, held an iPad Mini tablet in his hand next to a velvet rope at a tiny bridge that separated the cabanas and their private bar from the rest of the pool area. While I checked out the animal-print tattoo on his chiseled right arm, he was busy following the movements of a green neon mermaid, just like the ones I saw when I checked in, as she swam through the mini moat beneath the bridge. As I came closer, something on his tablet must've alerted him as he quickly gazed downward at the screen then up at me.

"Welcome to your adventure, Ms. Clay," he chimed with a clockwork smile as he stepped aside to allow me entrance to the cabana area just across the moat. "My name is Yuri. Allow me to show you to your cabana."

Yeah, I had the magic ticket all right with this bracelet. A regular princess on a budget.

While he led me, I noticed a pattern. Fine-ass men like him were responsible for attending to the female guests and vice versa. I guessed if someone was gay, they would cater to their requests too, but I was happy with my rugged, tattooed piece of man candy.

"So where are you from?" Yuri asked as a skinny bitch with tiny shorts carried a bottle of champagne by, holding it high like it was a trophy or something.

"Texas," I replied as I adjusted my sunglasses to check out this impressive brother with sandy brown dreads on the sly. He was coming out the pool all glistening after having cut a serious back flip. *Well, all right now.*

"Howdy then," Yuri said, like that shit would make me feel at home or something. "This here isn't as big as stuff back in Texas, but I hope you find it comfortable."

My cabana was one of the smaller ones, but like my suite, I felt a little lonely with no one to share it. Even with his small talk, I knew Yuri had other ladies to attend to and more tips to earn. "What would you like to drink?" he asked, even though my cabana was already stocked with fresh fruit and bottled water. Of course, he meant bottle service.

"Uh . . . I'll take a chocolate martini," I answered, knowing that's not what he meant.

"Anything else?" he added.

"No. I'll start with that. Long night. Trying to ease into it," I joked as I fanned myself.

"I understand. Well, anything I can do to make you more comfortable, just let me know. I'll be right back with your drink."

"Thank you," I responded. As he bopped away, whistling to himself over the loud music, I stepped out of the sun and took a seat to further give the impression I was nursing a hangover. While I waited on my drink, I bobbed my head to the beat of a new DJ who had taken over the elevated center stage in the middle of the four overlapping pools. Whatever hit song he put on, most of the people knew except for me. Some nonsense about making "that kitty purr fer a nigga, purr fer a nigga, pu-pu-pu-purrrr fer a nigga." What was that? 2Chainz? *Lawd, I'm too old for this scene,* I thought as regrets over being this reckless began to creep in yet again.

Of course, that NBA star Lake Scott and his boys were out here. Fools were rocking all-black wife beaters and shorts despite it being close to one hundred degrees. Even their towels were black. Daring the sun to win, I suppose. Fans and just your basic thirsty hoes of all colors had 'em surrounded like it was a feeding frenzy. One of his boys must've thought I was in awe as he took a bow in my direction and made a motion asking a sister if she wanted "The Great Lake's" auto-graph. Guess he preferred an ample woman, and

I ain't mad at him, but nah, nah, boo. I gave him the "I'm good" face at which he was surprised for a full second before turning his attention to the easier prey.

Maybe I should've called that driver Lowell and had him put me on a plane home.

"Uh . . . hello!" a familiar woman's voice yelled from outside my cabana, shaking me outta my funk. Someone had just walked by then doubled back when she saw me. "Why didn't you come get me?" Ladonna asked just as I recognized her. She was still in that royal blue bikini she was working to death, but had thrown on a hat big enough to graze someone's cornea if she made a sudden move. And why was she carrying a purse?

"I didn't know if you were busy," I replied truthfully. Didn't expect us to be best buds anyway since she'd mocked me and my free champagne earlier.

"And you got the last open cabana? *Really?*" she asked, mildly irritated while she fanned herself beneath her straw hat.

"Looks like it," I said with a smile and a shrug.

"Care to share?" she said, already barging in.

"I don't see why not," I said as I threw a bottled water to her, wondering what the markup might be on it. No point trying to pretend I had company coming, so I guessed making friends might make this trip better anyway.

"Well allow me to get this party started right . . . with the good stuff," she said as she chucked my water back at me. *Don't tell me she thinks Voss is too low-end as well.* "Can I get some service over here?" she shrieked, embarrassing me.

Yuri was just returning with my drink and smiled, despite Ladonna's attitude. Of course, when she saw him, she mellowed out kinda quick.

"Sir, we'd like two magnums of your best," she requested.

Magnums? If they were anything like the condoms, she was ordering some big-ass bottles. *Expensive. No, no, no!* "What are you doing?" I asked, visibly nervous. *My cabana, my tab.*

"What does it look like I'm doing? I'm buying friends," she said as she waved at a few men and rocked her slight hips. "Besides, these cabanas have a two-bottle minimum. What is it you do for a living anyway, Artemis?"

"A collection agency. A couple of locations back in Texas," I answered vaguely.

"Oh? Did you inherit it or built from the ground up?"

I laughed a hearty chuckle. "You obviously don't know my people. Ground up," I replied.

"A strong black woman. Good for you. My fortunes have been somewhat easier to come by. So, how big is your payroll? How many people do you employ?" she asked as she surveyed some of the beautiful bodies mingling nearby. Looked like she was car shopping and searching for just the right one, ready to kick the tires.

"About fifty between the two," I said with a semi-mumble, pulling a somewhat reasonable number outta my ass before I took a drink of my martini to force the lies back down my throat. Damn it tasted good. Was there anything they did just mediocre around here?

"Small business owner, eh?" she said, with whatever calculations she'd made in her head. "Drinks on me," she spat out without hesitation.

"You really don't have to do that," I said half-heartedly as my heart beat out of control. Someone like Ladonna could max my credit card out just by breathing.

"Oh shush. You can make it up to me later. Like maybe club hopping tonight? Or are you pacing yourself?" she said while mocking me with a fake sad face. "If you want me for a friend, you're gonna have to have stamina."

"Actually, I have dinner plans," I stated proudly. *Ha! Take that!*

"Oh. Is he expecting sex?" she asked without blinking.

"Excuse me?"

"Oooh, you dirty devil. You're the one expecting sex!"

"Noooo! Not from him," I replied, embarrassed while laughing out loud. Even though Julian Jackson was older, it's not like he was physically unappealing. "It's just dinner."

"You're gonna make me yawn, Artemis. Really," she chided. "Well, if you change your mind, make him use a condom. You can't trust the men out here. Well . . . actually you can't trust men anywhere. I learned that from my dearly departed daddy. Unless you're trying to get pregnant by him. Is he successful? Think about it. You could expand your business as he expands you."

"Ladonna. Please. Stop," I begged as I shook my head. This girl was too much.

"Does he stay here at Aquos?"

"Ladonna!" I yelled, waving my hands to get her to shush. I almost got up to physically cover her mouth.

"Because if he stays on our floor or higher, he's definitely successful. Or a criminal. Sometimes they're one in the same, y'know."

"Look . . . I appreciate your advice," I said, lying through my teeth. "But I'm not new to the rodeo," I uttered, groaning right after I said it. Texas through and through.

"Excuse me then, Miss Artemis," she clowned as two magnums of Perrier-Jouët rosé were delivered to us by Yuri and another one of the attendants.

"What do we do now?" I asked Ladonna as the rapper Pitbull proclaimed himself "Mr. World-wide" at the beginning of his latest song.

"We party. Pick some temporary friends, dear," she suggested as she gestured with her fingers for those who met her approval to join us.

I wondered what shape I would be in by the time dinner came around.

But fuck it, I thought as I motioned for the brother with the sandy dreads to join us if he chose. He certainly wouldn't die on me.

Right?

Chapter 11

"Artemis, do you really have to go?" Ladonna asked, almost pleading as I shoved her out the door along with the three eclectic stragglers we'd picked up from our cabana party downstairs: my man with the dreads from the pool, another guy who Ladonna described as the "Norwegian snowboarder with a big snowboard in his swim trunks," and a sister who was a Marine on leave from her base in California. As I got dressed for my dinner date with Julian, I couldn't just kick them out. I'd be lacking in my Southern hospitality. Especially since Ladonna fronted all the drinks at my cabana and saved me the embarrassment.

"Yes, but that doesn't mean the party stops. It just goes on without me," I replied with a laugh. I had fifteen minutes to put the finishing touches on my hair and makeup, which I was doing all by myself, and to sober up somewhat. But at least I wasn't driving tonight.

"Well, you look beautiful, girl. Just remember. Condom," she joked while simulating rolling one onto an imaginary penis.

Her motion brought a smile to the dread-headed panty remover whom I considered dead sexy when I was checking him out by the pool. I thought I might be ready for some harmless flirtation. But it was obvious by Ladonna's fourth magnum of champagne she ordered that he'd gravitated from my plump ass and thighs to her plump bank account. *Hey, do you, bro.* She was the one who said she wanted to buy some friends anyway, not me, so she could have him. Besides, all he woulda gotten from me on his very best day was some killer pussy.

Oooo. Poor word choice, I know.

But think of it as making progress.

After figuring out which elevator to take and which elevator to get off in this dang place, I arrived late to my dinner date with Julian. He'd selected Aquos's rooftop restaurant, Spire, with its panoramic view of the city for what I kept telling myself was going to be a friendly business powwow. And if I believed that shit deep down, then why did I wear my best evening gown? I'd luckily packed it on a whim, but it was fitting too snug in some spots for me. Well, it was dinner only and not dancing, so I figured I'd be straight as long as the lights were dim.

"Ms. Clay?" the maître d' asked before I could get out for who I was there.

"Yes," I answered, a little bit perplexed since I wasn't wearing my Aquos bracelet this time.

"Mr. Jackson is expecting you," he said, enjoying my surprise. "Right this way."

In the entire place there were only about seven people dining, but none were near where Julian was seated. For a place as exquisite as this, it didn't make any sense for it to be this empty unless the prices were really astronomical. When Julian spotted me, he stood up from his seat like a gentleman, then beckoned a waiter over.

"I thought you might stand me up," he said as he took my hand and gave me a soft kiss on my cheek before I could even think about objecting. *Decisive.*

"You took me away prematurely from some fun, so I did consider it," I stated, busting his chops. A habit I was getting used to.

"How did the maître d' know it was me?" I asked, only thinking the obvious being my race.

"Easy. I described you to him," he said kissing his fingertips for dramatic effect. "Knew you'd be looking lovely, so it was easy. That, and the fact that I bought out this entire section so we could be alone."

I'd be shitting you if I said the gesture didn't make my heart go all pitter-pat for a minute. Maybe he had a legitimate interest in me. But that might be as standard for this Julian cat to impress a woman as a regular brother buying roses or showing off his nice car.

As the waiter came over with an open bottle of wine, he flashed the label toward Julian then poured a little of the vino in both our glasses.

"You're so easy on the eyes," he said as those very eyes tried to avoid my bosom, but succumbed anyway.

"I can say the same about you, but you probably hear that from all your women," I said as I took in the basically elegant black suit that made him look like one of the old Rat Pack, or a slightly older Diddy.

"Oh? You're one of my women now?" he crowed, swirling his wine around before taking a sip.

"Shit, you wish," I clowned, perhaps being a little too loose if this was about business. *Artemis, you're outta your league, but don't you dare let it show, girl.*

Two servers came from the kitchen with these cute little square plates, each possessing a mound of what looked like either corned beef hash or dog food surrounded by pretty colors and a baby egg of some sort. Of course, I knew it wasn't dog food . . . I thought. Unless Julian was trying to prank a sister. But he knew better from our hallway exchange.

"The starter. I hope you like," he said as he waited for me to situate my napkin and utensils before beginning to eat.

I needed something to sop up the alcohol I'd been chugging, so I didn't waste any time trying to be too cute. "What is this? If you don't mind my asking," I said as I swirled the flavors around in my mouth, which I couldn't fully identify. Whatever it was, it was meaty and had some seasoning. Hell, I was still kinda drunk, so it could've been anything.

"Steak tartare with black truffle aioli and a quail egg," he answered as he identified the components on my tiny plate.

"Tartare? As in raw meat?" I said, fighting off the instinct to spit it into my napkin. I immediately stopped chewing as I looked around to see if anyone was watching.

"Of course. It's the only kind of tartare that I know of," he replied, looking confused.

"Uh . . . no offense, but I prefer my food fully cooked. Just call me an uncultured barbarian, I guess," I said with a half smile as I stared at the remainder on my plate. It sure looked pretty enough, but wasn't gonna happen. Couldn't believe this nigga had 'em serve me some raw damn meat. Not like it was sushi or something.

"Please. I'm not offended at all. It took me a minute to acquire the taste myself. I really should've waited for you before I ordered. That damn type A personality of mine asserting itself. No wonder I'm single," he added with a mocking sigh. "A soup then? Lobster bisque?"

"All right now! I can definitely work with that," I answered with joy. And if it came out with a live lobster kicking on top of a bowl I was so outta here.

After my soup, which was savory, Julian ordered our main course: a filet of Wagyu beef with foie gras topping and sautéed wild mushrooms for himself, and braised branzino with jasmine rice for me. Although being a little rushed and uptight at first, I found myself really enjoying Julian's company. Just days earlier, I never would've envisioned myself having dinner in a restaurant like this while soaking in a dazzling night view of the Las Vegas skyline. A moment I had to commit to memory fo' sho.

After my first glass of wine, I asked for water with lemon. "No more drinks for me. I had more than a few at the day club," I explained to him.

"With those kids?" he asked, his brow furrowing.

"Somebody had to supervise them, so I took it upon myself," I joked. "And believe me, there were plenty of us *responsible folk* down there, too. And, speaking of supervise, is this dinner more about your apology, or did you really get me all scrunched into this dress to probe me . . . about business."

Julian chuckled over my probe remark. "Nah. No business tonight. We can get to that later. I'm sure you didn't come to Vegas for that anyway."

"Nope. Just fun. Until I butted all in your conversation. What brought you here?"

"Some gambling and a change of scenery. I fancy myself a decent poker player back home in Connecticut. Too bad my winnings never reflect it. But I don't shy away from a challenge . . . of any kind. Besides, I've learned a lot about your management style just from this dinner."

"You don't say?" I said, suddenly feeling nervous. Sure, I talked shit. But that was because I had no responsibility and nothing else to lose.

"Yeah. You freely express your opinion, but know how to be forward yet non-offensive. You're not intimidated by the unfamiliar . . . well except for raw meat," he said, to which we both laughed. "But most importantly, you enjoy life."

"And that hasn't been too easy to do these days," I mumbled as I thought about my circumstances.

"Business, or personal?"

"Both," I said.

"Well, despite how I came across when we first met, I'm really not like that. I just play a convincing 'big, bad wolf' when I need to. If there's anything you need, I'm available, Artemis," he said as he reached his hand across and shook mine. "Even if it's just as a sounding board."

Well, that was so unexpected.

Besides finding my biological mom, spotting me a couple hundred grand, and promising to provide me good sex without dying on me, I thought I'd be straight.

But I ain't that chick.

And this world was filled with plenty dudes promising to make it better. Probably like my dad was doing right now with "the next one."

Not saying Julian was one of them, but . . .

Just sayin'.

"Thank you. I mean it. Really. And I'll keep that in mind, Julian," I responded.

"So are you ready for dessert then?"

"I am way too stuffed, but thank you."

"And here I thought I'd get a chance to feed you Bananas Foster or something," he teased, making my toes curl just a little beneath the table.

"And I love Bananas Foster, but I'm gonna take a pass tonight. Maybe we can work on that another time."

"Promise?"

"No. But I'll consider it."

"Fine then," he said as he signaled for the waiter to bring the check. No telling how many people we were cheating out of a night this nice and I did feel kind of guilty about it.

"I just need to stop in the powder room real quick," I told Julian as I moved my chair away from the table.

"I'll be here," he said as he got up from his seat to excuse me.

Inside the restroom, I slowed to smile at myself in the mirror. I'd handled my biz pretty well tonight and had allowed myself some serious moments of fun. Good for me. Definitely beat a day of collections back in Houston. Or, dealing with my mother and sister. But, after today's activities, that bed was gonna be nothin' nice.

And I could wake up whenever the fuck I wanted!

Sometimes it's the little things, ya dig.

I popped my clutch open to reapply some lipstick. I'd hurriedly transferred a few things to it from my purse before rushing here. Curiously, one of those items was the driver Lowell's business card.

"Oh shit!" I blurted out as I remembered that I promised to "Like" his business on Facebook. And if I didn't do it now, it wasn't gonna happen. Nothing I couldn't take care of with a few clicks on my phone, so I proceeded to find his car service and click the ubiquitous button. Feeling proud of delivering on my promise, I touched up my lips, did a quick once-over in the mirror, then merrily bounced.

When I came out, Julian was thanking the maître d' and entire staff for tonight.

"Thank you all," I added, knowing all too well how it is to slave away for someone else with no recognition or appreciation.

Julian took my hand as he led me to the elevators past a line of hungry folk ready to dine now that we were gone. Yet, something told me their experiences wouldn't be half as good as mine.

"What is it that you do back in Connecticut?" I asked to make small talk between us. When I agreed to this date, I never expected the conversation to go so easy with him.

"Besides yelling at people?" he teased, making fun of himself. "I own an advertising firm. Started off working for this nice Jewish guy. He was demanding, but fair. Opened a lot of doors for me that I couldn't have gotten in on my own. Anyway, he didn't really have any family, so when he prepared to retire, he made me an offer I couldn't pass up. A few years ago, I picked up a janitorial franchise to diversify in this economy. Now it's bringing in just as much as my first baby. But always room for improvement, y'know."

"Even though I was hard on you at first, I'm always proud of successful brothers," I said as I allowed myself to absently rub Julian's back. I was getting a little too comfortable.

"How long are you here?" he asked as the elevator opened, exposing the glass globe that was ever breathtaking.

"Just a few more days," I said softly. At which point I would be dragged away kicking and screaming while being accused of being a crazy woman.

"Y'know, it doesn't have to end right here. Allow me to walk you back to your suite. I do know the way after all," he joked.

"True, but I need to walk some of this meal off. But don't worry about me, Mr. Jackson. I'll be fine. I'm a big girl. I can handle myself."

"I noticed," he chimed before suddenly catching himself. "And before you think I'm going there, I don't have any problems with you being full figured. It's a preference of mine. Not that I'm assuming this dinner would be all I'd have to do to win you over or something."

"I gotcha. Ain't got no hang-ups on being me anyway."

"Good. And I don't even know if I could win you over. For all I know, you need to call someone back home and check in. Spouse, or anyone else?" he asked, testing me now.

"Nah. When I say a walk this meal off, I mean just that. I'm a widow. And my last relationship . . . ended suddenly," I said, holding a shudder at bay.

"Good," he said with a smile. "Not about your relationship ending suddenly, but . . ."

"Julian, relax. I got it," I said as I gave him a kiss on his cheek. "Thank you for redeeming yourself," I said before stepping on to the elevator.

"Y'know, Artemis," he called out before the doors closed to shuttle me away, "being fearless sometimes ain't bad."

"Oh, I ain't afraid of you, boy. But thanks for the advice," I commented with a wink.

I strolled through the hotel and casino for half an hour, getting a lay of the land while people-watching as I processed the evening's events. By the time I returned to my suite, I was dead ready for killer zzz's. But looking at Ladonna's door and Julian's even farther down the hall, I wondered what fabulousity was going on in their worlds right now.

"Girl, follow your first mind," I said to myself as I used my key card.

Just inside the door to my suite, I felt a buzz from my clutch. It was my phone, probably announcing a missed call from either my mother Ruth or my sister Anitra. They weren't going to ruin this though.

But it wasn't a missed call. It was a text.

I didn't recognize the number, but thought maybe it was Julian checking on me.

The message read:

> You like me, you really do! Well . . . really my business. Thanks, Ms. Clay. :-) -Lowell.

My wonderful driver. I grinned, forgetting he had my cell number on record and must've noticed my Facebook favor.

> Welcome. :-)

I texted back as I admired my suite once again on my way to the bedroom. After dinner tonight with Julian, I did feel a little odd carrying on a text conversation with my driver. But this was harmless.

Chapter 12

Last night's sleep was so complete that a bitch didn't even dream. A serious thread-count, pillow-top induced coma. The only thing I'd change was maybe having a nice man to wake up to. But I didn't know if Julian would be who I'd pick right now. Maybe somebody like Columbus Short from the ABC TV show *Scandal*. Shonda Rhimes knew exactly what she was doing when she cast him, for he could certainly do some "damage control" for me. And who knew? Maybe I'd be in need of a firm like the fictional Olivia Pope's once my misadventure was all said and done.

After a nice shower, I got my day underway with a little fresh fruit and Greek yogurt courtesy of room service. Then, while still nursing a slight hangover, I squeezed in a body scrub and hot stone massage in the hotel spa. The running tab of debt in my head had me wanting to dial back on the tips, but these people shouldn't have to suffer due to me. Still, I tried to keep everything around 20 percent and nothing higher.

It was close to lunchtime when I lazily strolled back to my room to determine what next lay in store. I didn't think I could handle another day at poolside in the hot sun pretending I could hang, so maybe blowing my complimentary chips in the casino might be more appealing. Who knew? Maybe I'd run into Julian at the poker table and see if any peculiar magic from last night's dinner still lingered? Hell, I probably was just looking for any experience to postpone the inevitable return home.

As I turned my phone back on, it began ringing. *Speak of the devil,* I thought as I saw the area code. Except it wasn't Julian. It was the same number that had texted me last night after dinner.

Lowell, the driver.

"I guess you're wanting my answer?" I asked, rather than greeting him. I didn't reply to his text last night because I was too tired and frankly didn't know what to say.

"Well, when you didn't reply, I assumed you were busy," Lowell offered.

"I was," I commented in a discrete voice as I walked past a loud group of men in even louder shirts. Dudes cared for their eyebrows and hair-care products way too much as they went about yapping like a bunch of women in the beauty shop.

"And now?" he pushed.

"Not so much," I replied, remembering those pretty green eyes of his from the airport that made me grin.

"Have you had lunch?" he followed up.

"No. I just left the spa and haven't even begun my day."

"Then you have to allow me to treat you to one of the best spots in Vegas," he insisted.

"What if I'm still too busy?" I countered. What was it with these men out here trying to woo me with food instead of diamonds 'n' furs? *It better not be a big-girl thang.*

"Too busy to be chauffeured around in style? Really? Like I said before, I'm at your beck and call. This one is totally on me."

"I don't know, Lowell," I said, my reluctance evident in my voice although I liked the idea of a free limo ride. "I'm not looking for anything overly pretentious or complicated today."

"Well if you want to 'slum it' for a change, then you're in luck," he stated with a haughty laugh. "Because, I'm talking barbecue, little lady. That is . . . unless a Texas girl like you is intimidated."

"Intimidated? By Vegas barbecue? Puh-lease! Bring it on," I crowed too loudly in the hallway as the elevator door opened to take me to my floor.

"Good. Knew that would get ya," he said smugly. "I'm downstairs in the lobby. Take your time getting ready. I'm off today. But dress comfortable. You can save your fancy designer clothes for another time."

"What if that's all I have?" I suggested, knowing full well I had less flashy clothes on hand for when I returned to my normal life with my head bowed in shame.

"The problems of the rich," he cracked. "Then I guess I'll just have to put up with you outshining me. This once."

"Whatever, boy. That's why I'm gonna take two hours getting dressed."

Thirty minutes later, I came down to the lobby wearing something between classy and basic: a plum-colored dress I'd bought on sale last year from Macy's with a pair of black sandals. The black Coach purse I carried on my arm was real. A gift several years ago from my husband, back when he was alive.

Even though he claimed to be off, Lowell stood at attention in his standard black uniform, just over the spot where mermaids usually swam by. When he saw me walking toward him, he intentionally looked me up and down for effect, then cast a thumbs-up as he held his watch up. Yeah, he was happy I didn't really take two hours. I returned the favor with a thumb of my own.

"Artemis?" someone called out as he shuffled toward the glass globe I'd just exited.

"Hello, Julian," I gushed before catching myself in front of Lowell's watchful eyes.

"I was wondering how you were after last night," he smoothly declared in his navy blue custom-tailored suit as he stepped away from the elevator. His powerful, commanding presence was on full display even when playing it leisurely.

"Doing very well, thank you. Told you I was a big girl," I quipped.

"I know, I know," he said with a quick smile. "Off somewhere?"

"Yes. Lunch," I provided succinctly as Lowell, seeing me standing there, approached. "That's my driver coming over to remind me," I said in advance of Lowell getting within earshot. Neither one needed to particularly know my business; even if most of my business was imaginary.

"He keeps you on a tight schedule, huh?" Julian said, paying Lowell no mind. To Julian, he was probably just one of those background folk who kept the world working for him.

"Yeah. I have a teleconference this afternoon, so . . ." I threw out in a language he'd understand.

"Okay," he said as he let a sigh escape his lips. "That reminds me. I have to check on my employees back home as well. But I'll be calmer this time. See how you inspire me, Artemis? Call me later?"

"Certainly," I said with a grin as I shook my head.

"Making friends?" Lowell asked as I watched Julian remove his cell phone from his pocket before he boarded the elevator. Even though I think he was sweet on me, that man was about his business furreal.

"Just inspiring folk to do better," I clarified as I turned to leave with him.

Instead of a limo, Lowell had a black SUV from his car service waiting for me outside. As he opened the rear door for me, I just stood there tapping my foot.

"What's wrong?" he asked, his face crinkling.

"If I'm slumming today, I'm riding up front with you," I replied with a wink.

"Okay . . . Artemis," he said, dropping the formality. "Let's get all slummy. Now get your ass in the Tahoe."

I laughed, then scooted my ass into the front passenger seat as instructed.

Lowell made a U-turn, heading back down the Strip, en route to our mystery barbecue place. After passing Caesars Palace, he made a left turn on to Flamingo. With some old Teena Marie playing on his Sirius satellite radio, he slowed in front of the Westin Las Vegas and lowered his window.

"See that over there?" he indicated, clearing his throat as if a tour guide. "That right there is where Tupac was shot. Not where he died though. After being shot here, Suge Knight drove the car back to the Strip and took a left. They stopped at Harmon near where the Cosmopolitan Hotel is now before Pac was transported to the hospital."

"One of the sadder Vegas moments," I commented.

"Yup," he uttered as he kept on driving. "You ever listen to his stuff?"

"Of course," I said.

"Dude ran the gamut with his music, from social commentary to thug standards to club bangers. Just so prolific. What were you big on in H-town back in the day, Ms. Clay?"

"Gheto Boys," I said with a chuckle. "Mr. Scarface, Willy Dee. Bushwick Bill."

"Your mind was *playin' tricks on ya?*" he teased.

"Still is, Lowell," I responded. "I'm riding with a stranger to a place he claims has good barbecue."

"Great, not 'good,'" Lowell corrected me as he took the on-ramp for I-15 North. "You'll see."

After another fifteen minutes of driving, we got off the freeway and passed another airport that I didn't even know Las Vegas had. I could see the mountains north of us getting closer in the distance. "If you're planning on burying me out in the desert, just remember I still got my cell phone on me," I taunted as I waved my iPhone in front of his face.

"And you 'Liked' my company on Facebook, so you know I ain't even thinking about disposing of you," he said, flashing those eyes at me just like I wanted. "And besides, we're almost there."

I didn't know how we could almost be there, for this looked to be a quiet residential area on the sleepy side of town. Lowell slowed down at one of those homes, except this one had a large private road on the side of it that led to a business in the rear.

"Isn't this a butcher shop?" I asked, incredulously as I read the business's sign. Was Lowell planning on buying the meat then cooking it himself?

"Yep. In the front. But what I'm interested in is in the back. Of the place, that is," he slyly replied as the Tahoe went through an open gate and we stopped beside several parked Harley-Davidson motorcycles. I'd gone from thinking we were at someone's house, to a butcher shop, now thinking he'd brought me to a hidden biker bar.

Lowell put the Tahoe in park, then calmly scanned me for my reaction. "You okay with this?" he asked.

"You know I'm from Texas, right? My dad rides horses, so not much different other than they might wear more leather. And besides, I've seen a few episodes of *Sons of Anarchy*."

Lowell erupted in laughter. "Good. 'Cause some of those inside there are my boys. I ride sometimes and trust me, we ain't running guns or killin' anybody like on TV."

Instead of a biker bar, this really was a barbecue joint like he'd promised. The place had a large outdoor patio area with picnic tables already filled with all kinds of people getting their grub on for lunch. A large raised bar connected to the meat market was where they took orders through a tiny window beneath a menu display. A pair of jeans would've been better for today, but I was gonna make the most of it.

True to my Texas roots, I went with the brisket and potato salad while Lowell had a pork rib plate with coleslaw and beans. I couldn't help but contrast in my head Lowell's letting me order for myself versus Julian's more controlled dinner last night. Of course, Lowell ordered Coronas with lime for both of us. I wasn't much of a beer drinker, but didn't complain.

"Whatcha thinkin' about?" Lowell asked, catching me being introspective.

"How this barbecue ain't bad," I said as I squirted more tangy sauce from the bottle onto my meat.

"That's all you're gonna give me? 'Ain't bad'?" he pushed, hunching his shoulders while turning up his beer.

"C'mon now! I'd be a traitor to my home state if I said anything more. But I do like it. Thank you, Lowell," I offered genuinely.

"You're welcome, Artemis," he stated with a smile as he wiped his napkin across his mouth. My eyes lingered on his lips as he licked them, the world briefly going mute for me. He was a successful professional who'd refused to allow all his edges to be smoothed. Yeah, Lowell definitely felt like somebody I'd kick it with back home. "Hope I didn't pressure you too much into going to lunch with me."

"No, you weren't bad. And this was very nice of you."

"I know. Five star, it ain't. But I figure you're used to five star on the regular, so I wanted to come at you differently. Show you a little of me in my downtime."

"Switching up the game?" I queried.

"Nah. No game. Just being me."

"Uh huh. But what if me being 'me' were flat broke and unemployed? How would you feel about that?" I posed.

"Cute," he said as he plopped his napkin on his finished plate and placed his elbows on the table. "I ain't ask for a balance sheet, woman. And I'm my own man. It's just lunch, Artemis. Loosen up."

"You're right," I admitted. "I'm sorry. Just a lot of stress in my life right now has me guarded." Well, that and two failed relationships that ended in the most final of ways.

"Which is why you came to Vegas, I assume. So live now, stress later," he offered as he placed his hand atop mine on the table. "Will you promise to give it a try?"

"Okay. I promise." I sighed, fighting back a tear forming in the corner of my eye. "Ooo. This sauce is spicy," I offered to hide my feelings as I wiped it away.

"It's got a little bit of a bite . . . if you're not prepared for it," he said in a way where I wasn't sure he was referring to barbecue sauce.

"So, you're a rider?" I asked, nodding toward the five grizzled black bikers in their leather vests carrying on boisterously among themselves at the picnic table in the far corner.

"Yeah. Them's my boys over there," he said proudly. To prove his point, he hoisted his Corona in the air to acknowledge them. All five yelled back at him with an unexpected name not his own. "Although I'm not an official member of their club, I'm affiliated and ride with 'em sometimes. They see I have my work clothes on . . . and a sexy woman with me, so they're keeping their distance."

"Who's 'Weasel'?" I asked, changing the subject so as to not blush over his compliment.

"Uh . . . that's my handle. Just a name they gave me."

"Should I ask?" I followed up with a smirk.

"Uh . . . no," he said, lowering his head in embarrassment. "And I think it's time to go."

Although going there took the same amount of time as coming back, I wanted the return trip to last longer. Of course, I didn't come out here looking for this, but this informal lunch felt more like a date than dinner from last night. And, knowing how things normally went in my life, I hadn't been honest with either of them. If I had, both would've turned into disasters.

Maybe that was a solution of a sort. To only share so much with each.

"Well, here we are," Lowell said as we arrived back on the Strip and at Hotel Aquos. He got a text on his phone that drew his attention. "Shit," he muttered as he put the Tahoe in park and read the screen.

"Something wrong?" I asked.

"Got a fare to pick up from the airport," he replied.

"I thought you were off today," I reminded him.

"I am. But one of my drivers just called in. No real 'time off' when you're your own boss. You know how it is."

"Yeah. I do," I mumbled as I looked away at my reflection in the window.

Lowell exited and went around to get my door for me. At the rear of the Tahoe, I could hear the vroom-vroom of a car as it pulled up behind us. *Somebody high on the floss scale no doubt.*

"Here you go, Ms. Clay," Lowell said, just as courteous as when he first delivered me here. If I hadn't been riding in the front, no one would even suspect we'd just been to lunch together.

As he took my hand, I gripped his a little tighter than usual. Sensing it too, Lowell smiled.

Those eyes, those eyes. Lawd, those eyes.

"There you are, bitch!" an all-too-familiar voice shrieked before any awkward words could be exchanged between Lowell and me. I didn't even bother hiding my eye-roll as I shuddered. "Artemis!" Ladonna screamed as she came running toward me in a bright yellow dress that clung to her toned shape.

Lowell stole a glance at her then turned back to me, his eyes saying he was at a loss for words. I shared his wide-eyed gaze as I realized it was Ladonna, in fact, in the sports car behind us.

"You, bitch! I thought you were just hiding out in your room when you didn't answer," Ladonna exclaimed all out of breath like she'd run a mile. Needless drama. "I wanted you to come car shopping with me," she said as she swung the massive orange purse around on her arm to allow me a better view of her toy. Whatever it was, it was black, shiny, and low to the ground.

"It's—" I went to say as I admired it.

"It's a Lotus!" she bellowed in my ear, cutting me off.

"Nice," Lowell said at the black curvy car. "Exige, right?" he asked. Of course Mr. Big, Bad Biker would know what it was.

"Yes! Bravo!" she responded, actually clapping like Lowell deserved a cookie.

"Ladonna, this is Lowell," I said, no longer delaying the introductions.

"Hello, Lowell the driver!" she said as she inappropriately hugged him then disengaged as if he were just that, my driver. Again, that damn purse of hers flew recklessly, walloping him across the back. Part of me was incensed, but she didn't know any better.

Lowell cut an awkward grin at me then waved bye.

As Lowell drove away, Ladonna was still blowing up my ear about the Lotus she'd bought out of boredom and how she wished I were there to see the fine men at the dealership fighting for her business. Money really was an afterthought to her. I was nodding, but tuning her out when she regained my attention.

"Uh . . . did I just see you get out the front seat of that Tahoe?" Ladonna posed to me with her hand on her hip.

"Yeah," I answered defensively.

"Uh huh. You and your driver kinda close?" she pressed as she dismissively handed her keys to the valet and gave them her room number. "I mean. I understand. He's cute . . . for a chauffeur."

"Nah. I just had a better view up front," I slyly replied as I walked inside.

Yeah. The barbecue sauce was spicy today.

Chapter 13

"You have to go for a spin with me, Artemis!" Ladonna gushed as we walked the halls of our floor. She just had to follow me upstairs, that mouth of hers just a-goin' on autopilot.

"Uh . . . girl, I don't think I can fit in that little windup toy of yours, but thanks," I proffered.

"Nonsense. You can definitely fit. They wouldn't make a car that expensive if people can't fit in it," she chimed in that airheaded way of hers. "And since you stood me up last night to have dinner with your handsome mystery man, we'll take it out to the clubs tonight."

Did she say "clubs"? Plural?

"Dang. You ain't got somebody else you can drag there? What happened to those people from the pool last night?" I asked, halfway joking.

"What do you think? We had an orgy! But no film," she said with a wide grin. "And condoms were in effect. I practice what I preach, bitch. Of course, they were as disposable as a condom, so I can't hang with them anymore. I have real friends like you for that."

"Ladonna, we barely know each other," I bluntly admitted as we stopped in front of her room door.

"But I wanna know you, dear. I find you interesting. What you want to know about me? Shoot," she instructed as she folded her arms, that big purse of hers still in the way.

"Uh . . ." I stuttered, not really wanting to know anything, but I guessed I was stuck with her as long as I was here. Friends and all that. "Where are you from?" I asked to get it out the way.

"Originally? Jamaica. But we moved to Manhattan when I was a little girl. Big city girl with island roots. I've also lived in London, Barcelona, Atlanta, and Fresno, California."

"*Fresno?*" I questioned, surprised.

"Don't ask. He had a big cock," she said with a shake of her head and roll of her eyes. "And you?"

"Texas," I responded. "That's it." Of course there was more, as I'd recently found out, but why bother?

"Knew it," she said smugly. Was it a real friendship if you wanted to slap the other person more than once in a day? "C'mon inside," she said as she waved her VIP bracelet to open her room door.

"What is it you do? For a living." I decided to ask since we were such friends. I had my own ideas, but figured I might as well confirm them.

"Besides live off my trust fund, divorce settlement, and investments? Let my money grow looong." She beamed as if happy I'd asked. "I know. Kinda boring, huh?"

"Totally," I deadpanned.

While my suite was a junior, hers was slightly larger. And God, she needed it. Shopping bags and boxes from stores that I never heard of were clustered in the corner of the living room, some of them untouched. Near them were handfuls of gift cards, too, scattered haphazardly across a table beside a closed laptop. Was I in a suite or a retail store?

"Early Christmas gifts?" I joked as I pointed to the gift cards.

"Those?" she responded as she worked her touch-screen virtual menu on the half wall faster than I could follow. I think she was adjusting her room temperature, scheduling a hair appointment, and purchasing concert tickets at the same damn time. And how did her virtual assistant look like a hot dude? "I hand them out in addition to tips sometimes. That is if the service is extra good. You'd be surprised how some people go crazy over them. One time at

Wolfgang Puck's, a fight broke out between my servers over who was going to get it. Makes me feel like Santa Claus, helping the less fortunate. Well . . . if Saint Nick were a girl and sexy like me. Take a few and try it out," she instructed as she walked over, grabbed several, and placed them in my hand.

My eyes must've been twinkling as I curiously asked, "How much are these?"

"I dunno. Five, I think," she muttered while moving on to her shopping bags to hastily dig for something.

"Five dollars each?"

She looked at me like I was stupid, breaking off her search. "Now what can someone do with five dollars? That ain't even enough for coffee. Those gift cards are for five *hundred* each, silly. Why do you think they fought over one at Puck's?"

I blinked hard and almost peed on myself with Ladonna's admission. This bitch was breaking off $500 in gift cards on a whim? I was so not worthy to be around here. One of these alone would pay two of my utility bills back home and she was tossing them around like leftover pennies in an ashtray.

"Oh, my God. You are throwing money around like a Saudi."

"Ha! That was my ex-husband. It was never going to work anyway. The whole 'racial' thing with his family," she commented, stunning me further.

"I couldn't," I mumbled softly about the gift cards I held.

"Oh please! They're a tax write-off to me. At least that's what my accountant tells me. Charitable contributions, or something."

"You sure about that?"

"Nope, but that's what I pay the Republican for." She giggled as she found the outfit she was looking for, tag still on it.

"I meant to do some shopping myself. I guess I could use a few . . . for tips like you said," I mentioned while hiding the tremble of my hand as I multiplied $500 by the number of cards I'd counted. The last gift card I held was one to Chili's mere days ago, a consolation prize for the bonus I'd earned. The cumulative amount of these gift cards put my bonus I was cheated out of to shame.

"Good. Well, take 'em and go," Ladonna instructed. "Because I just scheduled a chemical peel and hair appointment, so I must be getting downstairs to the salon. Give me your number so I can text you before we hook up tonight."

I walked back to my suite with my hands sweating. The plastic in my hands was worth more than I had in my name when I arrived. I shouldn't have been feeling that way, but I felt like a thief, wondering how comfortable Ladonna would be with me if she knew I was a broke woman. Still, I wasn't lying when I told her I planned on shopping. It was just going to be window shopping . . . until now.

"Breathe, girl. Breathe," I said aloud as I closed the door behind me and silently counted to ten. When no one knocked to tell me my charade was over, I smiled.

The suite's touch-screen display had a message flashing on it and the red button on the room phone was lit also. I strolled over to the glass panel and tapped it with my fingertip. My virtual assistant popped up as before, telling me there was a package waiting for me. I had no idea what it was, but chose to have it brought up. Perhaps it was a traditional welcome package from the hotel or something.

About five minutes later, there was a knock at my door.

"Ms. Clay, this was left at the front desk for you," the young man in black said with a bright smile. It was the same one who'd carried my luggage up yesterday.

"Oh," I exclaimed. "Do you know who left it?" I pressed, surprised by the lovely gift-wrapped box.

"No, ma'am. Perhaps somebody at the front desk knows more," he said.

"Okay. Thank you," I responded. As he went to leave, I stopped him. "What do you do besides work here?" I asked him.

"Ma'am?" he replied, caught off-guard by my question.

"Do you work another job or something?" I questioned intently.

"I attend school at CSN full time, so I can't work any other jobs," he admitted. He had goals. I liked that.

"Well, here. This is for you," I said as I placed one of Ladonna's gift cards in his hand. "I know how it was when I was a college student."

"Thank you. Thank you very much," he stated warmly. Once he found out how much the gift card was for, he'd really be excited.

I carried the present with me to the kitchen where I opened a bottle of sparkling water and set it atop the counter. I grinned, thinking maybe Lowell was lying when he said he had a fare to pick up. The sly fox probably just wanted to run somewhere to pick up a gift for me, I assumed.

As I carefully peeled back the red foil wrap, I began thinking about what I would say to Lowell when I called him. I guess our lunch affected him the same way it did me. The box underneath revealed it was from a dress shop, which made my stomach jump.

And the dress inside made me jump.

"Nooooo!" I crowed as I held the black draped cocktail dress up to my body. The designer was Tadashi Shoji and I'd be damned if it didn't look to be my size. Lowell's attention to detail impressed me even more.

Before trying it on, I decided to call Lowell first just to thank him. At this point, it didn't matter if it fit, for it's the thought that counts.

His phone was ringing when I noticed the card in the bottom of the box.

"Hello?" Lowell answered.

"Hey! I . . ." I said, pausing mid-sentence as I glanced over the note. And the signature at the end of it.

"Artemis, you there?" he called out.

"Yeah," I softly replied. "I . . . I was just checking to make sure you got to your fare in time," I added.

"Yes, I did. That was very considerate of you."

"Yeah," I said again, short with my words. "I'm considerate like that."

The signature at the end of the note wasn't Lowell's.

It was Julian's.

The dress was a gift from Julian.

Chapter 14

Julian's message read:

Artemis,
Thank you for putting me in my place when we first met. I'm not used to someone being so forthright and appreciate your bluntness, honesty, and beauty. Hope you don't mind this small token of my appreciation and remembrance of our brief time together last night. Even though our time here in Las Vegas has been short, I really hope to have many more moments in the future.
Julian

"Wow," I mouthed in a low tone with Lowell still on the phone.

"Something going on over there?" Lowell questioned.

"No. I'm sorry. I'm just a little distracted," I admitted as I admired the linen card etched with Julian's words. For all I knew, Julian had one of his people pick out the dress and address the note. Yet . . . it somehow didn't feel that way. Despite his claims of turning over a new leaf thanks to me, I didn't think he would be willing to share these kinds of thoughts with an employee of his.

"Is your unusual friend Ladonna around? I could see why she'd be a distraction," he admitted.

"Nah," I replied. "I managed to free myself of her. For a minute."

"Okay. Anything you want to share with me?" the Harley-riding, limo-driving brother whose friends called him "Weasel" for some reason asked.

What I wanted to share was my appreciation for the gorgeous, generous gift, except . . .

I was wrong.

Julian had sent it to me.

"Nah. That's it. Just making sure you got to your fare in time. Oh. The barbecue was great also. Thank you . . . again," I feebly offered Lowell in an effort to get off the phone.

"See! Your honesty is finally winning out," he clowned, probably thinking he was having a breakthrough with me. "I am really getting you to open up, Artemis."

"True." I giggled. "Well . . . guess I should go now."

"Okay, you go. But don't forget that I'm at your beck and call whenever you need me," Lowell casually reminded me oh so timely.

"Got another Facebook page for me to 'Like'? Because I've gotten good at clicking," I teased.

"Nah," he said. "But you can 'like' me if you want. I don't come with buttons though."

"Fine. I'll take that. But I thought for sure you had buttons for me to push, *Weasel*. It's a shame that you don't," I said coyly before catching myself. Had to keep telling myself flirtation like this was too soon. Yet it was hard to live by lofty goals with two very different yet equally appealing men vying for my time and attention. Who knew? Maybe, my heart and mind, too?

"Oh, now you wanna mess with my head. And on that note, I'm out," he crowed, abruptly hanging up on me.

I'm glad it worked.

Because I felt a bit dirty flirting with him while ogling over a dress bought for me by another man, and I didn't need to add that kind of guilt to my trip.

Guilt to my trip. Guilt trip. I made a funny off a non-funny.

But if I wanted a pity party, that could happen back home. Easy.

Resolute, I took my gift and went to the bedroom to try it on, away from potential prying eyes. I knew she wasn't real, but that virtual assistant was a little too lifelike if you asked me. Damn perfect smile and perfect hair and she was flaunting it. Was still wondering how Ladonna got hers to be a man though.

The Galleria back in Houston was no pushover, but I don't think I'd ever been a part of such an elegant and expensive shopping experience as this. Venturing out beyond Aquos's property, I strolled through the Forum Shops at Caesars, away from the hotel to avoid any embarrassment from my reluctance to indulge. The grandiose Roman style impressed me as much as the brand-name stores that had a sister wanting to drop to her knees and cry. I just wished these places would consider catering to women of more realistic sizes. I'd never be able to step inside the knockoff stores on Harwin Drive back home again without breaking out in hives. I was only window shopping, but those gift cards from Ladonna were quietly seducing me with their whispers from inside my purse.

I started on the first level, gazing up at its painted blue skies and billowy white clouds on the overhead ceiling as I walked along. From my dopey smile, some people probably thought I was high or something, but I was just high off the change of scenery. Just when I quit gawking, I'd walked up on a Disney-like show with life-like robots, *Fall of Atlantis,* that made me break out my phone to film it. On the second level, I was posing for a picture in front of a fountain, since I looked so good, when the man abruptly handed my phone back to me.

"Miss? Someone's calling you," he politely alerted me. At least he got my picture first.

"How did your teleconference go?" Julian asked when I answered. He never forgot anything.

Thank God my lies were small enough for me to remember.

"Splendid," I replied as I pressed my phone close to my ear so as to better hear him. The place was busy with real shoppers, their high-quality paper and plastic bags rustling against one another in passing like it was some obscene consumer orgy. "I'm actually out doing a little shopping," I stated, feeling odd with just my purse on my arm.

"My gift wasn't enough?" he asked, feigning hurt feelings.

"Julian, thank you!" I gushed. "It's so beautiful. I was stunned, but you didn't have to do that. Really."

"I know. It was my choice. Just like it was your choice to have dinner with me last night."

"I didn't *really* have a choice," I clowned him. "And the dress was your payoff?"

"No, no. Just like the note said, I wanted to do something nice for you," Julian assured me.

"It *and* the note were most definitely nice. I'll let you in on a secret. I'm wearing it now," I admitted, loving the way it made me feel so sexy and free. And expensive.

"Oh? Wow. It fits fine and everything?" he questioned.

"Totally. The way it feels. Oh my God. Mmmm," I moaned a little too loud. My memory of dancing in the bedroom mirror while running my hands over my curves hadn't faded. "Tell the truth. Did you have somebody break into my suite and get my size while I was out?" I asked him.

"No, definitely not. I kinda committed your body to memory," he said smoothly, his smile visible through the phone. "Then I found a woman with similar proportions and dared ask her for her dress size. Rude, huh?"

"You didn't!" I countered, embarrassed for him and imagining the beat down.

"I did," he admitted. "She was a good sport once she realized why I was asking. Told me you're lucky to have me. Uh . . . then I had to explain that we're not . . ."

"Oooh."

"Artemis, I'd love to see you again tonight. No pressure."

"Says the man who just bought me a totally overpriced dress," I jabbed. "I'd like that too. But I've been coerced by my friend Ladonna—she stays on our floor, by the way—to go club hopping tonight. Maybe I could see you somewhere along the way? I'm sure she'll be too drunk to even notice."

"So you're saying I have to hit the clubs in order to see you?"

"No. Just one club. I can't be in all of them at the same time. Or you can wait until I drag myself in. Whenever that might be." I giggled, feeling myself.

"If you're promising to make a late-night house call, that sounds kinda tempting, Artemis. Call me later and let me know where you're going to be, then we'll play it by ear."

"I will," I sang. Yeah, this dress he'd picked out had certainly unleashed something in me.

I was looking at which store to enter when Miss Nancy called me. As nothing could bring me down about now, I answered. Besides, she was my favorite coworker anyway.

"Girl, are you okay?" she asked, her voice cracking as if she was hoarse. "You ain't kill nobody and chop 'em up, huh?"

"No, girl. I'm okay," I replied with a false laugh and my newfound confidence tested.

"Do you plan on coming back to work?"

"Girl, I dunno," I said with a long sigh. "I'm trying to clear my head, s'all. I'm doing some shopping right now and you would not believe the sights out here."

I thought that would tantalize Miss Nancy, get her to loosen up and gab like we always do. Maybe demand to know where I was, but no. Instead she went stone-cold silent for a moment.

"Um . . . I don't know if you're aware, but HR came by your desk yesterday and boxed everything up. Then Rhonda held a meeting today and reassigned all your accounts. Girl, they fired you," she sobbed.

Chapter 15

"Did you hear me, Artemis?" Miss Nancy questioned after my pause.

"Yes, I heard you," I softly replied as I slowed in front of the Dolce & Gabbana store. My heart should've been beating like a jackhammer, but it wasn't. I knew this moment was coming. Knew from the moment I took my extended-indefinite-early lunch and went to Chili's.

Sure took them long enough.

"What are you going to do?" she stressed, her concern touching me. She was always there and, in a way, perhaps I let her down. "You always could file suit for workplace stress. We'll all back you up on that one."

"I'll deal with it another day," I answered. "We'll catch up when I'm back in town. Tell Rhonda and Marisol I'll miss working with them."

"Um . . . okay. You sure you're all right with this, Artemis?"

"Totally. I haven't felt this good in a while," I responded. "Oh. One more thing."

"Yeah, girl?" Miss Nancy commented, dread evident in her voice.

"Tell Karyn I said to fuck off."

Ooo, I wanted to high-five myself after that, but I got an Asian girl in a mini skirt to dap up the "crazy black girl" instead as she walked by. I couldn't let a moment like that go to waste without a little celebration. Not that Miss Nancy was gonna share my parting words with the office boss Karyn, but it still felt liberating.

I was a kite with a broken line, so I might as well soar in the wind until I came crashing down.

Or, got stuck in a tree.

And the Louboutin store just to my left had many branches in which to get tangled.

"May I help you?" the olive-skinned woman with large almond-shaped eyes offered as she welcomed me into the "land of the red bottoms" where girls' dreams come true.

"I'm looking for a pair of boots just like those in the display over there. But do you have them in a size ten?" I asked, imagining myself in possession of them already.

"I'm certain we can more than accommodate you, madam," she purred. I guess Julian's dress sufficed to command respect.

"Oh. I have one other question before you inconvenience yourself. It's a terrible habit of mine, but I don't like to use cash when I travel. Do you accept gift cards?" I asked with my brightest smile as I held one of Ladonna's many plastic buddies aloft in my hand.

This kite hadn't crashed just yet.

Gotta love retail therapy.

I left the Louboutin store with two pairs of shoes: some cute little black Chelita boots and a pair of sparkling ruby red platforms that looked like they'd been dipped in pure color. With my bag in hand, this warrior finally had the tools to fight off the other marauding shoppers. I swear, after this, I should have been on a first-name basis with Mr. Louboutin. Yeah. Stop by his crib and say, "Christian, baby, how do I look?" Then he would say, "You a regular *ciao bella,* Artemis." Yes, it was totally irresponsible, but not using my own money gave me a slight moral "out."

As I planned on finishing my window shopping tour and heading back to the hotel, I got a text from Ladonna.

Call me. ASAP

Oh no. What if she suddenly decided she needed her cards back? Or figured out I wasn't what I was pretending to be?

Better to call her back now than to risk her calling the cops on me.

"That was quick, bitch."

"Your text said it was urgent, so here I am."

"Where are you, bitch?"

"Just doing a little shopping at Caesars," I responded, mourning the loss of my beloved shoes already. And I hadn't even gotten a chance to take 'em for a spin.

"I knew it!" She cackled with that awful shrill laugh of hers. "You still there?"

"Yes. What's up?"

"Did you use any of those gift cards that I gave you yet?"

Uh-oh. Here it comes. Should've kept that shit in my purse, but nooooo. I had to test it out. "Uh . . . yeah. I just tipped a few people," I replied, ready to break out in a cold sweat.

"And?"

"They went crazy over them just like you said they would," I replied, in reality commenting about myself.

"Good! Toldja. But I'm glad you're still there."

"Why?"

"I decided we're gonna wear white tonight, Artemis. So you need to pick up something while you're out."

"Oh." I gasped followed by a major sigh of relief. I hurriedly checked how many remaining gift cards I had in my purse. Courtesy of my new employment status, some of these were now gonna have to be stretched to cover my bills back home. But I still had a few to spare, so I knew this darn mall better have a store with some white outfits for a plus size like me.

"I'm on it," I said, ready to add another shopping bag on my arm.

Chapter 16

"Well? How do I look?" I asked as I walked up.

"Gurrrrllll, look atcha!" Ladonna bellowed over the din of blaring horns and piped-in dance music from the concealed speakers around us. And we weren't even at the club yet. A steady procession of taxi cabs, limos, and hotel guests flowed tonight through the carport while we waited for the valet to retrieve her new sports car; the one with the name I still couldn't pronounce and which was too fast and too small for me.

I twirled around in my white suit skirt, arms extended and hair flowing in the dry desert air, showing off what I threw together on such short notice. Nothing like a little Ann Taylor to rein in my spending bug after Ladonna's scare, but I made it hard to tell with my overpriced accessories: the Louboutin boots I'd bought and my white leather Michael Kors fold-over clutch.

Okay! Okay! I bought the clutch after promising to myself to keep it reasonable. And I planned on sticking to that promise, too, except I just *haaad* to pass the Michael Kors store on my way out of Caesars. With so many people in there, I just had to see what was up. And that's where the clutch that would be sooo perfect with my outfit caught my eye inside the display case. Just like a new puppy waiting for somebody to take it home. I couldn't just let a puppy be homeless, could I? Besides, I still had enough of those gift cards of Ladonna's that one less couldn't hurt.

"Ooo, there's my baby!" Ladonna chirped as her car arrived.

"I don't think I'm gonna be too comfortable, Ladonna," I mildly groaned, growing accustomed to her blowing me off. "Of course, I told you that before when you first wanted to take me for a ride."

"Oh pipe down and get in, fussy-pants," Ladonna jokingly scolded as she hopped into the driver's seat and began fiddling with the buttons on the console. I doubt she had time to figure out what all they did. "We're not going to be in it that long. I just want to show it off to the foot traffic and plebeians in line outside the clubs when we pull up. And besides, you're the one who didn't want to use your driver tonight."

"I already told you I gave him the night off," I chided her as I squeezed into the tiny passenger space, cursing inside my head. Lowell was probably out riding with his biker boys or something and I didn't want to monopolize his time anyway. Maybe if I was honest, I'd admit I didn't want Ladonna getting too close again. That odd hug of hers when she met him still had me feeling a little stank.

"Whatever. That man is fine and has spectacular eyes, Artemis. I'd keep him on call *all* night long," she sang salaciously before adding, "if he weren't the help."

"There you go. I honestly can't tell if you're a bigger freak or a bigger snob, Ladonna," I noted while the limo in front of us pulled away.

"Definitely higher on the freak scale. The snobbery is for my amusement," she admitted as she slipped the valet a twenty-dollar tip. With a quick adjustment of her breasts perched atop her white party dress, she assessed herself in the rearview mirror and pouted her lips like she wanted to kiss herself. "You all situated, Amiss?" she asked.

"*Amiss?*" I repeated, not quite sure if Ladonna was just slurring her words. If she was, bitch had no business behind the wheel.

"Term of endearment I came up with for you. It's still Artemis, just minus the unimportant stuff. Ain't it cute?" she asked me.

Before I could express just how cute I thought
it was, she jammed her foot down on the acceler-
ator, forcing me back into my seat as we zipped
away from the hotel, leaving the smell of burnt
rubber in our aftermath.

We were only two blocks away from Aquos
with Ladonna recklessly switching lanes as she
horribly rapped along with the song on the radio, when she got a call. As she recognized the
number, her expression changed to joy and she
lowered the blaring song invoking, "Deez niggas
won't hold me back" over and over again on her
radio. I figured I'd use my brief reprieve from her
chatter to check my phone as well. Maybe I had
a call from Lowell among the three missed calls
I'd intentionally avoided, two of which were the
familiar numbers of creditors.

No. No call from Lowell. Maybe he was put off
by the odd way I was acting earlier when I still
basked in the shock of Julian's gift. More likely,
he was the kind of man to let a woman make up
her own mind with no pressure. He was a busy
man after all.

Beside us, a limo like the one in which Lowell
first picked me up was abruptly stopped along
the curb in front of the Gucci store at City Centre,

probably to let one of its passengers throw up. As we overtook it, I grinned, hoping the driver might be Lowell, of whom I was thinking. But when he turned to catch me grinning, it was another brother. I still granted him a sweet wave of my hand as the black girls in the all-black car dressed in all white sped along with the impatient traffic.

"Nooo! Get the fuck outta here!" Ladonna remarked to whomever she was speaking, making me cringe.

Who knows what that was about. I decided to check my voice mail real quick and at least attend to one message before my friend reclaimed my attention.

"Miss Clay," the droning voice on my message began, making my stomach twitch. My now former occupation made me more despondent being on the receiving end of these types of calls, but they'd become commonplace this year. I hoped I wasn't that obnoxious when pursuing the money. "We are attempting to speak with you regarding your delinquent account. Please call us back at—"

I deleted it before another word was spoken. They'd call back though.

"Good news?" Ladonna asked, having ended her call.

"Just some bullshit back home," I admitted. "And yours?" I questioned, unable to not notice her wide grin. *Somebody must've left her another pot of gold or something.* These people, I tell ya. Like the rapper was now droning in a lowered volume, "Deez hoes be actin' up." Or something like that.

"Change of plans, Amiss," Ladonna said as she put her turn signal on and slowed.

"Why? Where are we going now?" I asked. Funny, because I didn't know where we were heading in the first place, just that it was supposed to be the hottest spot in town.

"Back," she said.

"Back to the hotel?" I quipped.

"Yes, we are!" she whooped in a manner way too happy for that kind of change of plans. "Bitch, that was my hookup coming through. We got something better to do than club hop. And you will not believe it. We are going see Royal T. . . . in private concert!"

Chapter 17

Technically, we didn't go back to our hotel, so Ladonna got a chance to show off her ride anyway. We drove back to the property, but instead of returning to Aquos, we went to its sister property, Stratus, the one all about the sky 'n' stuff.

The valets were kinda the same as at our place, except they greeted us with, "Welcome to your dreams. Welcome to Stratus." Well, my dreams had long been crushed, so I was all about the "adventure." *Guess I'll stick with Aquos.*

"Fortune has smiled on us, Artemis," Ladonna said as she exhaled.

I was just glad she'd dropped her nickname for me, however briefly. It reminded me too much of Carlos's nickname for me, Artie, except unlike him Ladonna wasn't gonna die in bed with me like him. No matter how pissy drunk I got.

"We got an invite to one of the hottest tickets in town tonight."

"That was one of your friends who called you, huh?"

"Of course not," she admitted, her face going deadpan. "Just one of the concierges from our hotel. Of course, she thinks we're best buds, so that helped getting us into the show as last-minute additions."

"Gift card tip?" I joked, not really joking.

"No. Of course not," she corrected me, speaking deliberately as if behind a lectern in community college or something. "Because if I really tipped her then she'd realize she's not actually my friend and just the help. Duh. Stick with me and you'll get the rules down before you go back to Texas."

I shook my head and followed, admittedly enjoying the way people stared at us. We were like a couple of stars, or at least reality show stars, depending on who was doing the watching. And I'll be damned, we were really going see Royal T. Daniels in concert. My sister Anitra loved her some "Royal T." as everybody called him these days. If I got close enough, I'd be sure to get a picture with him just to irk the living hell outta her. Even though I'd learned she was only my half sister, I could still give her full grief.

From what Ladonna shared with me, this was a private concert for about fifty people, us being fifty-one and fifty-two. When we exited the private VIP elevator on the top floor, Ladonna got the gawkers she wanted as we were escorted past them inside the theatre and seated at a plush curved bench in a prime spot near the stage.

As the rest of the concertgoers filed into the horseshoe-shaped theatre, I read the tiny invitation on our table by candlelight. It wasn't just Royal T. in concert tonight, but his special guest Natalia. Now this was some unexpected shit, for I'd followed Natalia since she won the US Icon singing competition years back.

"Oh, my God! Natalia's here, too," I hissed giddily as I grabbed Ladonna by her arm.

It felt good to see a homegirl from H-town going platinum and winning Grammys. I mean, besides Beyoncé. Kelly Rowland also had done good since going off to Europe, but she was really from the ATL. I had all of Natalia's albums and used to dance by myself to her video for "All Is Love."

"Why yes. I forgot. Isn't she from Texas too? Heh. You're practically homegirls," Ladonna commented with a chuckle as she got the attention of one of the premium hostesses. "A magnum of your finest champagne please. None of the cheap stuff. Oh. And a couple tequila shots too. Top shelf," she requested with a flip of her hair that drew the attention of more than a few gentlemen in attendance with their dates.

"Do you ever get tired of spending money? Or drinking?" I asked softly so as to not ruffle her feathers. After all, Ladonna was responsible for me being able to party so much harder on this trip. And she didn't know it, but she'd given me a tiny lifeline with some of those gift cards of hers.

"Not in the least, Amiss," she asserted, making the s's sound like z's at the end. "The more I spend, the more I help folk. And the more I drink, the more I spend. Thus I serve a purpose in the big wheel, dear. When you grow your business and move up a tax bracket or so, you'll probably feel more philanthropic yourself."

How in the hell did she succeed in making me feel guilty over not being as reckless a spender as she? As the lights began to dim and the emcee took the stage, I quickly took out my phone before everything popped off.

Change of plans for 2nite. Next door @ Stratus. A private concert on top of the world. Will let you know when it's over.

I texted Julian, feeling a little something about wanting to keep tonight's excitement going. I only had one more night here and maybe

personally thanking him for his gift might bene-
fit both of us. Did he take charge behind closed
doors as he did in public? A girl could wonder.

> Good. Now I don't have to chase you
> down. Have fun.

Julian replied, making me a little anxious as
my feet fidgeted beneath the table.

"Have you gotten laid since you been here,
girl?" Ladonna dared to ask. Of course she'd
dare.

"Not yet," I said smartly with my mind on the
future.

"Yet, huh?" she said with a wink, casting her
eyes at my phone as I stored it. "Well, here's to
ending that," she toasted with a raised shot glass
as the night's entertainment began.

I almost coughed from the tequila's burn,
but fought it. Savoring the heat going down as
Natalia took the stage and told everyone to get
up on their feet, I obeyed.

Natalia went through a medley of her hit songs
with most of the people up and dancing, some
yelling at the top of their lungs to the words of their
favorites. The kids could have their overstuffed
party scene on the Strip without me tonight. My
own private concert with one of my favorite sing-

ers no more than six feet away was more than I ever could ask for. It was enough to have a sister speaking in tongues, but that was probably just the combination of endorphins and bubbly.

Before she began her final number, Natalia took a moment to thank her best friend Amelia back in Houston for writing some of her most recent number-one hits. When she asked if anybody else was from H-town, I was the one who dared to holler. I'll never forget her pointing at and me and saying, "Well all right now!" before going into her last song of the night . . . "All Is Love."

Oh my God. Did she read my mind?

Just kill me now.

My skirt suit had enough give in it to allow me to attempt my dance moves from when I was . . . *ahem* . . . a few sizes smaller. And ain't nobody telling me I didn't nail 'em either. When her two backup dancers saw me matching their moves (at least in my mind), they actually paused to come off the stage and dance with me.

All the people on our side of the theatre, including Ladonna, began cheering me on as Natalia sang her ass off, extending her notes and riffing better than Beyoncé at an awards show complete with a hair-blowing wind machine. When she wrapped it up and brought the house down, I was out of breath, but still found the energy to clap and jump for my girl.

"Bitch, I did not know you could move like that," Ladonna proudly admitted as we returned to our seats for the brief set change and emcee segment. "I need to find you back in Texas after all this is over. Maybe we could hit up Miami for a weekend."

"Yeah . . . whooo . . . that . . . would be nice," I huffed while dabbing the perspiration from my forehead. I was messing up my makeup, but fuck it. "As long as you don't call me 'Amiss' ever again."

"It's a deal, Artemis," she agreed with a nod and wink as she signaled for more drinks and a few more napkins to our table. "But I'm still calling you 'bitch,' bitch."

Before Royal T. came out, Natalia returned to mingle with the concertgoers, smiling and posing for pictures as the camera phones came out in full force. *So this is how a private concert of this caliber goes. No limo to whisk the people away, but actually kickin' it with folk?* If Ladonna didn't give that concierge one of her $500 gift cards, I was gonna find her and give one of mine.

"Do you want me to take a picture of you with Natalia if she comes around?" Ladonna asked, seeing my star-struck eyes.

"Yes. But only if she comes nearby. I don't want to act like a groupie," I instructed her.

"Hey, H-town," a woman's voice called out from behind me. I knew it from interviews on *Entertainment Tonight* and numerous awards shows, usually during acceptance speeches.

As I went wide-eyed, Ladonna smirked and motioned for me to fork over my phone.

"She close enough now, bitch?" she joked in a low voice.

Chapter 18

"Thanks, y'all, for coming out tonight," Natalia said as she shook both our hands. Up close, she was just as cute and pretty as she looked in her videos. "I know this is Royal T.'s gig tonight and I'm just a special guest, but I appreciate the love from fans like you."

"Are y'all on tour together?" I dared to ask, trying to rein in my curiosity. So many questions I wanted to ask of someone whose life probably wasn't a whole lot different than mine growing up. It's just that I'd never come so close to speaking with a celebrity before. That is, other than Mattress Mack who did the TV spots back home for his store, Gallery Furniture. And that's when I went there with my mother to pick out a sectional and he gave us a good deal. Okay. Rambling. I'ma shut up.

"Talking about it," the songstress admitted with a nod of her head and wry smile. "It's a matter of our schedules syncing. And the money being right, of course."

"I know that's right," Ladonna interjected at the mention of money. Of course she would. "I'll bet tonight's appearance fee was quite lovely."

"I ain't gonna complain. Vegas isn't really my scene nowadays, but it's a business, so I do what I do. Besides, Royal T. lives out here, so it made sense."

"A business. I know how that is," I groaned. I'd been doing my job while hating it simply because I had to. Just like being cheated out of my hard-earned bonus back home, it was a business decision.

"Oh? What is it you do, Artemis?" Natalia asked.

Holy shit, she called me by my first name. "I . . ." I began, wanting to be perfectly honest with Natalia. What I did would be past tense now because I hadn't a job to which to return.

"Artemis owns a collection agency. Soon to be Fortune 500, but she hates to brag," Ladonna matter-of-factly volunteered before I could decide on what to say.

"Well go 'head on, girl! It's so uplifting to see a sister making it, especially one from back home. Keep up the good work and I'll have to look you up next time I'm in H-town."

"Uh . . . okay!" I gushed, still pissed at Ladonna for embellishing what was already a lie.

As Royal T. was about ready to make his appearance, I quickly took another picture with Natalia, even daring to post it to Facebook and Instagram for all the people worrying about me back home to choke on it. Natalia provided me with her assistant's number then hustled away to snag a seat at the back of the theatre to watch Royal T.'s number. I was still in hella disbelief over Natalia just kicking it at our table and being as genuine and natural as can be.

The lights went black as the anticipation for Royal T. built. I stifled a giggle as some of the women jockeyed for position close to the stage. Even in the dark, I could make out Ladonna adjusting them damn breasts again and checking her breath. Didn't Royal T. have a pregnant fiancée anyway?

When the lights came back on, Royal T. stood there with three dancers, opening up with "Where Dem Hands At?" his high-energy dance track that kicked the party into overdrive. I loved his "Smooth Criminal" style though with that little fedora of his, electric dance moves, and those full lips. If I got a picture with him too, people back home were gonna be too through with me.

Like Natalia, Royal T. went through a medley of his biggest songs, hopping off the stage and dancing through the crowd with his dancers in tow. When he strutted by us with a spin move, Ladonna clumsily bumped against him, her breasts coming menacingly close to putting an eye out. All intentional, of course.

"Yeah. He might get it tonight," Ladonna presumptuously declared to me, visually stalking the singer/actor/performer in the darkened theatre with her squinty eyes. *No wonder she was so eager to drop a night of club hopping for this. I ain't mad at her because if he were to take me by the hand and offer to bounce, I'd be like flubber.*

"Ladies and gentlemen, it's been my pleasure to spend this night with you, but for my last number, I . . . I'm having a little difficulty with my throat," he said, hamming it up with his acting ability and charm.

On cue, the audience let out a collective "awwwww" as his dancers fawned over him, faking concern for his imaginary ailment.

"So I'ma do my best to finish strong . . . but would like one of you ladies to join me on stage and help me out."

"Me! Me! Pick me!" Ladonna screamed, joining the chorus of other roaring women who were in near riot mode. All that was missing was a pair of panties to go flying through the air. I just chuckled as I assumed Royal T. had somebody already singled out by his boys or from when he danced through the audience.

"Now, it's my understanding that my girl Natalia found out she had an extra backup dancer among y'all. Is that sexy, sexy lady still out there?" Royal T. asked as he cocked his fedora back. How did that hat stay on his head when he was moving? As Ladonna scowled at me, I suddenly felt flush.

"Well, pretty miss in the white skirt?" Royal T. asked as a spotlight suddenly shone on me. "What I wanna know is . . . can you sang, too?"

Chapter 19

"Uh . . . you do know the words to this song, right?" he teased me. "I mean . . . because if you know Natalia's stuff and don't know mine, my feelings will be really, really hurt."

"I know your songs, Royal T.! I wanna have your baby!" somebody yelled from the audience.

"Easy, lady! It's just a concert!" he yelled back, causing everyone but the girl to laugh.

"Are we up here to sing or what?" I pressed as I guided Royal T.'s arm closer so I could speak into his mic, joking now as I loosened up. My knees had quit knocking, but my palms were still sweaty. And I wasn't about wipe them on white.

"You heard the lady," he said to the anonymous, unseen people working the controls. "Let's go!"

The sudden eruption of colors and sounds on cue startled me to where I almost fell in my Louboutins. But Royal T., being the consummate showman, was swift and caught me just in time in those powerful arms of his as if the whole routine were planned. He performed most of his final song, "You Know You Wanna," with me awkwardly standing there looking pretty and shaking my hips while he danced around me, a cyclone of swagger and sexiness. As I nervously joined in to sing the words to the chorus with him, I spied an impeccably dressed man standing alone who wasn't there a moment earlier. Once my eyes adjusted to the lights, I recognized him.

Julian Jackson.

My persistent gentleman was somehow here. He grinned as if overcome with a mixture of surprise and amusement, bringing a blush to my cheeks.

When we mercifully finished our duet, Royal T. had me take a bow to my own share of applause, then gave me a warm embrace and kiss on the cheek before ushering me back from whence I came.

"I seriously can't bring you anywhere, Miss Wallflower," Ladonna jealously taunted in a good-natured way as I rejoined her to watch the finale from our seats. "You're a regular star magnet, ain't ya, my friend?"

"So that's why you keep me around, huh?" I teased as everyone in the place stood to applaud Royal T.'s amazing performance.

Julian came upon our table as the clapping faded to be replaced with the mumbles of people milling about, looking to leave, network, or "get another drink in this bitch" as I overheard somebody say.

"Artemis, I had no idea," was all he said, his mouth agape as he took both my hands firmly in his and kissed me on the cheek opposite the one Royal T. had graced with his full lips.

"Neither did I," Ladonna added as she inspected Julian then winked at me.

"Julian, this is my friend Ladonna. Ladonna, Julian," I offered.

"Julian Jackson. Pleased to meet you, Ladonna," he said as he stuck his hand out to shake hers.

"Do tell," she replied as she awkwardly hugged him instead, another one of her oversized purses almost assaulting the man's back in the process. Damn thing didn't even go with her outfit, but who was I to say. I was surviving off her kindness in the most.

"How'd you get in?" I asked, remembering what Ladonna had said.

"When you texted me where you were, it wasn't hard to figure out. Especially once I saw you up there. Wow," he marveled, pointing toward the stage where Royal T. had just performed. "It was a private occasion, but I desperately wanted to see you and got impatient. And as you know, I'm not without my means. I'm a VIP member at *both* Aquos and Stratus, sooo . . ."

"See, Artemis, this is certainly the right kind of man for you. Well, for anyone in their right mind," Ladonna said, feigning a swoon.

"I don't know now. How can I compete with someone as accomplished as Royal T.? I mean . . . music *and* movies? I certainly saw a different side of you tonight. Should I be jealous, Artemis?" Julian asked, his eyes blazing with an intense fire that felt more desirous than controlling. Nothing like seeing another man covet something you want—even if faked for a song—to get the blood flowing.

"Jealous? Only if you're insecure, babe," I said, back to jousting with Julian as I liked. Think he liked it too because he kept coming back for more.

"Touché," he remarked. "I think we need a round of shots," he called aloud as he sat with us. Amazing how both he and Ladonna were used to people doing things at the mere sound of their raised voice.

As the waiter delivered another round of shots, Royal T.'s people hastily set up a line for those in attendance for a short meet 'n' greet.

"You better hurry and get in line," I implored Ladonna after downing my last shot for the night. It no longer burned at this point, but seeing Julian looking all good 'n' shit was generating some heat in another place.

"For a photo with Royal T.? Why? I have plenty already of him, except you're in all of them," she jabbed with a roll of her eyes. "Lines aren't my thing. I'll just cut later or he'll send his people over. But right now I need to go powder my nose. You coming, dear?"

"Be right back," I said to Julian, squeezing his knee as I stood up. He reciprocated, his palm drifting over my calf as I left with a grin.

On our way to the restroom, Ladonna bumped people with her purse all along the way, apologizing to some at least. Somebody was gonna yank it off her arm and stomp on it if she wasn't careful. I had no idea of the brand, but it couldn't be worth less than a grand based on her standard of living.

"I assume that was your dinner date from the other night," Ladonna said in the mirror as I washed my hands beside her.

"Guilty as charged," I replied. "He stays on our floor back at the hotel."

"He seems adequate enough. And certainly handsome. What does he do?" she posed as she wiped a lipstick smudge off her teeth.

"He owns a janitorial franchise," I answered first. I did that on purpose just to watch her try to hide her grimace. "Oh. And an advertising firm."

"Okay. More than adequate for a starter such as yourself. You are fucking him before you go back, right?" she asked, or maybe stated. Hell, I'm not sure.

"Ladonna, we need to clear up some things before we go any further. I know you don't mean that much harm, but I don't like being referred to as a 'starter,' whatever in the hell that means. Got it?"

"Fine, bitch. You are a 'finisher' then. Better? Especially after all the attention you've been getting tonight. Royal T., Natalia, your gentleman friend out there," she said, counting on her fingers and still not getting it. "And by the way, that girl Natalia is gay. She wanted to order off the 'late-night menu' and you probably didn't even know it. I ain't stupid. But you still didn't answer my question. Are you fucking your man candy out there?"

"We'll see," I said with a flip of my hair as I stepped smartly out the restroom. And this shit about Natalia being a lesbian? She'd dated that rapper Penny Antnee and he was all man. Ladonna obviously had one too many shots.

The line to meet Royal T. was well formed by the time we came out. Some of them recognized me as the girl who got called on stage, smiling and striking up small talk as I walked by. What I was not expecting was to recognize one of them myself.

Let alone someone like that.

A petite, stunning woman in a black evening gown with a sparkling diamond pendant froze me in my tracks. She hadn't noticed me staring as she waited to meet Royal T. because she was distracted by the older man who was her date for the night. He obviously wasn't her husband. Not because of the obvious age disparity, because it certainly was there, but because he was married to someone else.

I knew this from the man's annual Christmas card sent via e-mail last year to everyone in the company. Or, should I say, *his company*.

Bram-Lect. The place that fired me two days ago.

Roy Bramlett, the real owner and president of the kind of company I pretended to own was here in Vegas and less than ten feet from me. Besides being obviously younger than him, his date looked like she might be Eritrean or something. I attended college at SFA with a few of them, so was familiar with their features. From their family Christmas

card, Roy's wife looked to be Midwestern like him
and just as challenged in the pigment department.
Oh yeah. And Mrs. Bramlett was probably at least
twenty years older than the sweet thang on which
Our Boy Roy was heaping all his affection and
attention. I assumed this concert was his way of
showing her he was "pretty fly for a white guy."
But she seemed disinterested in him and whatever
corny nothings he was whispering in her ear;
bored enough to catch me staring at her, which
she didn't particularly like. I should've looked
away and kept it moving, but I was too stunned,
hoping that maybe her date just bore a passing
resemblance to Roy. That whole "everybody has a
twin somewhere" spiel. But nah, it was so Our Boy
Roy and he was so busted. That motherfucker who
denied me my bonus while out here cheating on his
wife. Hell, part of my bonus was probably tied up
in that diamond pendant of hers.

When Roy must've asked her what was wrong,
she pointed at me. At first, he must've dismissed
me as the plump girl who made a fool out of herself onstage with Royal T., but he wasn't stupid.
After he mouthed something to her probably
about ignoring me, he stole another glance. Then
it clicked for him. Like I said, he wasn't stupid.
He probably had a good memory for faces, too,
in his line of work; especially if the face looked
like it wanted to kill him.

The faint color he possessed fled his features as he placed my face that had no business being here in his select world.

"Artemis, do you know them?" Ladonna asked, probably wondering what the holdup was on my part. And why I was mean-mugging the tall white dude with the lovely exotic sister on his arm.

"No," I replied as I gave Roy a forceful middle finger and nodded my head. "He's just another inconsiderate asshole with a mistress."

"Then this is the perfect town for him, for he can pretend to be the opposite of that," she said, moving me along before things became any more uncomfortable. "Because you're sure pretending like you know him."

We rejoined Julian, but by now, my heart was racing as my active imagination began considering some dismal possibilities: What if Roy and his mistress were staying here at Stratus? Worse yet, what if they were staying at my hotel Aquos? What if Julian somehow knew Roy Bramlett? Or, what if Roy were to tell him and Ladonna who I really was: just an unemployed collector with barely a penny to her name?

"I'm about to leave," I abruptly announced to both Julian and Ladonna.

"Why? What's wrong?" Julian asked. "Did something happen?"

"Some cornball back there was making eyes at Artemis and got her all pissed off," Ladonna answered for me. I don't know if that's what she really believed about my incident with Roy, but it sounded good enough to me.

"Where is he?" Julian roared, looking in the direction of the people in line to see Royal T. Last thing I needed was a confrontation and the chance that Julian learn the real deal.

"Let it go, Julian. Please," I urged as I blocked his path and held him by the arm. "I've had too much fun tonight and want to end on a positive note with no drama."

"Matter of fact, why don't you escort her back to Aquos next door, Julian?" Ladonna asked on my behalf before I knew it. "I have my car valet parked here, so I need to move it whenever I'm done."

"Ladonna, I can't just leave you here," I objected.

"Nonsense. I'm going to get my picture with Royal T., remember? And if I have my way, that may extend into the rest of the night," she boasted. "You two enjoy your midnight stroll," she teasingly sang as she strolled herself back toward the object of her desire.

With no further coaxing, we left the theatre. Julian escorted me to the elevator, reminding me of the note on which our dinner ended. Up until my seeing Roy, this wasn't how I envisioned tonight going.

"Is this going to end like it did last night? Different hotel, but same outcome? With you breaking off on your own again and leaving me standing here? Y'know, I'm still upset that we didn't have our dessert."

"Yes, I remember all too well," I said, feeling relieved the farther away we got from the theatre and that awful confrontation.

Taking charge, Julian grabbed me and brought his lips to mine. Our delicate formality evaporated, consumed in the flames spouting between us. "Well, you need to let me correct that. So why not now?" he asked as the VIP elevator's doors parted. It was empty and just waiting for someone . . . anyone.

"You know what? You're right," I agreed as I gazed longingly into Julian's eyes, my lips and mouth still hungry. I had only one more night left and everything I'd lost I didn't know if I ever wanted to reclaim. "Why not now," I seductively recited back at him, batting my eyelashes as I pulled him closer to me again. I whispered in his ear, "A little dessert might be just what I need. I'll even let you order. Want to see what's on the menu?"

Julian smiled and stepped on to the elevator with me.

As the doors began to close, a man came rushing up at the last minute to get on.

"Catch another one, my man," Julian sternly instructed him. "This elevator is occupied."

Chapter 20

After the doors shut, Julian pulled a card of some sort from his wallet and inserted it in a slot just above the floor buttons.

"What is that?" I asked, curious as to whether it might grant us access to a secret floor or something.

"My VIP card," he calmly replied as he pushed an unnumbered button, which brought the elevator to a screeching halt. "I let you escape from me last night on an elevator. Not this time."

"It's like that?" I asked as I braced myself against the rail of the rear elevator wall.

"Yeah. Like exactly like that," he replied. "At least for the next ten or fifteen minutes."

"I hope I didn't take you away from anything tonight," I nervously stammered as I became acutely aware of where this was going and what we were about to do. *Calm down, girl. Nobody's dying on you. This isn't even your real life, so you can't hurt anybody.*

"No. Just impatiently waiting for you," he uttered, breathing heavily as he held me steady by my waist. My negativity subsided as my passion rose.

"Hope I was worth it," I said breathlessly as I ran my finger across his belt buckle and left it there, using it as a hook from whence he couldn't escape. Just below my hand, the outline of Julian's hardened dick was prominent through his black slacks.

Prominent and impressive. Hey now.

He dipped his head down to kiss me and because of my heels, he didn't have far to go. As we hungrily kissed, he slid his hands away from my waist and down my thighs, grasping the bottom of my skirt.

I shuddered and closed my eyes as Julian began hiking it up, the fabric reluctantly yielding against my hips as it slid along.

"Julian, the . . . the camera," I gasped, second thoughts making me tentative as he tugged and pulled like a man possessed, biting on my neck at the same time. "They . . . they can see us."

"It's okay, Artemis," Julian said he paused, his eyes still afire. "They're trained to practice discretion on these kinds of elevators. From the moment my card key was used, it's been just me and you in here. No eyes for now," he explained as he reached between my legs. "Just me . . . and you."

I gasped at his knuckles against my inner thighs as he nudged his hand against my clit through my panties. He nuzzled and worked his fingers around and around, teasing me so much that I begged. By the time he moved my moist panties aside and slid his digits inside to finger me, my legs were writhing to where I could hardly stand.

Time was ticking though and I wanted more, so I hastened things and unbuckled his belt. Julian finished by unzipping his slacks and dropped them and his underwear to his ankles. I took my jacket off as I allowed him to slide my panties off, then bent down to retrieve a condom from my purse.

Since I was already there, I sucked and stroked Julian right before tearing the foil package and rolling the condom on to his dick with my mouth.

After sliding my skirt up farther, I propped myself onto the elevator rail in the corner and cocked one leg to the side.

"I'm ready for that dessert now," I offered to Julian with a wily grin. He was more than happy to fuck a woman he thought he knew ever so briefly. As he entered me, I wrapped my arms around his neck and kissed him heartily. Getting fucked right on an elevator was never on my list of things to do, but I could merrily cross it off now.

I squeezed my hips, holding on for dear life at Julian's upstrokes so as to not lose my balance. My older lover was exquisite in his technique, each change in direction and pace only enhancing my desire. Our bodies pressed so close together that our breathing began to match, panting and moaning in time.

"Yes!" I screamed, no cares in the world except for the pleasure that Julian was giving me. The camera in the upper corner of the elevator didn't matter anymore and perhaps its presence was turning me on more. But as I climaxed, something made Julian pause, stopping his manic rhythm. "Are . . . are you okay?" I asked.

He didn't answer. Instead he retreated, clearing space between us. As he reached in his jacket and grabbed his chest, I was overcome with grief.

The memory of Carlos dying on me was too fresh. The wounds of what I'd learned about my real mother were too deep. My own emotional state, playing this charade, was too fragile.

I was a broken basket case on an elevator in Las Vegas.

And another man was dying on me.

"I'm sorry! I'm so sorry!" I screamed, tears steady flowing as Julian withdrew from inside me, his hand still inside his jacket. "I did it again! Oh Lord, I did it again!"

"Artemis? What are you doing?" Julian let out as I darted past him and rushed toward the elevator controls. I removed his VIP card from the slot and frantically began pushing buttons to get the elevator to move or open up.

"I'm sorry. I'm . . . I'm so sorry," I told him.

"About what? What is wrong with you, woman?"

"Your chest! You're grabbing your chest!" I shouted, my hands trembling now as I scampered to put my panties back on and grab my jacket before the doors opened.

"No, you're mistaken. I was grabbing this," he advised as he dangled something in front of my blurry, tear-filled vision. "My cell phone. It was vibrating against my chest and startled me. That's all," he said softly, probably trying to calm me down as he slowly approached.

Julian wasn't dying on me and I'd been foolish. But the painful memories besieging me were as real as anything.

The elevator doors parted, delivering us on a floor filled with waiting guests, puzzled looks etched on their faces.

Eric Pete

"Artemis! Wait! Where are you going?" Julian begged of me as I abandoned him and fled into the crowd.

"Ma'am, are you all right? Did something happen?" a member of hotel security asked as I bumped into him, barely able to breathe.

I wasn't hearing that as I was too busy suffering an anxiety attack.

Chapter 21

All day, I'd remained holed up in my room. The epic highs of yesterday and last night were erased in an instant as I let a silly misunderstanding get the best of me and take me to a really bad place. Before I could fully flee into the night, the security staff over at Stratus made me see their on-staff nurse. Of course, I did what I'd done this entire time.

I lied to the sweet lady, claiming I'd merely suffered a panic attack after the elevator took too long to get to my floor. It was none of their business what I was doing on the elevator at the time, so I left that part out. Poor Julian must've thought I was certifiable after that display. Luckily, I disappeared before he could get his pants up. I sincerely hoped I didn't embarrass him too much, but would talk with him when I was ready.

Someone knocked on my door, but I didn't bother to get up. The Do Not Disturb sign told them all they needed to know. It was either

Ladonna or Julian, no doubt, after I hadn't answered my phone. One wanting to know if I got laid and the other wondering why I stopped in the middle of getting laid. This bed was too comfortable to allow me to deal with that right now. And besides, I had my virtual assistant to keep me company. I'd even given her a name while hidden from the world.

Fancy.

Yeah, good ol' Fancy would keep the monsters away while allowing me to order room service, too. You can't beat that, right?

But tomorrow, I had to go.

Back to life. Back to reality.

And my Vegas problems were nothing compared to my Houston problems.

I groaned as I bothered to read my texts.

I guess you're still w/ him. Must b good, bitch. *Ladonna's text.*

Plz call me. Don't understand. *Julian's text.*

Call Momma. *My sister Anitra's text.*

Saw pic on FB. Was that really u wit Natalia or Photoshopped? Where wuz that? *Anitra's second text.*

You've won a prize. Click here to claim it http:xfssew. *Spam. Duh.*

Wait. You took a picture wit Royal T??? Call me! *Anitra's third text.*

Was it something I did? Let me know you're all right. *Julian's second text.*

I deleted those, but what stuck out, besides my feeling bad about Julian, was noticeable by its absence. Nothing from Lowell.

Another call was coming in from a collector. Figuring I might as well deal with it now, I answered.

"Hello?" I groaned, my head aching at the very sound of my voice. Last night's drinks had taken a toll on me, too.

"Ms. Artemis Clay?"

"Yes, this is she," I replied as I sat up in the bed, one eye feeling like it was glued shut and unwilling to cooperate with my brain.

"How are you doing today, ma'am?" the man from some noisy call center dared to ask.

"Can you please get on with it?" I barked. Fuck the niceties.

"I'm calling on behalf of your delinquent account with GE Capital. This call is an attempt to collect a debt and may be recorded for quality assurance purposes," he recited with his soulless voice.

"You want me to pay, right?" I snarked.

"Yes. Are you ready to make a payment today?"

"I guess so. I'm speaking to you. Can I use a gift card to make a payment?" I asked, realizing I was going to have to walk into the living room to get my purse. Might as well start tackling my real problems now, and this would make for a good transition back to the real Artemis.

After an extended, stress-free session in the soaker tub, I lotioned up and ordered some hot tea and fresh fruit from room service. Tightening the belt on my robe, I turned on the TV to catch up on what was going on in the world.

As I texted Ladonna back, Julian called. I stopped mid-text as he was a priority at this moment.

"Hello," I said with false cheer after clearing my throat. After the concern evident in his texts, he deserved some relief.

"Whoa. Didn't expect you to sound like this after last night," Julian reacted. "Are you in your room? Everything better with you?"

"Yes and yes." I chuckled. "And I apologize for flaking out last night. I was enjoying myself. *Really* enjoying myself."

"Whew. So it wasn't me?" he asked.

"Not in the least," I assured him, thinking about the more pleasurable parts of that elevator ride.

"So what's the deal with your running off? I looked everywhere for you. Even went back upstairs at Stratus, thinking you might be with your friend Ladonna. She was no help," Julian offered.

"Oh. That," I muttered. "I was suffering from too much champagne and vodka shots. Also, had a crazy anxiety attack from out of nowhere. I haven't had those since I was teenager," I lied.

"Might be time for some Xanax or something," he semi-jested. My run-off was pretty extreme. "We don't have to pick up right where we left off. But our time is short and I do want to see more of you."

"I think you saw quite a bit last night," I joked.

"You know what I mean. But speaking of that, it was kind of limited. I normally hate being on the clock. I like to take my time . . . make love to the woman I'm feeling."

"Oh? If you're trying to impress me, mission accomplished."

"Artemis?"

"Yeah, Julian?"

"When you freaked out, you said something about 'doing it again'. Is some of this related to your last relationship?" he questioned.

"Okay. You might say that," I admitted. "Which is kinda why I can be a little prickly to deal with." Everything from that moment was such a blur that I probably left a lot of clues for Julian to pick up on; so much for making up shit about teenage anxiety disorders.

"Just admitting that is big," he noted. "Look . . . I'm getting a notice from my bank that I need to call them immediately, so . . ."

"Go on and handle your business. I'll be fine. Holler at me later."

"So if I knock you might answer this time?"

"If I'm here," I mocked, being coy. I had no plans and it was probably best for the world at large if I spent my final night alone in my suite renting On Demand movies.

And right on time, there popped up a text from Lowell.

Where to? was his simple message.

Chapter 22

Lowell promised to only take up an hour of my time, but gave the ominous warning to dress comfortably. This time when I came down to the lobby, I couldn't find him.

I texted him. U here?

"Yes, I am," a cordial, deep voice replied in my ear from behind me almost immediately after sending the text.

"Boy, that shit ain't funny!" I yelped, startled by the stealth moves he'd put on me. As I went to playfully slap him on his shoulder, I was stunned by the full view I got of Lowell. No wonder I didn't spot him, as I'd come downstairs expecting to see his black driver's suit as always. Instead, he switched things up, pretty appealing in his jeans, black biker boots, and patched leather vest. If he wasn't a member of the Village People, he most certainly was a rider then.

"Glad to see you still gracing our lovely manufactured city," he said as he removed his Ray-Ban sunglasses in his leather-gloved hand. Those green eyes of his were just so fun to get lost in.

"You're in luck. This is my last night," I offered as I gave him a warm hug and nervously allowed him a kiss on my cheek, but was struck with those conflicting feelings again. Despite what went down with Julian last night, neither one of us had expressed it to be anything more than a spontaneous hookup. And, frankly, after my panicky "hit and run," I imagined, despite his talk, Julian probably classified it in kind.

But if that was the case, why did letting Lowell kiss me in a place where Julian might catch me seem shady? I guess this person I was pretending to be had a scandalous nature to her, kind of how my sister Anitra probably envisioned me anyway for sleeping with "her man," Carlos.

"I figured as much," he stated. "Sorry I didn't reach out to you last night, but somebody got a hold of my credit card data and ran up a shitload of charges. I've been busy closing my account and trying to figure when it happened. Just finished this morning."

"That's so awful," I exclaimed. "I hate thieves. Any leads?"

"I don't think it happened online, so I guess maybe when I took you out for barbecue. Funny," he said, pausing to reflect, "because I've been going there for years. Thought I could trust them. Did you notice anything strange that day?"

"Other than those guys calling you 'Weasel'? No," I admitted.

"Oh well," he said with a shrug as I checked him out and his rugged look. The Weasel comment didn't even faze him this time, so the credit card thing must've pissed him off more than he let on. I guess if I had money, I'd be too through also.

"What did you do anyway last night?" he asked, moving on from that which pissed him off.

"It was major," I bragged. "I went with my friend Ladonna to a concert at the top of Stratus. If you go on my Facebook page, you can see some of the pics I posted from my phone."

"You're talking about that private show with Royal T. and Natalia?"

"Yes! That was it!" I beamed. "Were you planning on being there?"

"Ooooh no," he piped. "Those 'one night only' private affairs are a little too pricey for my liking, but because of my job, I gotta be aware of all the happenings."

"I not only danced with Natalia's backup dancers, I got to go on stage with Royal T.," I crowed like some thirsty, basic chick.

"Now . . . see, you're taking your Las Vegas experience and maximizing the hell outta it," Lowell teased with a huge smile, not letting me figure out if he was mocking me.

"True. Who woulda thought. But it's good to see you not working for a change," I told him as I stole another glance at his muscular legs poured into those jeans.

"And I'm glad to see you listened to me and dressed comfortably," he said, eyeing my attire: a blue and white Nike jogging suit that I normally wore on weekends.

"I can listen sometimes, but what do you have planned?"

"Ever been on a motorcycle?" He grinned.

"Oh my gawd, oh my gawd, oh my gawd!" I yelled, my heart pumping and arms clamped tight around Lowell's waist like an iron vise. I'd spent most of the adrenaline-packed ride to Lake Mead with my face buried in the patch on the back of his black leather vest that said WEASEL.

"Are you all right?" Lowell asked as he looked back at me, his hands still resting on the bike's handlebars as he revved the throttle.

It was hard to hear over the loud rumble of the Harley-Davidson's pipes down by my feet. "Yes! Shit yeah!" I squealed as I finally relaxed my grip. I'd held on so hard, you'd think I was performing

the Heimlich on him. It didn't hurt that Lowell
had stopped to let me enjoy the stunning view of
the Las Vegas Valley from up here. The trip to the
north summit went so insanely fast that it felt like
we made it in mere minutes. I don't think I'd ever
been so scared, yet so exhilarated, in my life.

"Like I said. Just an hour of your time. Too
bad it took ten minutes of that convincing you
the helmet wouldn't mess up your hair . . . that
much," he clowned as he turned off his motorcycle. The man definitely knew how to ride.

"You're just lucky I'm not vain . . . that much," I
countered, stifling a giggle as I got off the hog and
carefully removed Lowell's helmet. "Ride up here
a lot?" I asked, letting my ears hear normally.

"I could show you so much more, but don't
want to monopolize your limited time. Maybe
next time you're out here? Or when I take a road
trip to Texas?" he suggested as he dismounted
from the large-engine bike.

"You're making the very big assumption that
I found this fun. And that I like your company,"
I posed, leaving him to mull that over. I walked
across the loose desert gravel for a better look
at the mountains and manmade lake around us.
This view alone was worth my trip.

Without responding to my taunt, Lowell came
up behind me and reciprocated, wrapping his
arms around my waist for this part of the road
trip. For a long, deep moment, the two of us just

took in the view without speaking. Feeling him
pressed so firmly up against my ass did make my
mind shift from *natural wonders* to *wondering*
how he'd *naturally* feel hitting it from the back.

"What is your truth, Artemis?" he asked, breaking the silence. With us so close, his bellowing
voice resonated through my body like an echo
chamber.

"In what way?" I responded. "This have to do
with what happened to your credit card?"

"It was more open-ended and philosophical
than that, but if that's where your mind takes
you . . ."

"Look . . . you don't know me like that, but . . ."

"But I want to know you like that. Can't you
tell?" he asked, still holding me tight. Part of me
wondered if it was to not let me escape in case I
confessed and he had to call the cops.

"You want the truth?" I asked him.

"The better question is, do you?"

I reached back, comfortably placing my hand
on the back of his neck where I caressed it, but
kept my gaze fixed on the beyond. "I am from
Katy, but I don't own any company. Hell, I don't
even own a job right now. I am beyond dead
broke and drowning in debt, but what I do know
is that I never stole anything a day in my life.
Well . . . that is until I stole your heart today."

"Funny," Lowell deadpanned.

"Hee. Hee," I shot back.

Chapter 23

Lowell delivered me back to Aquos on his Harley, but a little past the hour in which he'd promised. That was my fault for getting chatty out at Lake Mead like I was high inside a smoky cave or something and on a vision quest. But I felt better for it.

Thing is, after spilling my guts, I didn't truly know whether Lowell believed all or even just a portion of my 4-1-1.

"Don't forget. I got you for tomorrow. Text me your flight info later," he reminded me as I got off his bike and handed his helmet back. With his motorcycle still running and rumbling, we kissed. It was a slow, deliberate burn between us with our lips as an introduction. An introduction hinting what might come later.

Lowell took my hand and placed it to his chest just inside his vest. "Feel that?" he asked.

"Yes," I replied, admiring his firm muscle tone.

"I had a physical last month and get checked out annually, Artemis. Part of my benefits coverage through my company. And I work out. Don't worry. I'm nothing like your last boyfriend or your deceased husband," he offered.

"So you believe me?" I asked, smiling wildly with relief.

"I have to. Nobody would make up a story about bad luck like that," he said with a chuckle. "But might be something we hypothetically revisit maybe next time I'm your way."

Lowell rode off, the valets admiring his Harley, as I walked toward the front door and the smiling greeter eager and ready to "welcome me to my adventure." But in the door reflection, I saw a police car. I looked back out of curiosity and saw what the officers were doing.

The two of them were signing paperwork for a flatbed tow truck driver. And on that flatbed was Ladonna's black sports car. It was unmistakable, for I'd remember those tiny-ass seats for the rest of my life. Images of Ladonna improperly parking it came to mind, but she could afford the ticket.

Inside the hotel lobby, the mermaids still swam beneath me. I was going up to my suite to begin packing for my trip home, but decided to check my most recent balance at the front desk.

"Hello, Ms. Clay. How may I help you?" the woman said as I walked up. I hesitated, knowing she couldn't have memorized my face and name like that. That was before realizing my VIP bracelet was inside my purse. It must've still given off a signal.

"I leave in the morning and just wanted to confirm my current bill total," I lied. I could get that off my little touch screen up in the suite. What I really wanted to see if they had any issues with my credit card's limit beforehand.

"Uh . . . Ms. Clay, could I see your bracelet?" she asked. "We're having some issues of some-one possibly counterfeiting our bracelets and accessing our system. So we're checking each guest's to make sure they're working properly."

"Um . . . sure," I said as I reached in my purse and retrieved my accessory for her. Just over her shoulder, a man was kinda lurking. He stood out by not wearing the uniforms like everybody else. Maybe he was a corporate auditor, quality control or something, because he was watching not just me, but all the customers who approached the desk. After checking my bracelet and comparing it to something on her glass screen, she handed it back to me with a warm apology, then gave me my bill balance. With room service, the spa, and everything else, my card had barely enough to cover it. But I still had Ladonna's gift cards.

On my way to the grand ol' bubble elevator to magically take me to my floor, a woman in a white baseball cap and baggy pink cotton warm-ups whistled to herself while wrestling with three large bags of rolling luggage. Minding my own business and feeling a little melancholy about my adventure rapidly coming to an end, I kept on walking.

Until she whistled again.

At me.

"Amiss," she hissed.

I did a double take, but nobody else would call me that.

"Ladonna?" I asked, confused by my friend's sudden unimpressive fashion sense. At least she still had one of her signature "big-ass bags" on her arm. "What are you doing?"

"I moved to another hotel and just transferring my stuff," she said as she moved close to one of the nosier waterfalls in this place rather than in my direction. It was very anti-social of her, even for dealing with me.

"Why?" I asked as I walked to her instead.

"They took issue with some of my partying and said I made disparaging remarks to the staff. They really need to reevaluate how they award five stars to some of these places. How was your night with Mr. Julian?" she asked, still struggling with all her luggage.

"It didn't end quite as planned," I replied, shaking my head. "Need a hand?"

"Would you please, dear?" she asked. I frowned, remembering her only calling me "dear" one other time as opposed to "bitch" or "Amiss." That was at the club and in front of Julian.

"Looking a little underwhelming, aren't you?" I asked Ladonna.

"If you must know, I'm feeling under the weather and also don't want my new hotel trying to gouge me based on my fabulousness either," was her reasoning.

"If you say so," I responded with a shrug. "Do you know they just towed your car away?" I asked before I forgot about it.

"Yeah, I know," she moaned. "When it rains, it pours. I'll get it out of impound later. I have one small favor . . . before you help me carry this stuff out."

"Sure. Whatcha need?"

"Could you let me borrow your bracelet?" she asked.

"Uh . . . why would you need mine?" I questioned.

"Because when I got into it with the staff and they told me to leave, they took mine. Now, I have several more bags in my suite, but no way to access my floor without it."

"Um . . . okay. I guess," I said as I tried to figure out why she didn't just use a dolly from the concierge. Maybe when a hotel kicked you out, they really cut you off. And she did have a ton of shopping bags up there.

"Great! Stay right here with my stuff and I'll be right back down with the remainder," she instructed me.

I sat on a sofa nearest Ladonna's luggage and tried to guestimate how many more bags she was going to bring down. While I waited, I retrieved my phone to see if Julian had texted me.

"Ma'am, may I ask what you're doing?" a man asked as he approached me.

"Waiting on a friend. This is her luggage," I matter-of-factly offered as I went back to looking at my phone.

"Do you have your hotel bracelet?" he continued.

Damn, man. Go on. Find someone else to hassle. "My friend has it. She'll be right down," I replied right at the moment I realized he wasn't wearing the standard black uniform of the hotel staff. He was that same man I'd seen earlier lurking by the front desk. And he wasn't smiling.

I went to get off the lobby sofa when two powerful sets of hands grabbed me by my shoulders. It was two more men who'd joined us, sneaking up behind me.

The police officers from outside the hotel.

As one whispered into his radio, the other one addressed me. "Ma'am, you are under arrest. You have the right to remain silent. You also have the right to an attorney," he began reciting.

"What do you mean? I didn't do anything!" I yelled as I tried to move out from under the too-firm hand on my shoulder. When I did that, they threw me to the floor and handcuffed my hands behind my back.

I kept protesting, but it was like they were suddenly deaf, acting all antsy and stuff like I was a big deal or something. And there, from on my stomach, I spied Ladonna.

She scurried along the far wall, bypassing the commotion with my hotel bracelet on her arm.

She stole one quick glance toward me, seeing the fear and surprise in my eyes.

Then kept walking.

Chapter 24

"Credit card fraud and theft? What the fuck is this all about?" I yelled, reciting the charges they'd told me before throwing me in the police van.

She didn't speak. Instead, she just sat there across from me, stoic.

Not me. I was stressing in a major way.

"And why did you try leaving me there?" I asked Ladonna. If I wasn't restrained, I'd have put dem hands on her.

This bitch tried to get away back at Aquos, but ran right into two more officers who were just waiting for her to try to escape.

And now, my stupid ass was caught up in whatever this was by coincidence. Guilt by association.

"Ladonna, say something!" I snarled. "Or I swear I will—"

"My name ain't Ladonna," she finally replied, cutting me off in a completely different accent than I'd ever heard escape her lips. This one sounded deep, syrupy South. "And this ain't gonna turn out too nice."

Chapter 25

"Stay right there! I'm on my way!" Lowell yelled.

I wasn't going anywhere.

Except on my flight outta here.

Home couldn't come fast enough.

"I can't miss my flight," I said to him as a taxicab stopped right in front of me to unload its passengers.

For once, my luck held. That and Ladonna taking pity on me are what got me off the hook with a warning, courtesy of LVPD, to choose my friends more carefully in the future. The girl I thought was my friend had a criminal record in five different states as long as my arm and was actively engaging in credit card fraud and identity theft the whole time she was at Aquos. Nothing she'd told me about herself was true, which is fitting, I guess, seeing as I'd been less than honest too. The police first pinpointed where she might be operating as hotel guests in our general area began complaining about somebody stealing their info and running up charges. Those big-ass purses of hers actually had skimmers sewn into their lining to steal people's credit card data when she walked by, or bumped into them. It explained how and why she'd inappropriately hugged both Julian and Lowell and how both wound up getting their card info stolen. She then was selling that stolen data to organizations while using some of it herself to support her extravagant lifestyle, including massive purchases of gift cards to hide the money trail.

Hiding in plain sight, and even her Aquos bracelet was as much a fraud as she.

One of the last things Ladonna—I mean, "Sherlitha Dix of Jackson, Tennessee"—told me before they took us off the van and hauled us to separate rooms was that she saw my account balance when she first swiped my credit card data. The bitch said she felt sorry for me when she realized I had zip, which is why she splurged so much on me.

Well, that and her "wanting someone to share the fun with."

The final treat for me she shared was that, at the concert, she realized I knew Roy Bramlett from the way I was acting. And, that there was no love lost. When I left the concert with Julian, she was sure to bump Roy and his mistress with her purse skimmer and did an "extra special" job on his credit; things that would lead to questions by his wife back home in Illinois. Questions that Roy would have trouble answering. I guess maybe Our Boy Roy really should've given me that bonus after all.

As I'd worried about going to jail as part of Sherlitha's scheme, her last words to me in Ladonna's accent had been, "Don't worry. I got ya. Us broke bitches gotta stick together." She assured me she was going to accept full responsibility and was true to her word, as good as that was.

I was lucky to have my return flight ticket already because all those remaining magical $500 gift cards of hers, including those I had, were seized by the police as evidence.

Embarrassed was what I felt. But Lowell was different. Upon my release, I'd shared with him what had happened and that I was going straight to the airport. I didn't think Julian would be quite so sympathetic or understanding about my issues, so we would just have our memories to look back on.

"Look, I've got a fare for the airport, so I'm heading your way as we speak," Lowell repeated to make sure I could hear him over the traffic noise. "Wait for me outside, okay? I'm almost there, so don't leave without me saying good-bye, Artemis."

"Okay. I'm not moving. I'm in front of the United terminal right now."

"That's where my fare is heading. And they're in a rush too, so this is perfect," he stated before he hung up.

Over the next five minutes, several limos came and went. I watched them all, checking my watch, as general boarding for my flight was scheduled to begin soon.

As I checked the limo drivers for Lowell's familiar face, one of the passengers exiting a recently arrived one walked briskly in my direction.

"Artemis!" the man in the charcoal sport coat and slacks called out before I could check his driver.

"Julian?" I called back in surprise upon recognizing him. "What . . . what are you doing here?" I asked in disbelief.

"You haven't answered your phone since yesterday," he stated, sounding out of breath. Upon spotting me, he'd hopped out of his car before the driver had a chance to come around and open his door. "Then this morning, the hotel said you checked out and had left, so I rushed over to check the departures for Houston, hoping to catch you before you got past security. And here you are, standing right here. It was a crazy, desperate gamble, but I couldn't let you leave without a proper good-bye. Or without telling you I really want to see you again . . . outside of Las Vegas. Even if I have to fly from Connecticut to Houston to see you, or vice versa. What do you say?"

"Oh Julian . . . wow," I said, equally stunned and flattered. But I was outside the terminal looking for Lowell, who was supposed to be arriving with his fare right about now. I was so busy focusing my eyes downfield at the limos coming toward me . . .

"Artemis?"

That I hadn't bothered to check the limo in which Julian had just arrived.

"Lowell," I gasped as he stood in the open driver's door, staring at the two of us.

One of my issues when I came to Vegas had been my reluctance with relationships because of the two men who died on me. Now my problem was with two men again.

Except both were very much alive.
How do I know?
Because they both were staring at me.
Oops.